Forbidden Whispers

Secrets of Whispering Pines, Volume 3

Holly Bowne

Published by Write Expressions Ink, 2024.

This is a work of fiction. Similarities to real people, places, or events are entirely coincidental.

FORBIDDEN WHISPERS

First edition. June 2, 2024.

Copyright © 2024 Holly Bowne.

ISBN: 979-8227568830

Written by Holly Bowne.

Chapter 1

It felt like he was swimming through mud, struggling to fight his way to the surface. Eventually, he was able to pry open one eye, then the other. It was as if grains of sand were scraping against the inside of his eyelids. He tried to move, but his arms and legs were leaden. He took several slow, deep breaths, and then, with a monumental effort, forced himself into a sitting position. A moan of pain escaped his lips with the effort. He blinked several times as his surroundings came into focus.

It appeared to be a spacious living room. But it was in shambles. There was a white leather sofa across from him, its stuffing poking up from slashes in the cushions. A sleek, black chair stood at one side of the sofa, its mate lay opposite, toppled onto its side. The sofa sat at a strange angle before a large window, currently obscured by vertical blinds. Slivers of sunlight seeped out from the top and bottom, letting him know that it was daylight outside. In front of the sofa, the shards from a broken glass-top table were scattered across the thick, Arctic shag rug which lay beneath.

He lifted his gaze to slowly sweep over the rest of the room and noted more overturned furnishings and items scattered about. A cracked crystal vase lay on its side; the bouquet of fresh flowers that had clearly once been inside it now lay wilted and crushed in a puddle of water on the hardwood floor. Artwork that was still on the walls hung askew, the rest lay in broken frames on the floor.

The floor plan of the space was open, and he could see the dining area from where he sat. A marble dining table held a partially empty bottle of wine and two wine glasses. Beside them sat what must have once been a charcuterie tray. He could see the dried-up remains of cheeses and crackers poking up from the edges of it.

He could tell that the decor of the place was luxurious, high end. But he didn't recognize any of it. And the silence of the place was profound.

"Hello?" His voice came out like a croak. He squeezed his eyes shut against the sudden pain that rocked through his head as he spoke. He struggled to his feet and cleared his throat, trying again. "Hello, is anyone here?"

His words were met with silence. Confusion clouded his mind as he tried to piece together how he'd ended up in this unfamiliar, disarrayed space.

He surveyed the room once more, and his eyes fell on a large, gilt sunburst mirror that had somehow escaped the destruction. He stumbled his way across the room toward it, feeling strangely uncoordinated. It was as if his feet were having difficulty translating the message from his brain telling them to move.

He reached the mirror and gasped as he took in his reflection. A pair of extremely bloodshot gray eyes stared back at him. His thick, dark curls, normally combed neatly back, now stood on end, framing a face that sported a colorful bruise on his left cheekbone. He could see a bit of dried blood around his nose and there were a few drips on his rumpled white polo shirt. He lifted his fingertips to gently touch the tender bruise.

His head was really beginning to ache now and he was starting to feel nauseous. He moved to the black chair that was still in place and sat down hard on it, dropping his head between his knees. He took several deep breaths, trying to think what to do. He had no idea where he was. And he had no memory of how he'd gotten here.

He searched through the fog of his mind, trying to recall any details from the night before. Suddenly, a memory popped into his head, making him sit bolt upright, then he winced as the room spun. He remembered now. He'd been on his first date with Valentina last night. They'd met at Lakeside Latté for coffee. But he couldn't recall anything after that. Was this her home? And if so, why did he have no recollection of coming here? And even more concerning, where was she?

He glanced again at the dining room table, the two wine glasses, and the open bottle of wine. He frowned. There was no way that he drank anything last night. Was there?

He stood again and walked through the entire place, calling Valentina's name as he entered each room. In one bedroom, he spied a photograph by the bed. He walked over and picked it up. The picture confirmed that this must be Valentina's home. The girl in the photo was clearly a young Valentina, maybe around the age of ten, and she was smiling up at a woman who looked similar to her. Her mother? He set the photograph back down and moved on, searching every room in the place. But it was soon clear that he was alone.

He felt in his pocket and pulled out his cell phone. His first instinct was to call his brother Wade, a member of the Whispering Pines police force. Then he remembered Wade was out of town. He hesitated for a moment longer, debating. Then he checked his cell phone contacts, selected a name, and dialed a different number instead.

Maggie Milena sat in Lakeside Latté across the table from her potential client, Sandra, her expression sympathetic. Maggie had heard similar versions of Sandra's story many times, and she knew from experience that step one was simply letting the person feel heard.

Sandra had been divorced for over three years and she was in her early forties. She'd tried three different online dating services, but the matches were always horrendous. She hated the whole process of "virtual dating" before the real dating even began. It just wasn't working out well for her. And the last man she'd been paired with had been the final straw.

"He was not interested in learning about me at all," Sandra said, setting down her oversized mug with a clatter. "In fact, I have no idea how those algorithms put us together in the first place because we shared zero interests in common. He talked the entire night about himself and his impressive," here she rolled her eyes, "portfolio of investments. And then, can you even believe it? He had the gall to ask me to pay for both our dinners, claiming he was just respecting me as an independent woman!"

Maggie shook her head. "Well, that's something that would never happen when you're on a Matches by Maggie date."

Sandra lifted her mug again and took a sip of her coffee, then broke off a piece of the lemon and blueberry scone on the plate in front of her. "Can you explain to me a bit more about your program and how it works?"

"Certainly," Maggie said. "As a certified matchmaker, I create a dating experience that's personalized just for you. It will be completely private, with no online dating profile for the world to see."

Sandra nodded approvingly and popped the bite of scone into her mouth.

"In addition, nobody will ghost you or present a false image that's a far cry from reality," Maggie said, warming to her subject. "The Matches by Maggie process starts with you and I having a confidential, in-depth conversation where I get to know you. I learn all about your life experiences, personal interests, hobbies, dating history, and relationship goals. I find out what you're looking for in a potential partner, what's worked for you in past relationships, and just as importantly, what hasn't worked.

"Then you sit back and relax while I combine my matchmaker skills with the information I've gathered from you during our conversation. I personally handle everything from match selection to booking reservations and arranging everything necessary for your first date. I become your dating concierge. That way you spend your time dating instead of searching for hours through online profiles and swiping screens."

Sandra smiled at this as Maggie continued.

"We don't do anything virtual. You'll go on real face-to-face dates because that's the only way to tell if there's chemistry. It's personal, it's private, it's effective, and it's off-line. After I select your match, I call you and share with you details about who I've chosen. I always respect your confidentiality and only share your name, never your address, phone number, email address, or where you work.

"As for the date itself, I do all in my power to create an environment that makes getting to know your match as easy and fun as possible. I can even provide some effective conversation starter prompts to help your conversation flow smoothly."

Maggie leaned forward, her gaze intent as she concluded her sales pitch. "Selecting your match isn't just my job, Sandra, it's my passion. I'm here to help you find that special someone. To help you achieve your very own happily ever after."

Sandra sat back in her chair and looked pleased. "All of that sounds wonderful. And I must say, with only a few exceptions, your reviews speak for themselves!"

Maggie kept the easy smile on her face but inwardly seethed at the reminder of the mysterious negative reviews that had recently popped up online.

"What happens after that first date?" Sandra asked.

"Well, I chat with you both to get feedback. If things went well, and you've already made plans to get together again, great! If not, it's important that I get good feedback on your impressions, likes and dislikes, so that I can fine-tune future matches."

Their conversation continued a bit longer as Maggie answered a few more questions. But in less than half an hour, she had another signed contract in her hand. She stood to bid Sandra farewell and then sat back down in the booth, ready to relax and enjoy her own coffee and the rest of her cinnamon roll. But just as she lifted the delicious confection to her lips, her phone buzzed with a call.

She grinned, answering it with a tap. "It's great to hear from you, Noah! Are you calling to tell me how great it went with Valentina last night? I had such a good feeling about you two."

Chapter 2

Maggie stood beside Noah Riley at the entrance to Valentina's condo with her mouth hanging open. Her gaze moved from him to the trashed living room and back to him again. She'd already been there for two full minutes and hadn't yet said a word.

Then, just as he opened his mouth to speak, she started to sputter, "Wha...wha...what happened?"

When he didn't answer right away, she turned the full force of her wide-eyed, golden-brown gaze on him.

He gave a small shrug. "I don't know."

She gaped at him. "You don't know? What do you mean you don't know?"

"I'm sorry. But I just don't know. For some reason, I can't remember anything from last night," he said. "I wasn't even certain where I was until I saw a picture of Valentina beside her bed when I searched the place."

Maggie's gaze scanned the room again, falling on the wine and glasses on the dining table. She looked at him accusingly. "Did you get so drunk last night that you blacked out?"

Noah shook his head. "I don't drink."

"Uh-huh," Maggie said, looking doubtful. Her eyes swept once again over his messy hair, bloodshot eyes, bruised face, and rumpled clothing. "And where is Valentina?"

"I don't know."

Maggie took a deep breath and ran a hand over her face, clearly thinking. "You say you've searched the entire condo?"

He nodded. "Every room."

"What about...other places in here."

He looked confused. "Other places?"

She cleared her throat. "Clearly something happened here, Noah. Something...violent." Her eyes flicked over the room again. She swallowed, then continued. "A friend of mine has had me listen to a few true crime podcasts with her, and sometimes people aren't always where you might expect them to be."

Noah felt lightheaded. "Are you talking about a dead body stuffed in a closet or something?"

Maggie winced at his words. "It's...possible."

A lump of panic rose in his throat, bringing with it the nausea he'd felt earlier. He raced into the kitchen and heaved over the sink. He was mortified to see out of the corner of his eye that Maggie had followed him. Her look of concern did nothing to assuage the embarrassment he felt.

He turned on the faucet and swished out his mouth for several long minutes.

"Would you like a piece of gum?" Maggie asked.

"Uh...yeah, that would be great."

He dried his hands on the decorative towel hanging from Valentina's pristine oven while Maggie rummaged through her purse. She pulled out a stick of gum and handed it to him. The crisp, clean flavor of peppermint filled his mouth, the scent of it helping to calm his nerves.

"So, I'm thinking we should probably go through the rooms more carefully then," Maggie said, looking apologetic.

A feeling of dread rose in him, but he gave a small nod. "Okay," he said. "Let's do this."

Together, they moved from the kitchen down the hallway leading to the other rooms. First, they checked the laundry room, then the bathroom. A peek behind the shower curtain revealed nothing more incriminating than a sparkling clean white tile shower.

Next, they stepped inside the master bedroom. Maggie dropped to the floor and peeked under the bed. She gave a sigh of relief. "It's clear, except for a few dust bunnies."

"Great," Noah said, and turned to look at the closet with a feeling of distaste. He reached for the closet door handle and slowly opened it. Maggie was behind him, peeking around his shoulder.

The two sides of the walk-in closet held rows of women's clothing that were organized by color from light to dark. There was an empty laundry basket and shelves that held a few neatly arranged pairs of women's shoes. Nothing more.

Noah sighed with relief and shut the door.

They moved on to the final room, the second bedroom. After Maggie's look under the bed, Noah started to feel himself relax a little. He opened this bedroom's closet door more easily than he had the first. But he gave a sudden cry of shock and stumbled backward against Maggie as a large dog came bounding out from inside.

The dog made a beeline for the front door of the condo and began to whine.

Noah and Maggie exchanged a look and then raced after him. The dog appeared to be some type of German Shepherd mix, with a glossy coat of black, cream, and gold fur. One of his ears pointed straight upright, but the other was cocked at a forty-five degree angle. His long nose was pointed directly at the door. He wasn't interested in them at all. He just continued to whine and began pawing at the door. A blue leash trailed from the collar around his neck.

"Maybe he needs to go to the bathroom?" Maggie suggested.

"Oookay," Noah said. He picked up the leash and opened the front door. The dog bolted through it, pulling Noah along with him. He bounded down the steps of the small front porch and stopped at the fire hydrant in front of the building, lifting his leg.

Maggie stood at the front door watching while Noah waited, and waited, and waited for the dog to finish. His mission finally complete, the dog trotted back to sit in front of Noah. His soft, milk-chocolate brown eyes were expectant.

"I'm sorry, boy, but I don't have anything for you," Noah said. He reached out a tentative hand and let the dog sniff him. Then he scratched him behind his flopped-over ear.

Maggie spoke from the open doorway. "He seems to know you."

Noah looked at her helplessly.

She sighed. "I know, I know. You don't remember. I wonder what his name is."

"He's got a tag." Noah slipped his hand to the dog's collar and lifted the small, silver circle at its center. "Boon," he said, and looked at the dog's face. "Well, Boon. Feel better now?"

Boon licked Noah's palm.

Noah looked back at Maggie, bemused, and shrugged one shoulder. She gave him a half smile back and shook her head. Her soft blond curls bobbed around her face and shoulders, looking like a halo of gold in the morning sunlight. Despite the utter craziness of the situation, he was struck afresh with how beautiful she was.

As he led Boon back up the porch steps, his thoughts drifted back to when they'd attended high school together. He'd had the most massive crush on the curvy, petite Maggie Milena. Actually, it was more than a crush. He'd been completely in love with her. But she never knew.

They'd met at the start of their junior year when he'd signed up to get an honor society member to tutor him in chemistry. Maggie was a total brainiac, ending up as their class valedictorian. And she had been an incredible tutor. She'd helped him pass that dreaded class. And during the time they'd spent together, he'd fallen head over heels for her. She was sweet, talented, and beautiful. And he dreamed about a relationship with her. But unfortunately, she was already taken. She dated the football team's quarterback—the most popular guy in school—for all of her junior year and part of her senior year. So, he'd settled for the friend zone.

As a result, he'd focused all his energy on making music and getting gigs with his band. He and Maggie had remained close until the end of their senior year. But then they'd gone to different colleges. He'd tried to keep the friendship going, but Maggie hadn't responded to his emails or texts, and he eventually gave up, believing he'd never see her again.

When his sister-in-law Alex had suggested using a matchmaking service to help him overcome his ongoing reign of dating disasters, he'd hesitated. But she'd insisted that friends of hers had experienced great luck with Matches by Maggie, so he'd let her arrange his initial interview. At the time, he'd had no idea it was *his* Maggie.

When he'd walked into the coffee shop for their first meeting and saw her, he'd almost turned around and walked right back out. But she'd spotted him in an instant, waving him over to her table. She had been friendly and polite, but barely acknowledged their former friendship from a decade ago. She simply assured him that she'd work hard to find him his perfect match.

However, from the moment he saw her again, the secret feelings he'd harbored for her came bubbling back to the surface. Recognizing how he still felt had made him feel awkward when it came time to share his dating background with her. And there was no way he was going to tell her the whole truth about the issues he'd been having in the dating arena. Not Maggie Milena! So, he'd played down the real reason that he needed professional help getting dates, simply telling her that since he had recently started his own business, he preferred the convenience of keeping his personal life offline.

Noah and Boon reached the door, and Maggie stepped aside to let them back in, shutting and locking it behind them. Then she turned to face Noah, her eyes snagging his. "So, what do we do now?"

"Uh...maybe we should go back and look in that closet where we found Boon," Noah suggested. "There might be a clue in there that will help me remember something."

Maggie agreed, and Noah, still holding Boon on his leash, led the three of them back to the second bedroom. The closet for this bedroom was much smaller than the master bedroom's spacious walk-in closet. There was a simple rod with a couple of men's shirts and pants hanging on one side. A large black suitcase lay on the shelf overhead. But the closet held nothing else.

"Anything spark a memory?" Maggie asked.

Noah shook his head. "Nope. And those are not my clo–"

He was shocked into silence by the sound of sudden, loud banging at the front door of the condo. "We know you're in there, Tina! Let us in! NOW!"

Maggie and Noah looked at each other, eyes wide. Boon began to growl.

"Tina!" More banging.

Noah shushed the dog, uncertain what to do.

The banging stopped and the voice grew softer, yet somehow sounding more dangerous. "You and your boyfriend are gonna pay for what you did, Tina. Going to the cops like that. And you never should have lied to Papa Dom about your bachelorette getaway. Next time, make sure you let all your little girlfriends in on your plan. He knows the truth now and he's not happy, Tina. And even worse for you, *I'm* not happy. If you open the door now, it'll go easier for you. At least, I promise not to leave any visible marks." A pause. "I'm not making the same promise for your boyfriend."

Noah watched Maggie's face grow pale, and he quickly put his arm around her waist to support her sagging legs.

"What's happening?" she whispered. "Who is that guy?"

The voice came again, barely above a whisper now but clearly audible in the quiet of the condo. "Last chance, Tina. Open it, or I'm busting it down."

A couple of seconds of dead silence ticked past and then there was the sound of violent kicks against the door.

Noah made a split-second decision. "C'mon!" he whispered, pulling Boon and Maggie with him through the open closet door. Boon growled again. "Shhh, no!" he commanded the dog in a firm whisper. He pulled the closet door shut just as the sound of the cracking doorframe shattered the air.

Chapter 3

Noah held his breath in the darkness. He could feel Maggie trembling against the curve of his arm. He pulled her closer against him. The feel of her soft body tight against his and her delicious, enticing scent momentarily distracted him despite the imminent danger they suddenly found themselves in.

Footsteps clomped against the hardwood floor, then suddenly stopped. "What the—"

"Where is she?" This was another voice, deeper with a more gravelly timbre than the first.

Noah could hear the two men as they began moving through the living room and dining area, then down the hallway, clearly searching the rooms for Valentina.

In the darkness of the closet, Noah patted the dog's head to help keep him calm while also trying to give Maggie a reassuring squeeze. Even as he tried to soothe them both through these actions, he was terrified. He had no idea what he'd do if they were discovered.

The two men now stood in the hallway just outside the bedroom where they hid.

"Do you think it's the boyfriend? Did he do something to her?" This was gravel voice.

"I don't know." A long pause. "Something doesn't feel right about all this though. Something's off."

"No kidding, Nick!" Gravel's voice was sarcastic. "The place is trashed, Tina's missing, and she's not answering her cell!"

"That's not what I mean," the man called Nick replied in a growl. "First, there was the whole thing with Clarissa claiming she knew nothing about any bachelorette party vacation. And now..." There was another long pause, then, "We need to give Dom an update. We'll start with that and go from there."

The sound of the two men's footsteps grew quieter as they made their way back through the condo and then out the front door.

Noah continued patting the dog and kept his arm firmly around Maggie. "Just wait." He breathed the words, not trusting that the two intruders were truly gone.

Eventually, all that remained was an eerie stillness.

Several long moments of silence passed before Noah finally whispered, "I think it's safe to get out of here now."

Slowly, he turned the door handle of the closet and swung it open. The three of them stepped out of the closet, and he heard Maggie let out her breath at the same time that he did.

Boon looked up at them accusingly.

"I'm sorry, buddy!" Noah said, giving the dog a scratch behind his flopped-over ear. I know you've got to be sick of that closet." The pup seemed to accept his apology without hesitation, offering a quick lick in response.

Maggie was still visibly shaking. She moved over to sink onto the bed, covering her face with her hands.

"Are you okay?" Noah said softly.

"No, I'm not okay!" she hissed, still keeping her voice quiet. "Who were those men?"

Noah looked helpless.

"Arrrghh!" Maggie groaned, shaking her head and frowning. "I can't even believe this is happening. Do you think we should—" Her words were abruptly cut off as Boon suddenly jumped up onto the bed and climbed onto Maggie, forcing her backward on the bed by laying his furry body across hers.

Maggie was only a smidgeon over five feet tall. Her bare legs and sandal-clad feet dangled over the edge of the bed as she lay there sputtering protests at the dog's fervent attempts to lick her face.

Noah choked down his urge to laugh at the sight of tiny Maggie lying there beneath an eighty-pound dog who looked like a thick, fuzzy blanket thrown over the top of her.

He approached the bed, about to make a joke. But instead, Noah felt conflicting emotions swell inside him as he looked down at her. She was so undeniably beautiful, her amber eyes wide, golden curls splayed out across the bed, framing her delicate features. She took his breath away. And part of him wanted to tell her so. But a much bigger part of him held back, uncertain how his words would be received.

While he stood there, Maggie made several failed attempts to move the massive dog off her prone body, her face growing red with effort. Finally, she looked at the frozen Noah. "Uh...a little help, please?"

"Oh, sorry!" He snapped out of his reverie and picked up Boon's leash. "C'mon, boy, off!"

Boon instantly obeyed, jumping back onto the floor. He sat down quietly next to Noah as if nothing unusual had happened. But he was still watching Maggie, and she was eyeing him back with uncertainty.

"What was that about?" she said.

"I dunno. Maybe he thought you could use a hug?" Noah offered.

"Hmph." Maggie stood up and began brushing the dog fur off her dress. "What I was going to say is, do you think we should call the police?"

"Oh. Uhhh..."

She looked up, clearly surprised at his reaction. "I mean, it's clear that Valentina is missing, right?"

Noah nodded slowly.

"And it's also clear that something," she waved her hand to encompass the entire condo, "er, bad happened here..." she trailed off.

Something bad. Right. Noah didn't need to hear her say out loud what they were both thinking. *What if he'd done something to Valentina?*

Now, it was his turn to sink onto the bed.

"Are you sure you can't remember anything from last night?" Maggie asked, genuine concern etched on her face.

He closed his eyes and ran a hand through his already mussed-up hair. Then he looked up at her. "I remember meeting Valentina at Lakeside Latté yesterday at three-thirty. We had coffee, and I remember thinking that our date wasn't going so great. But then..." Here he frowned.

"Then what?" Maggie said.

"Then..." He squeezed his eyes shut for several long moments before opening them and lifting his palms. "Then nothing. It's just a big blank."

Maggie stood looking at him, lips compressed as she thought. He felt helpless, wishing he could ease the worry he saw flickering in her eyes. Several long moments ticked past. Finally, keeping her eye on Boon, she eased herself down to sit beside him on the edge of the bed.

"Noah," she said, her voice quiet. "I know what you're thinking, but there's no way you did anything harmful to Valentina."

"You don't know that. I told you I can't remember anything. What if I..." He couldn't finish the sentence.

"Noah, you are the kindest person I've ever known. Remember when you stood up to that mammoth-sized senior in the cafeteria during our junior year? He was bullying that super skinny kid from the Robotics team, and you stepped in the middle of it all, separating them. Then the jerk started threatening you, pushing you, trying to get you to fight with him. Yet somehow, without resorting to anything physical, you managed to completely defuse the situation. You even had the guy apologizing to the kid by the end of it all." She shook her head in wonder. "You were amazing, Noah. And I just don't believe the man who did that would ever willingly hurt another soul. It just wouldn't happen."

Noah was in shock. Not only did he not recall the situation Maggie had just described, but he was stunned by the fact that she was able to recall it in such detail.

He turned his head to face her and met soft, brown eyes that were now gazing at him in a way that made his heart beat faster in his chest. He wished he didn't have any doubts himself. But with no memory of what he'd said or done, anything could have happened.

He knew, however, that what Maggie was suggesting was the right thing to do. And normally, he wouldn't have hesitated, especially considering the fact that his brother Wade and new sister-in-law Cassie were both on the Whispering Pines police force. But as of two days ago, they weren't in town or even in the country. Cassie had joined the force a year ago, and she'd finally earned enough vacation so they could go on their two-week honeymoon to Greece. Without Wade in his corner, he felt much more nervous about involving the police, particularly in light of his apparent amnesia.

He took a deep breath. "Look, I know we need to call the police, but I'd like to make another phone call first."

Maggie tilted her head quizzically. "To whom?"

"A man named Hugo Garcia."

Hugo stood in the busted-out doorway of the small condo wearing a very similar expression to the one Maggie had worn when she'd first arrived. However, he recovered more quickly than she had.

Noah watched as Hugo's gaze swept the room with a practiced eye, then returned to examine Noah's appearance for the second time.

Hugo was his brother Wade's former beat partner and a close family friend. He was in his late fifties and had retired from the police force a year ago to spend more time with his newly adopted teenage daughter, Ani. Noah decided to call Hugo before contacting the police because he knew the situation didn't look good for him, and he also knew he could completely trust Hugo.

Noah noticed that Hugo had lost a bit of weight since the last time he'd seen him, no longer sporting the rounded belly on his stocky frame. He still wore his thick salt-and-pepper hair in a short, cropped style, and as usual, despite the circumstances, his dark eyes were kind.

"Okay, *amigo*, tell me what happened," Hugo said.

Noah related everything he'd already shared with Maggie, who now stood silently by his side, her hand absently petting the top of Boon's head.

"And the door?" Hugo asked, glancing back at the splintered doorframe.

Maggie shared that bit of the story, describing how they'd hidden in the bedroom closet and everything that they'd overheard the men say to each other. Hugo pulled out his phone and tapped out notes into it.

When Noah and Maggie had both finished, Hugo gave a nod, then pulled out a pair of blue latex gloves and put them on his hands. "Stay here," he ordered. "I'm going to do an inspection of the place."

Noah, Maggie, and Boon stood in silence while Hugo made his meticulous way through each room.

Twenty minutes later, he returned to them. "Well, there's a few things that don't add up. First of all, Valentina's closet is full of newly purchased clothing with the tags still on them. It doesn't look like she's ever worn anything hanging in there. Second, aside from this room," he waved a hand to indicate the space where they stood, "this place is neat as a pin. There's only one roll of toilet paper in the bathroom, and quite honestly, judging by the layers of dust everywhere, it doesn't look like anyone actually lives here."

Noah frowned and saw a similar look of perplexity on Maggie's face.

Hugo removed his gloves and shoved them into the pockets of his jeans. "Plus, aside from the photograph in the bedroom and a couple of items in the fridge, I don't see any personal items for Valentina anywhere. No purse, no cell phone, no pens, no paper, nothing."

Noah's frown deepened. "What does all that mean?"

Hugo gave a shrug. "I don't know yet." Then he looked at Boon. "Another thing, I doubt that's her dog. If it is, she has no dog supplies here at all, either. No food or dog dishes."

"His tag only has his name on it," Noah offered absently, his mind whirring.

"There are a lot of unanswered questions here," Hugo said. "Not the least of which is why you have no memory of what happened." Hugo pointed his chin in the direction of the partially drunk bottle of wine and glasses on the dining room table. "Because I know there's no way *that* was the cause."

Noah felt rather than saw Maggie's surprised look at him in response to Hugo's statement, but he said nothing. He felt overwhelmed, frustrated, and if he was being totally honest, a little scared. He had no idea what his next step should be, and although the nausea had now abated, the ache in his head was getting stronger. He lifted his fingertips to his temples.

"What's that?" Hugo's voice was sharp.

"What?"

"That!" Hugo reached for Noah's right hand and flipped it palm-side down. There was a smudge of dark blue ink on the back of his hand in a roughly rectangular shape with some illegible words printed inside it.

Noah looked at it in surprise. "I feel like...there's something familiar about it, but I'm not sure." He stared at it in confusion another moment, then with a resigned sigh, resumed massaging his temples.

"So, what do you think we should do now?" Maggie asked.

"To be honest, I think your first instinct was the right one, Ms. Milena," Hugo replied. "We need to call the police."

Chapter 4

Noah's heart sank. "I'm going to jail, aren't I." It wasn't a question.

A small smile tugged at one corner of Hugo's mouth. "Probably not today, *hermano*."

"Is that because of the rule about waiting twenty-four hours before someone is officially considered missing?" Maggie asked.

Hugo's smile broadened. "That's a bit of a myth, Ms. Milena."

"Please, just call me Maggie. And really?"

"Yes, Maggie. While it's true that a police department may wait to take your report about a suspected missing person, that doesn't apply to people suspected of being a victim of foul play, which is potentially what we're dealing with here."

Noah groaned.

Hugo gripped Noah's shoulder and gave him a reassuring look. "Don't worry. At least not yet. Like I said, there's a lot of things I'm seeing here that just don't add up. For all we know, Valentina left of her own accord. But first, we need some officers to really comb this place for evidence. The police will also contact Valentina's family and friends to see if anyone has heard from her."

Hugo's gaze swung between them, "As a matter of fact, have either of you tried calling her?"

"I don't have her number," Noah mumbled.

Hugo looked confused. "I thought you had a date with her last night?"

"I did, but..." Noah's face reddened. "It was a setup by a matchmaking service."

"My matchmaking service," Maggie said. "Matches by Maggie. But it's our policy not to share personal information such as phone numbers or addresses with our clients. We simply arrange their first date, and after that, it's up to them what they feel comfortable sharing."

"Ahhh." Hugo's face cleared.

"I have her number," Maggie added, pulling her cell phone out of her purse. She made a few taps on her screen and then held the phone to her ear.

Her hopeful expression turned to dismay a few seconds later. "Her voicemail is full."

With a grim expression, Hugo pulled out his own cell phone and placed a call to the Whispering Pines Police Department.

It wasn't long before two officers arrived. Noah, Maggie, and Hugo answered all their questions. It was particularly frustrating for Noah to realize how little he could recall about the previous evening, including how he'd ended up in Valentina's condo.

After they were questioned, the officers had the three of them wait near the entrance while they examined each room, took photographs, lifted fingerprints, and packaged up the wine and glasses.

Finally, the officers finished and everyone stepped outside while one officer placed a bright yellow police banner over the condo's front door.

A feeling of unreality washed over Noah as one officer told him not to leave town. He let Noah know they might need to bring him into the station for more questioning. Then the officers left them all to go speak with the management team of the complex.

"Look, I've got to go pick up Ani," Hugo said, glancing at his watch. "But I'll keep you updated on the investigation."

Noah's expression was bleak.

Hugo gave him a pat on the back. "Don't sweat it, Noah. Our police force may be small, but they're a smart bunch. I'm sure they'll find Valentina alive and well."

"And if they don't?"

"We'll cross that bridge when we come to it. In the meantime, you should probably go get checked by a doctor to figure out why you can't remember anything. Maybe it has something to do with that bruise on your face. Maybe you hit your head last night."

"Yeah, I guess," Noah mumbled. Then Hugo bid them both farewell and headed toward the parking lot.

Maggie turned to face Noah. "Hugo's right," she said, a look of concern on her face.

"I know. But, Maggie, all I want to do right now is find Valentina."

"I get it. I feel the same way."

"Maybe if I try retracing my steps from last night…"

"But you only remember the start of your date at the coffee shop," Maggie said. "And that's the only thing I arranged for you, so I don't have any additional information either."

"Well, I can start there, at least. Maybe I said something to Olivia, or maybe she'll remember something."

He was referring to the friendly owner of Lakeside Latté, Whispering Pines' most popular coffee shop.

Noah looked down at Boon. He'd taken the dog's leash back from Maggie when they'd exited the condo. "What am I going to do with you, though?"

The dog cocked his head, looking up at him with liquid brown eyes.

Noah sighed deeply and slid a sideways glance at Maggie. Her brows were furrowed, and there was a little crinkle over her nose. This was a familiar sight to Noah from back when they were in high school. He recalled how the crinkle always appeared whenever she was deep in thought. Despite the stressful situation, she looked absolutely adorable, and Noah felt an overpowering urge to lean over and kiss that crinkle away. He cleared his throat. "Look, Maggie, I'm really sorry about all of this. And I want you to know how much I appreciate you coming so quickly when I called this morning. I hate that I ended up involving you."

"Don't be silly! Of course I'm involved. We're friends, Noah. And besides, all this happened while you were on a Matches by Maggie date. I care about you and Valentina. I need to know that you're both okay. Besides, like Hugo said, we don't even know exactly what happened yet."

He was touched by her efforts to keep a positive spin on it all. But as he looked back up at the yellow tape draped across Valentina's door, he couldn't quite shake a feeling of impending doom. He sighed. "Well, I guess we should go now."

"Do you need a ride?" Maggie asked.

"Uh...maybe?" He frowned and glanced toward the condo parking lot. "Like I told the police, I know I drove to the coffee shop for the start of the date. But I have no memory of driving here last night. And it's scary to think I might have." He ran a hand over his face. "But man! I really hope my car is here."

"Let's go see," Maggie said.

The two of them walked along the sidewalk that led to the small lot in the back of the building. The neatly painted white lines offered enough spaces for about two dozen cars. Noah's eyes swept over the colorful array of parked vehicles. He should have been able to easily spot his Trailblazer, but he didn't see it.

He frowned and dug his hand into the pocket of his pants to pull out the key to his car. He planned to hit the lock button so his headlights would light up. Instead, what he found in his hand was a slim, black key fob with a fancy red-and-gold logo etched into the top of it. "What the—"

Maggie looked down at his hand and then back at his face with a surprised look. "Seriously? You drive a Porsche?"

Noah's eyes were wide. "No, I don't drive a Porsche!"

She arched a brow. "Then why does your key fob have the Porsche logo on it?"

"I don't—"

She quickly pressed her fingertips against his lips. "Please don't say 'I don't know' again!"

He couldn't resist smiling at her beneath the light pressure of her fingers, but then returned his gaze to the mysterious key fob. Giving a little shrug, he lifted it and aimed it toward the lot full of cars. He saw lights flash from the middle of the lot.

He pulled Boon along as he immediately started walking toward it, Maggie trailing behind them. He arrived at the spot where the lights had flashed and stopped short, Maggie bumping into him.

She stepped around him and then sucked in her breath. "Nice!" she breathed, walking toward the sleek, silver Porsche 911 Turbo S Cabriolet. Noah stood frozen, his mouth hanging open.

Maggie pressed her face against the tinted window. "I can't see anything," she said.

Recovering, Noah hit the unlock button, and she pulled open the passenger-side door. "Oooh, I wouldn't have pegged you for a red-leather interior kind of guy."

"I'm not!" Noah protested as she slipped into the passenger seat. "Maggie, this is *not* my car."

He circled the car like it was a dangerous animal about to strike. What was he doing with the keys to this Porsche in his pocket? And where was his car?

He took in the vehicle's sleek lines and pristine condition, finally stopping at the hood to stare down at the unmistakable Porsche shield emblem with the prancing black horse at its center. It perfectly matched the one on the key fob he held in his hand.

Still holding Boon's leash, he walked back to the driver's side door, commanded the dog to sit, and slid in beside Maggie. She was busy rifling through the glove box.

"I don't understand," Noah said, shaking his head. "I promise you that I do not own this Porsche."

Maggie was studying one of the documents that she'd pulled from the glove box. Then she glanced up at him, brows slightly raised. "Um, apparently you do."

"What?"

"Read these," she said, handing several pieces of paper to him.

Noah's mouth fell open again as he flipped through the registration, insurance, and title papers to the car, all clearly showing one Noah Riley as the owner.

"I bought a Porsche last night?" he shouted.

Suddenly Boon, who had been sitting quietly next to the open driver's side door, leaped into the car and onto Noah's lap. He filled the entire front of the vehicle as he pressed his large body against Noah, his doggie face now eye-to-eye with Maggie.

"Boon!" Noah exclaimed, getting a mouthful of fur. "What are you doing? Get down, boy! Off!"

A lot of wriggling, twisting, and nudging ensued, resulting in Boon eventually sitting in the tiny, low-slung back seat, his furry head poking between Maggie and Noah in the front.

"Start it up!" Maggie said, her face flushed with excitement.

Noah hesitated, uncertain. But then he reluctantly obeyed, and the engine purred to life. His eyes moved from the standard tachometer centered behind the steering wheel to the glowing digital displays that showed speed and car status information floating along each side of it.

Maggie instantly tapped at the large touchscreen that lit up in the center of the instrument panel. She scrolled through options for navigation, entertainment, and vehicle settings. She tapped a button and gave a delighted squeal as the atmospheric drums and heavy bass of a dubstep tune poured through the Bose surround sound system. She started swaying to the beat in her seat before catching Noah's eye. He was staring at her.

"I'm glad you're enjoying this," he said.

Maggie looked back at him, barely managing an apologetic look. "I'm sorry, but...c'mon! We're in a Porsche!"

"But where is *my* car?" he said. "And don't say this is my car!" he quickly added when he saw her open her mouth.

She closed it.

He shut his eyes and leaned back against the soft leather of the deep bucket seat. He tried to deep breathe and think. But it was useless, his memory of last night was still a blank slate. And his headache was pounding out a relentless drumbeat against his temples. When he opened his eyes, he found a genuinely contrite Maggie looking back at him.

"I really am sorry," she said. "I can't imagine all you must be feeling right now. I know you said you want to try and retrace your steps to find Valentina. I want to help."

Noah sighed, then sat back up and shook his head. "It could be dangerous, Maggie. Think about what happened with those guys breaking into—" She held up a hand, cutting him off.

"I *want* to help! This matters to me, too, Noah. Valentina was my client, and I'm just as concerned about what might have happened to her. Let me help you retrace your steps."

He looked uncertain. "Are you sure?"

"Absolutely."

He surveyed the Porsche's stylish interior, still trying to process how it was possible that this luxury vehicle had somehow ended up in his possession. Despite his reservations, he let out a resigned sigh.

"Okay then," he said with reluctance, and started to adjust the mirrors. "I guess we should start with a visit to Lakeside Latté. You can follow me in your car."

"Uh…"

He looked over at her. "What?"

"Don't you think maybe you should change first?"

He'd completely forgotten about his disheveled appearance and blood-stained shirt. He glanced at his face in the rearview mirror and groaned. "Yeah, I guess that's probably a good idea."

"Look, my car is over there." She indicated an old burgundy Subaru a few rows away. "I'll drive home and get Valentina's file info off my computer while you go freshen up. Then maybe you can pick me up at my place?"

"What about him?" Noah said as Boon once again poked his head through the gap between their seats, his exploration of the back seats apparently complete.

"I think we should just keep him with us for now," Maggie said, leaning sideways to avoid his probing wet nose. "I mean, maybe Hugo's wrong and Boon really is Valentina's dog. He might even be a help."

Noah glanced between her and the dog with a doubtful look, then gave a little shrug. "Okay, it sounds like a plan."

Chapter 5

The printer in Maggie's apartment spat out the final page of Valentina Romano's interview results. Maggie lifted out the stack of paper and began scanning pages for any potential information that might serve as a clue to Valentina's whereabouts. Seconds later, her phone buzzed.

She glanced at the screen and smiled at the name lighting it up.

"Hey, girlfriend," she said, answering it. "I've got you on speakerphone."

"Why? Is my dad there?" The voice of her best friend since elementary school, Jaime, filled the room.

"No, he doesn't normally work on Saturdays."

When Maggie had officially started her matchmaking service a couple of years ago, Jaime had begged Maggie to hire her father, George Fairfax. Not that the reserved gentleman had any real knowledge of or interest in the matchmaking business, but he'd been floundering with what to do with his life after losing Jaime's mom to heart disease. As a retired corporate executive, his business acumen and financial knowledge had been a huge help to Maggie as he took on the role of her company's business manager. There was also the added bonus that for now, he was willing to work without pay.

"You'd better not be working either, missy," Jaime said in her best mom voice, making Maggie smile. "I was calling to see if you wanted to meet for lunch. I need a break from your precious, little namesake here, so Jack is going to watch her for a few hours."

Jaime was referring to one-year-old Emma, Jaime and her husband Jack's little girl.

Maggie laughed. "Since my name is Maggie, I'm not sure if Emma qualifies as my namesake."

"You have and always will be an 'Emma' to me!" Jaime said, referring to Maggie's college nickname. It was based on the title character of the popular

Jane Austen novel who fancied herself a matchmaker. Although, Maggie had found much greater success than Jane Austen's quirky character ever did.

Jaime and Jack Knightly had been one of Maggie's best success stories. Jack was a well-established nerd who hadn't even had a dream of a chance with her gorgeous blond friend. Until Maggie that is. Maggie had seen the relationship potential when they were all in college together, and she'd used her skills to successfully connect the two of them.

Maggie sighed. "I'd really love to meet you, my friend, but I can't. I've got a crisis on my hands."

"What crisis?"

Maggie proceeded to tell Jaime about everything that had happened that morning.

"No way!" Jaime cried. "That all sounds more like one of my true crime podcasts than real life. And are you talking about *the* Noah Riley? Like your super-secret crush from high school, Noah Riley? As in the 'he's so hot, but he doesn't think of me that way' Noah Riley?"

"Cut it out!" Even though Maggie was alone in her apartment, she felt her face redden. "And yes, that Noah."

"What are you going to do?"

"We've got to find her, Jaime. I'm freaking out! You know I can't afford any more bad press. It's been hard enough getting my business off the ground while battling against those random bad social media reviews that keep popping up."

"Have you figured out which of your clients is leaving them?"

"No, it's so strange," Maggie said. "You know I always ask for feedback from every client. And unless someone is lying to me, so far, everyone has been really pleased with the process and the results."

"Of course they have," her friend answered loyally. "Just keep doing what you're doing, Maggie. You're bound to overcome a few negative comments."

"Unless one of my clients ends up...murdered." Maggie could barely get the last word out.

"I'm sure that won't be the case. That police officer was probably right and she just went off somewhere on her own. You'll find her."

"I hope so."

After promising to get together soon, they disconnected. Maggie resumed her perusal of Valentina's file but didn't find anything enlightening. She looked at her phone again to check the time and realized that Noah would be returning for her soon. She stuffed the pages into a file folder and then ran into the bathroom to check her appearance.

For her morning appointment, she'd selected a pretty, sky-blue summer dress. She knew it complimented her figure well. The length was short without being too short—showing off just the right amount of leg.

She freshened up her eye makeup and lip color, then critically analyzed the mass of blond corkscrew curls that framed her face and hung past her shoulders. Dampening her fingertips, she twirled a few of them to smooth out the frizz that had developed during her morning adventure with Noah. She thought about exchanging her understated necklace and earrings for something a bit more flashy but then gave herself a mental smack. *What was she doing? This wasn't a date. It was a rescue mission. Keep your head in the game, Milena!*

But doing that was going to be quite the challenge around gorgeous Noah Riley. He was even better looking now than he'd been in high school. And he could still make her heart skip a beat when he turned those smoky gray eyes in her direction.

Not that he ever knew.

Even though they'd become close friends in high school, he'd spent most of his time jamming with his band and hanging out with his fellow music-loving friends—always with a different girl on his arm—while she'd ultimately wasted her time trying to make her long-term relationship with Joe work. She shook her head at the memory. She'd been loyal to a fault with Joe. No matter how many times he'd cheated on her, she'd always caved and taken him back, determined to make it work.

When she'd finally found the courage to break up with Joe for good during their senior year, it was Noah who had brought her solace. He'd stumbled across her in an empty classroom with tears streaming down her face. Without words, he'd pulled her into a tight embrace and allowed her to cry until she'd run dry.

"I just thought if I tried hard enough, showed him enough love, I could make it work. Make us work," Maggie had confessed between sobs. "I feel like such a failure."

"Oh, Mags," Noah had said, pulling back so he could look down into her tear-stained face. "This is not on you. You are not a failure. True love should never be one-sided, where one person has to constantly fight to keep it alive. It should be effortless, like slipping on silk or gliding on waves. And it should make your soul sing, not weep in the quiet corners of empty classrooms."

Maggie had smiled through her tears. "That sounds like the lyrics to one of your songs."

Noah had grinned at that, gently wiping away her tears with his thumbs. Then his face had grown serious. "Joe is a total narcissist, Maggie. He never treated you the way you deserved. To be totally honest, he's not good enough for you. You are worthy of...so much more than someone like him could possibly give."

She'd almost imagined a choked sound to Noah's voice when he'd said that last bit. And when she'd lifted her head to look back up at him, she saw something enigmatic glimmering in the depths of his eyes.

Over the next several months, they started spending more and more time together. Going out "just as friends." And it wasn't long before Maggie realized that her feelings for Noah ran much deeper than friendship. Maybe they had for a long time. But she'd been too wrapped up in trying to make her broken relationship work to notice.

Just before graduation, she'd finally decided to risk their friendship by telling Noah how she felt. She'd talked Jaime into coming with her to attend his band's final gig before summer vacation, determined to talk with him at the end of the performance. But when a girl from his band wrapped her body around his and put him in a lip lock in the middle of the performance, she realized how ridiculous her idea was. He'd always been a good friend, but he'd never made a move beyond that. It was clear that he just wasn't interested in her in that way. The crowd had cheered like crazy at the kiss, and any hope she'd had of a romantic relationship with Noah evaporated with that applause.

After that, he'd left town for the summer and she'd begun distancing herself from him because she knew that she could never go back to being just friends with him again. Then in the fall, they'd headed off to different colleges, providing the perfect opportunity to simply drift apart. It was painful at first to ignore his texts and emails. But after a while, they stopped coming, and she tried to forget about him and move on with her life.

Needless to say, she was shocked when he'd turned up requesting her matchmaking services. She doubted any woman around was immune to his charms and still couldn't believe that he needed any help in that department.

Plus, finding the perfect woman for the man she had been in love with was about the last thing she wanted to do. But she squelched her personal feelings, determined to be a true professional with him and do her job.

The ring of her doorbell snapped her sharply out of her memories.

She gave herself one final glance in the mirror and then ran to the door. Swinging it wide, she sucked in a quiet breath as the handsome face of her imaginings looked down at her. He definitely cleaned up well. His deep, gray eyes were fringed with thick, dark lashes that most women would envy. The light bruise on his cheekbone didn't do anything to detract from the strength of his chiseled jawline or the tantalizing dimple at the center of his chin, which almost seemed to beg for a kiss. His dark curls were still damp from his shower and combed back from his face. And he'd changed into a pair of jeans and a navy blue polo shirt.

"Can I come in?"

"What?" She felt a little dazed. "Oh, sorry! Yes, of course." She moved back and he stepped inside, filling her small entrance with his lean, muscular frame.

She walked over to her kitchen table and picked up the file with Valentina's paperwork. "I've gone through it but I didn't find anything helpful."

He looked disappointed. "Well then, I guess the best thing for us to do is 'begin at the beginning,' as Lewis Carroll famously wrote."

"You know *Alice in Wonderland?*" she said with surprise.

"Sure," he said with a grin. "I may not have been as brainy as you were in high school, but I love a lot of the classics. And you have to admit, it's an appropriate story for where I'm at mentally right now."

She laughed. "Okay, let me grab my purse, and we can begin at the beginning with Lakeside Latté."

They pulled into the small parking lot of the popular Whispering Pines icon. It was full of cars, as usual.

Noah pulled out a black extendable leash from the center console storage area and, twisting in his seat, reached behind to attach it to Boon's collar.

"Where'd you get that?" Maggie asked.

"My family are a bunch of dog people. I borrowed it from one of my brothers. I know this place is dog friendly, so we can just bring him inside with us."

Maggie remembered that Noah had two brothers—one older, one younger—and that it had been his brother Jake's wife, Alex, who had contacted her on Noah's behalf to arrange for the matchmaking service. Jake and Noah looked a lot alike, both tall and lean with that dark, curly hair. The main difference was that where Jake's eyes were almost black in color, Noah's were a soft gray that seemed to change shades depending on his mood.

As the three of them walked toward the door, Boon easily kept pace. The graceful way his long, slim body moved reminded Maggie of a gazelle. She smiled as Noah quickly scooted behind her so that he could reach to open the door for her. Once they stepped inside the cozy shop, Maggie breathed in the delicious aroma of fresh-brewed coffee and baked goods. She hoped Noah didn't hear her stomach rumble in response. In her morning rush to Noah's aid, she hadn't been able to finish her pastry or even her mug of coffee.

The shop walls were exposed brick and shiny metal piping ran along the ceiling overhead. A polished wooden floor gleamed beneath cozy groupings of overstuffed chairs and low tables. Pendant lights with warmly lit Edison bulbs hung down over rectangular high-top tables that lined both walls. Almost every space was filled with people sipping beverages, chatting or working on laptops.

Lakeside Latté was the most popular coffee shop in town, thanks in large part to the warm, welcoming personality of its owner, Olivia Wooldridge. Maggie often chose it as the location for morning and early afternoon dates that she arranged for her clients due to its comfortable vibe. Olivia was a third-generation citizen of Whispering Pines. She knew pretty much everyone in town, and everyone knew her. She was always a great source of information concerning anything happening in the area.

Maggie led the way toward the back of the shop, passing by glass cases filled with the source of the delicious baking aromas.

"Hi, Olivia," Noah and Maggie said in unison.

The full-figured brunette shop owner laughed from behind the cash register. "How's it going, you two? Especially you!" She lifted a brow and smirked at Noah.

"Why did you say it like that?" Noah asked with a slight frown as he sat down on a stool in front of the counter. Just then, Boon poked his head over the countertop. Both of his pointed ears were standing straight up at attention now, his black nose wriggling as he inhaled the delicious, new smells.

"Well, hello to you, pretty boy," Olivia said, distracted from answering. She reached across the counter to pat Boon on the head and scratch him behind his ears. The dog closed his eyes in bliss. "Is he yours?" she asked Noah.

"Er, no," he said awkwardly. "It's kind of a long story."

Olivia looked up, quizzical. "Anything to do with yesterday afternoon?"

"Maybe? But before we explain," Noah said, "can I get one of your delicious café lattes with oat milk and an Asiago cheese bagel with cream cheese? I feel like I need caffeine and protein." He turned to Maggie. "Would you like coffee or anything?"

"Actually, that would be wonderful! I'd love one of your cinnamon rolls and a caramel mocha with two extra pumps of caramel, please."

Noah stared at her for a beat.

"What?"

"That's not coffee, Maggie. That's dessert."

"What can I say, I like sweet things."

"Maybe that's why you're so sweet," Olivia laughed, pulling on a pair of gloves and turning to fill their orders.

"Thanks, Olivia," Maggie said, flashing Noah a smug look. "Now, about yesterday, can we ask you some questions concerning anything you remember about the date Noah had here?"

"Sure!" she said as her hands worked the espresso machine. "But give me a bit, I have another worker coming in, in about fifteen or twenty minutes, and I can take a short break then."

Noah, Maggie, and Boon stepped aside as some new customers approached the counter to place their orders.

Noah still held onto Boon's leash, so Maggie grabbed their orders when they came up. "We should get a table," she suggested.

"I noticed a couple of empty ones outside when we walked in," Noah said.

They walked back through the shop and outside to claim the table. The late-June sunshine bathed the area in light and warmth, and Boon lay down comfortably on the ground beside them.

Noah held out a chair for Maggie before slipping into the one across from her. She recalled how even back in high school, he'd exhibited old-fashioned gentlemanly manners like this. She knew some women might find it offensive. But in truth, she liked it. It made her feel special. A breeze ruffled the now-dry curls on top of his head and when he turned his eyes on her, her breath caught in her chest. There was an inexplicable heat and intensity in the way he looked at her. It made her feel as if he could see right through her.

She took a sip of her drink and decided to change the direction of her thoughts by slipping into one of her most comfortable roles: the professional interviewer.

She cleared her throat. "So, Noah, I know all about your dating history, of course." She was surprised to note a light flush suffuse his cheeks at her mention of this, but she continued. "But I'm wondering, what inspired you to make your recent move from Grand Rapids to Whispering Pines?"

Noah had already polished off nearly half his bagel. He followed it up with a long swallow of coffee before responding. "I moved here in part because of my brothers' and grandfather's nagging," he grinned. "But in all honesty, it didn't take much persuading. I've always loved this area. Even though, as you know, we grew up in Grand Rapids, we spent every summer here with our grandparents for as long as I can remember."

"Your whole family?"

He shifted in his seat. "No, just me and my brothers, Jake and Wade. You remember that my mom died when I was pretty young?"

She nodded.

"Well, it was really after that. It kind of became a tradition. My dad was always really busy with his construction business. I think he felt he didn't have the time—or if I'm being completely honest, the interest—in spending time with us the way our mom had."

Maggie frowned at this.

"But hey, I managed to grow up all right, didn't I?" Noah seemed to rush to lighten the mood. "I mean, I know it wasn't great on my dad's part." He looked away. "I feel like he just never really got over my mom's death. And his solution was to bury himself in his work. But I had my brothers and my grandparents, and we're all pretty close."

Maggie nodded with understanding.

"Anyway, both Jake and Wade have moved here. They really wanted all three of us to be together again and near Pops, our grandfather. Our Nana died several years ago and Pops remarried a wonderful local woman. It's been really good to live near family again."

He closed his eyes and tipped his face toward the sun, taking in a deep breath. "Plus, I really do love this town with incredible Lake Michigan right here and the state park with its acres and acres of trails and sand dunes. And, of course, the people here are great." He opened his eyes and winked at her. "So, once I started my business, my brothers knew I was able to work remotely from anywhere, and I had no excuse not to join them here in Whispering Pines. So here I am."

Maggie dabbed at the remaining crumbs of her cinnamon roll. "I know from the forms you filled out that your business involves marketing, but what exactly do you do?"

He gave her a sort of shy smile. "There's a bit of a story to it if you really want to know."

"I do!"

"Well, as you likely recall from when we were in high school, I've always been into music."

An image of the last time she'd heard him perform—and the girl kissing him—popped into her mind. This time the light flush was staining her own cheeks. She hoped he didn't notice. And she shoved the memory away.

He continued. "I actually developed my love of music from spending time here with my Nana. She was a gifted pianist and she gave me lessons whenever we stayed with them over the summer. My mother played as well, so we had a piano at our house in Grand Rapids, too. I would practice on it during the school year. It sort of helped me feel a connection with my mom, just knowing that her fingers had once touched the same keys."

Maggie noticed how Noah's eyes grew a little misty as he shared this memory. But then he refocused his gaze on her. "Over time, I expanded into other instruments, like guitar, saxophone, and drums. I had dreams of making it big one day. By the time I got to college, though, I realized that making it as a professional musician probably wasn't in my cards. However, music has remained a passion of mine. So, after a few years in the corporate world, I eventually figured out a way to combine what I love with my experience in marketing."

"How so?" Maggie asked, tilting her head.

"I now provide freelance marketing services for a couple of venture capital firms that specialize in investing in music tech startups. The startups are run by techies who believe in their products and hope to get acquired by name brand companies. But they're not marketers. I help them create a marketing strategy. And I write a lot of their marketing content for them, like website copy, ebooks, customer success stories, stuff like that."

"That's unique," Maggie commented, taking a sip of her caramel mocha. "Definitely not your run-of-the-mill marketing job."

"Nope." Noah flashed her a dazzling smile.

Maggie smiled back. "So, do you still make music?"

"Mostly just for my own pleasure," Noah said. "Although, thanks to my grandfather's bragging, I've been able to play a few gigs at some local venues here in town. But that's about the extent of it, besides volunteering for Whispering Pines JAMZ."

"What's that?"

"A music school for lower-income kids in the area. We work with young kids up to older teens, anyone who has musical aspirations, regardless of skill level, age, or musical ability. I firmly believe everyone can use more music in their lives."

"That sounds fantastic," she said, genuinely impressed. "I'm sure the kids love it." This was the Noah she remembered from high school. Kind and thoughtful, always doing things to help others. It warmed her heart to see he hadn't changed much in that regard.

"They do," Noah said with a grin. "And I have to admit, I love it too. It gives me such a great feeling to see their faces light up when they learn something new or accomplish something they didn't think was possible."

Listening to him, Maggie couldn't help but admire him even more. Not only was he talented, an entrepreneur, and incredibly good-looking, but he had a big heart as well. She wondered why it was so difficult for him to find a woman who appreciated him for who he was.

"You know," Maggie said, peeking at him over the top of her coffee mug. "I always loved hearing your band play when we were in high school. I don't think I missed a single performance you gave. You guys were good!"

"You were a very supportive friend," Noah said.

She sighed inwardly at his use of the annoying "F" word.

"I still can't believe you took time out of your busy schedule of studying, tutoring, student counseling, and participating on the debate team to come hear little ol' me and my band play."

"I wasn't *that* busy," she mumbled, secretly flattered that he recalled all her former activities with such ease.

Noah laughed. "Yes, you were." At her expression, he rushed to add, "But that's a good thing! You were way more organized, motivated, and goal-oriented than I ever was. That's why I know your business will be a great success, Maggie. Despite this, er, setback."

Maggie sighed deeply and put her mug down. "I really hope you're right, Noah, for both of our sakes."

"Okay, your turn," he said. "Why matchmaking?"

She smiled and glanced away, unable to meet his eyes as she searched for the right way to explain it all. Finally, she said, "I guess I have a story, too. One that goes back to before we were in high school.

Noah's brows lifted at this.

"I'm sure you recall the tragic connection we share from our childhoods, how I lost both of my parents in a car accident when I was ten."

She glanced up briefly to see acknowledgment and sympathy reflected in Noah's eyes. But she dropped her gaze again to continue.

"From my earliest memories, my parents were always so in love with each other and with me. But everything changed dramatically for me after they died. I was sent to live with my aunt and uncle, whom I'm sure my parents thought would be the best guardians for me. But it wasn't a happy home. They had a terrible marriage and fought constantly. I never understood why they stayed together. It was a toxic environment completely devoid of love. To escape from it all, I began immersing myself in romance novels."

Noah smiled at this. "So, that's where your love for matchmaking came from?" he asked, intrigued.

"Partially," Maggie said. "Reading all those love stories sort of planted the seed. But then it kind of grew from there. You probably didn't know this, but in high school I successfully set up a few of my friends, and their relationships worked out surprisingly well. When I got to college, I had more successes and realized I had a knack for it. Even a passion for it. I encountered so many people struggling in unhappy relationships or unable to find love at all. And it was so fulfilling to help them find the same kind of loving connection that my parents had.

"Of course, at first, I never thought about trying to earn a living out of making love matches." She chuckled. "So, after graduating with my double major in human resources and psychology, I followed the traditional path and got a job at a large recruitment agency where I worked for a few years."

"Hmmm...isn't that kind of like matchmaking for businesses?" Noah said. "I mean you're matching the right people to the right companies."

Maggie laughed. "I suppose you're right. I never thought about it like that."

Noah's expression grew curious. "So, how did you make the shift from matchmaking for businesses to matchmaking for individuals?"

"Well," she said. "I became aware of how much my friends, and friends of friends, were struggling with online dating apps in their efforts to find the right person to share their lives with."

"Online dating is the worst!" Noah said.

"Exactly." Maggie leaned forward, her passion growing as she spoke. "Tech companies and algorithms are completely impersonal, plus they're not totally devoid of the biases of the programmers who create them. They can't measure chemistry or gut feelings or love connections. I just knew I could offer a more personalized and effective solution. So, after a few more success stories under my belt from playing matchmaker for friends, I did some research and ultimately took the plunge to turn it into a business venture."

"That's a great story," Noah said. "Your business is definitely not run-of-the-mill either. Before my sister-in-law Alex found your service, I thought real-life matchmakers were only for the rich and famous."

Maggie laughed.

Then Noah surprised her by reaching across the table and gently lifting her left hand. "What about you, though, Maggie? You've had success with so many couples now. Why don't I see a ring on your finger?"

She hoped he didn't notice the goosebumps that rippled up her arm as his warm fingers gently enveloped hers. She didn't respond right away as he continued holding her hand and gazing into her eyes with that blasted smoldering intensity again. His touch was so distracting that any response she could have mustered instantly flew out of her head.

"Oh, honey, I wouldn't if I were you!"

Maggie looked up to see a gorgeous strawberry-blond gazing down at their clasped hands.

"Excuse me?" Maggie said, quickly pulling her hand away.

"Hello, Susanna," Noah said. Maggie noticed that his face had turned a deep shade of crimson.

"Noah." Susanna nodded with a half-smile that didn't quite reach her eyes.

Maggie observed that Susanna was wearing a Lakeside Latté apron. She must have been the worker that Olivia was waiting for.

"Let me give you some free advice," Susanna said, her attention back on Maggie. "If you're hoping for a good time with someone who makes you feel interesting and special," she jerked a thumb toward Noah, "stay away from this one."

"Susanna, I already told you how sorry I was," Noah said. Impossibly, the flush on his face seemed to grow even darker. "It was an accident."

"Uh-huh." Susan was already turning away to head for the coffee shop entrance.

Maggie frowned. "What was that about?"

"I...uh, went out with her once after I moved here and...uh, sort of fell asleep while she was talking."

"What?"

"It really was an accident!" Noah cried. "I'd done an especially grueling weight workout earlier that day and I'd pulled a muscle. I accidentally took a pain medication that included an ingredient to help you fall asleep faster. It literally knocked me out."

Maggie's mouth was still hanging open when the coffee shop door opened and Olivia stepped outside. "Am I interrupting something?"

Maggie closed her mouth and cleared her throat. "No, no, of course not. We were just discussing business."

Olivia set her coffee down on their table and pulled a chair away from another empty table to sit on. She closed her eyes and took a sip of her coffee, then sighed with bliss. "Okay, I'm ready now. You said you have some questions about Noah's coffee date yesterday? Fire away!"

Noah seemed to have collected himself. "So, you remember me coming in with my date yesterday, right?"

"Yup, a hot brunette with the kind of figure other women would kill for? Hard to miss."

"Uh...right. Anyway, I remember we sat at a table near the register, right?"

Olivia nodded, taking another sip of her coffee.

"But after that, I have no memory of what happened."

Olivia set down her coffee cup. "Really? Like amnesia or something?"

"Yes," Noah said. "I can't remember anything about the date, what we talked about, where we went afterward, nothing."

"Wow, that's so bizarre!" Olivia's eyes were wide. "Sooo, does that have anything to do with why you're not sure what the story is about this sweet pup?"

Boon had risen and was resting his head on Olivia's lap to enjoy more of her ear scratching.

"That's right," Noah said. "Can you tell me anything about what happened on my date yesterday? Anything at all?"

"Well," Olivia looked off into space while she continued to run her hands over Boon's silky black and gold head. "The start of the date was typical for you. A complete disaster."

"What?" Maggie cried.

Olivia focused on her with a grin. "Ever since Noah moved to Whispering Pines, I've had the pleasure of witnessing him on a couple dates here, including one with Susanna." She tipped her head toward the shop. "They never seemed to go very well."

Noah's face was red once again. "Uh…could we forget about all that for now? Let's just focus on yesterday."

"Right, yesterday. Let's see…after you picked up your coffee orders, you sat down together at a table near me, just like you said. It looked like the conversation wasn't really flowing well because she wasn't really looking at you, and she was texting on her phone a lot. To your credit, Noah, it looked like you were really trying to engage her. But then, you spilled your coffee. And she lost it! Her reaction seemed over the top to me. She ranted at you for several minutes. It was painful to watch."

"Really?" Maggie was surprised. Valentina had seemed so sweet and mellow throughout all their interactions.

Olivia nodded. "It was weird, actually, because it wasn't like any of the coffee got on her fancy clothes or anything. Noah just accidentally knocked it off the table, and it went all over the floor."

"I'm so sorry!" Noah said.

Olivia smiled and patted his arm. "That's what you said yesterday, too. Even offered to clean it up for me."

"Good," Noah said.

"Anyway, while you and I were mopping it all up, your date stepped outside. I could see her pacing in front of the shop window, talking on her cell phone. Just as we finished up, she came back in and you both sat back down again. But then this is where it got even more weird."

"How so?" Maggie asked.

"Remember how I said that his date didn't really seem into it at all, like not really paying attention to Noah and more focused on her phone?"

"Yeah."

"Well, all of a sudden, she turned on the charm. She put her phone away and started acting super flirty, tossing her hair, laughing at everything Noah said, touching his hands on the table. It was kind of like a switch got flipped or something."

Olivia looked at Noah. "After a bit, I saw you pull out your phone and I heard you say, 'Dinner sounds like a great idea! I'll see if I can get us a reservation.'"

"Then what?" Noah asked.

Olivia shrugged. "I heard your date say that she insisted on driving. But then you guys left."

"Did I mention what restaurant I made reservations at?"

Olivia shook her head. "Sorry, honey, I didn't hear it if you did."

Noah's face fell.

"Wait a minute!" Maggie said excitedly, turning toward Olivia. "You said Noah made the reservation? From his cell phone?"

"Yes."

She looked at Noah. "Just check your recent calls!"

"Of course! My brain still isn't operating at full capacity, I guess." Noah pulled his phone out of his pocket and tapped the screen.

Then he dialed a number and put the phone to his ear. "Hello? Uh...I was wondering if I could get a reservation for lunch today? Oh?" He was quiet for a few beats. "Well, how about dinner then? What time do you open? Perfect! Can I reserve a table for...two?" Here he shot Maggie a questioning look, and she nodded vigorously. "Under the name Riley, please. Great, thank you."

He laid his phone on the table. "The restaurant doesn't open until five o'clock. But we now have a waterside table reserved at Oasis on the Water."

"Oooh!" Olivia said. "I'm jealous! I love that place."

Maggie battled with her conflicting emotions as she tried to ignore the flutter of delight rippling through her. She was excited to realize that she was finally going on a date with the gorgeous man seated across from her. But then she immediately scolded herself. *Remember what this is really about, Milena!*

It was about the safety of a young woman and helping Noah clear his name. She needed to get any unrealistic romantic dreams out of her head. They had to focus on finding Valentina.

Chapter 6

"So, he truly doesn't remember anything?" Jaime asked. She was sitting on the floor of her living room across from Maggie while fourteen-month-old Emma toddled between them. Emma was busily pulling toys out of the toybox beside Jaime and carrying them over to drop into Maggie's lap.

Maggie had texted Jaime the minute Noah dropped her off at her apartment after their coffee shop visit. Finding out that her friend was free, Maggie had rushed over to discuss the latest development in the situation with Noah.

"Nothing," Maggie said, blowing a stray curl out of her eyes and wrapping her arms around the chubby little girl, making her giggle by showering kisses all over her soft, pink cheeks.

"What could make that happen?" Jaime addressed her husband, Jack, who was seated in a nearby recliner, his face buried in a thick book. He lifted his head and looked at his wife. "What did you say, hon?"

Jaime smiled and shook her head. "It's the weekend, babe. That means you don't have to read about the latest in environmental science restoration plans or whatever that massive textbook is about!"

Jack gave his wife a bemused smile as he often did. Maggie reflected on how opposite, yet how perfect they were for each other.

Jaime was the kind of woman other women loved to hate. She was tall with a perfect, hourglass figure—even post-baby—and wide-set bluer-than-blue eyes. Her luxurious blond hair was currently twisted into a messy bun atop her head. But even with that, and the old joggers and T-shirt she wore, one flash of that dazzling smile could find even the most oblivious man falling over himself to do whatever she asked. And her husband was no exception.

Maggie switched her gaze to Jack. His lanky frame barely filled out the fashionable khaki shorts and short-sleeved button-down shirt that his wife had bought him. He was two inches shorter than Jaime, with kind brown eyes and a mop of dark hair that always looked like it needed to be combed. His nose was just a bit too large for his thin face and the square, black hipster eyeglasses he wore—another selection by his wife—were currently balanced at the end of it. He pushed them up with one finger. "I never have time during the week to read for fun like this," he defended himself.

"Fun?" Jaime shot Maggie a look that made her press her lips together to stop a laugh from erupting.

Jack marked his spot with a bookmark and set the massive tome on the table beside him. "You have my full attention now, my love."

Jaime flashed him one of her heart-melting smiles then summarized her conversation with Maggie and repeated her question.

Jack frowned and rubbed a finger up and down his long nose. "Some people experience a blackout effect from too much alcohol. That can lead to a type of amnesia known as Wernicke-Korsakoff's psychosis."

Maggie shook her head. "Apparently, he doesn't drink."

"Hmmm, well, it could be drugs. Or a hit on the head? You said he had a bruise on his face?"

"Yes, I tried to get him to go see a doctor, but he refused," Maggie said. "He just wants to focus on finding Valentina."

"He probably should get checked out, because it's really hard to guess how it may have happened without a medical diagnosis. However, most amnesia does usually resolve without treatment. I'm sure your efforts to retrace his steps could help his memory return."

He turned his attention back to Jaime. "Would you like me to take our little angel and put her down for her nap?"

Emma was snuggled onto Jaime's lap now, eyes drooping as her head lay against her mother's chest. Jaime nodded. "Yes, please."

He gently lifted the sleepy child and, cradling her against him, carried her out of the room.

Jaime got up and pulled Maggie to her feet, leading her over to the sofa beneath the room's large picture window. She plopped down on it, tucking her legs beneath her and angling toward her friend. "Enough about his amnesia. Let's get back to the more important part of this conversation," Jaime said. "Your date tonight."

"It's not exactly a date," Maggie said, feeling uncomfortable.

"Uh, you and your high school crush are going out to eat at one of the nicest restaurants in Whispering Pines," Jaime said. "It's a date."

"Jaime, our goal is to find Valentina!"

"Yeah, yeah, I get all that. But what are you going to wear?" She leaned toward Maggie with a mischievous glint in her eyes.

Maggie tossed up her hands in exasperation. "I don't know, I haven't thought about it."

Jaime gave her a look. "Lie!"

"Oh, all right," Maggie grumbled. "I've thought about it."

"That red, ruched bodycon dress with the low back?"

"That seems a bit much," Maggie said doubtfully.

"Oooh! I know. You should wear that black spaghetti-strap V-neck dress with the skater-style skirt. It's a nice blend of casual and classy. Plus, it shows off your great legs." Here Jaime reached over to pinch one of Maggie's calves.

"Cut it out!" Maggie laughed, slapping Jaime's hand away and curling her legs under her for protection. "Seriously, Jaime, you know that I can't think of this as a true date. It's business."

This time it was Jaime who threw up her hands. "You do such an incredible job of creating perfect dates and love matches for your friends and your clients. But I've got to be honest with you, Maggie, you're an epic fail when it comes to turning your famous skills on yourself. When I think about that loser you dated in high school, and then those two jerks from our freshman and sophomore years of college..." Jaime trailed off, shaking her head.

"Jaime, you know a big part of the problem with those relationships was my—"

"I still don't buy that!" Jaime said, cutting her off. "I'm not denying what you've told me about your own issues. But those guys were egotistical jerks—totally into themselves—and they never treated you well."

Maggie's face flushed. She wanted to deny her friend's words, but she couldn't. She had bent over backward to be a great girlfriend to every guy she'd dated. But in return, she'd been taken for granted, used, and cheated on. All she ever wanted was to be romanced and to feel loved.

"Maybe you just need to look at yourself more objectively, think of yourself as another client," Jaime said. "Look at Jack and me. We would never have gotten our happily ever after if it wasn't for you and your mad skills, *Emma.*" Jaime put an extra emphasis on Maggie's nickname.

Jaime and Maggie had met super nerd Jack Knightly at the same time, standing next to him at a party they'd attended their junior year of college. Jack was an environmental scientist going for his PhD. He'd been talked into attending the party by a fun-loving roommate who had promptly abandoned him upon arrival. Maggie had chatted with him for a bit and recognized his struggle with social skills. She'd noticed a box of conversation starter questions on a nearby table, and for fun she'd engaged with Jack by asking him the questions while Jaime had sipped her drink and searched for someone more interesting to talk to.

Maggie had been intrigued by Jack's answers, and after Jaime had wandered off, they'd continued talking. Due to Maggie's skills at connecting with people and drawing them out, Jack finally ended up confessing that he'd had a crush on Jaime for a while. He saw her every afternoon in the University Food Court and it was the highlight of each day. Like most men, he'd been struck by her beauty, but was too shy to ever approach her. "Besides," he'd added. "A guy like me? And a girl like her? Never in a million years."

But Maggie knew a potential love match when she saw one and set out to play Cupid for the couple. She remembered what Jack had said about the University Food Court, and for the next several days, she finagled for the two of them to run into Jack there. They had several conversations with just the three of them. But once it became apparent that Jaime and Jack actually enjoyed each other's company, Maggie smoothly removed herself from the equation. Maggie was the Maid of Honor at their wedding and now godmother to baby Emma.

Maggie refocused on her friend's face and sighed. "I know you're right, and it's frustrating. But the fact is, I'm great at playing matchmaker for everyone but myself."

"Look, I may not know matchmaking, but I know fashion," Jaime said. "And I order you to wear that little black dress tonight!"

Chapter 7

Noah took a deep breath and slowly let it out before lifting his finger to ring Maggie's doorbell. He couldn't believe he was about to take Maggie Milena out to dinner. This was something he'd dreamed about doing since he was sixteen years old. But it wasn't a date, he reminded himself sternly, as much for Maggie's protection as for his own. If she ever discovered the real reason he needed dating help, she'd not only drop him as a client, but most likely get as far away from him as possible.

"Coming!" he heard her voice call from inside.

The door opened and she held onto it with one hand while she hopped on one foot, trying to slip on a strappy black sandal to match the other one she already had on. "I'm almost ready," she said, slightly breathless, and then a look of concern crossed her face. "Is something wrong?"

Noah realized his mouth was hanging open. He promptly closed it. "No, no, you look…really nice."

A small smile played at her soft pink lips. "Thank you."

Nice was an understatement. Her sunlight and cinnamon curls spiraled softly around her face and brushed against her bare shoulders. The simple black dress she wore accentuated her tan and clung nicely to her curves before flaring out into a short skirt that left plenty of her shapely legs visible beneath it.

"You look nice, too," she said, indicating his khakis and black button-front Henley shirt. She grabbed a small purse from a table beside the door. "Okay, I'm ready. Let's go find Valentina!"

"Right. Find Valentina." He offered her his arm, and with another small smile, she took it. He couldn't deny the electric jolt that ran through him as her fingertips slipped around his upper arm. The sensation was like a fiery current racing through his veins, igniting every nerve ending.

He led her to the Porsche and opened the door for her. She slipped inside, giving him another nice glimpse of her legs as she gracefully swung them into the car.

He walked quickly around to get behind the driver's seat.

"Where's Boon?" she asked, looking into the back seat.

"I didn't think it was practical to bring him along tonight. My brother Jake and his wife Alex have a dog already. Plus, they're dog sitting our other brother's dog already. So, they offered to watch him for me tonight for a doggie play date."

"Awwww, that's sweet." Maggie straightened in her seat and put on the seatbelt, then looked at him with a bright smile. "Let's take Lakeshore Drive."

"For the view?"

"No! I want you to open this baby up. Let's see what it can do!"

He rolled his eyes. "I'm not doing that. The last thing I need now is a speeding ticket."

"Party pooper."

He grinned. "Would you like to drive?"

She looked at him, her face glowing with excitement. "Can I?"

"Sure, apparently it's my car."

They each got out and switched seats.

She started the engine. "Can I ask you a favor?"

"What?"

"Can you open the timer on your phone?"

"Uh...okay." He pulled out his cell phone and opened the timer app.

"Now, can you hit start?"

"Sure, *whyyyyyyy!!!!*" The car exploded forward on the street as she jammed the accelerator to the floor.

"Hit stop!" she shouted, slamming the brakes. She looked over at him. "What does it say?"

"It says you're crazy, lady!"

"C'mon, seriously! I read that this car can hit sixty miles per hour in 2.6 seconds."

Noah looked down at his phone. "It was actually 2.2 seconds." He unbuckled his seat belt. "But now we're switching back, because I'm too young to die."

They arrived at the restaurant and Noah offered her his arm again as they strolled up the boardwalk to the front door. Because it was a lovely summer evening, the exterior walls of the restaurant were removed and gentle lake breezes drifted through the establishment. Tables of different sizes were arranged around the floor and on the outdoor deck overlooking the lake. Tiny white lights covered the interior ceiling and the outdoor railing, giving the entire place a fairy-tale ambiance.

"We have a reservation under Riley," Noah said to the hostess.

The young woman behind the stand checked her iPad screen and nodded. "Yes, sir, I see it here. Follow me, please."

She led them to a table for two overlooking the white-crested waves of Lake Michigan and handed them both menus.

"Excuse me," Noah said to the hostess. "Were you working here last night?"

"No, sir."

"How about any of the other staff?"

"Our manager was working yesterday evening."

"Do you think we can speak with him or her?"

"Sure." The girl shrugged. "I know she's tied up doing an interview right now, but she should be free in an hour or so. I'll let her know."

"Thank you," Noah said. Then he looked at Maggie. "In the meantime, let's order. Even though I was here last night, I don't remember it. And I've heard this place has delicious food."

Maggie chuckled.

When the waitress came to take their drink orders, Maggie ordered a glass of red wine while Noah ordered an iced tea.

They both looked over their menus, but after a moment, Maggie set hers on the table. He looked up to find her studying him. Her eyes seemed more gold than brown against the backdrop of wide blue sky and dark waves.

"So," she said, "between what you told me and Hugo's reaction to the wine bottle in Valentina's condo, I'm getting the definite impression that you don't drink alcohol."

Even though she'd said it as a statement, Noah could tell it was a question.

He reached for his water glass and took a sip. "That's true, I don't."

She tilted her head in inquiry. "Is there any special reason?"

He hesitated for a moment, but he knew he could trust Maggie with this intimate detail of his background. "You know that my mom died in a car accident when I was young, just like your parents did. But I don't think I ever told you how it happened." He took a breath and continued. "The fact is, she was killed by a drunk driver. It was the middle of the afternoon. She'd just picked up my brothers and me from school."

"Oh no, Noah! I'm so sorry!" Maggie immediately began scanning the room. "Let me call the waitress back. I don't need that glass of wine with dinner. I'd hate to do anything to make you feel uncomfortable."

Noah reached over and laid his hand on top of hers, and she immediately stilled. He wondered if she felt the same scintillating heat that he felt whenever their skin connected. "Please don't worry about it. It's just a pact between my brothers and me. We promised each other we'd never drink so that there was never even a possibility that we'd play a role in another family losing a parent for the same reason we did. Besides," he added. "After your little stunt earlier, I'm going to be the only one driving tonight anyway."

Maggie laughed, and he kept his hand over hers as long as he dared, regretfully removing it when the waitress arrived with their drinks and to take their orders.

Conversation flowed comfortably between them throughout their meal, just as it used to when they were in high school together. And Noah couldn't remember a time when he'd felt so at ease on a date. Of course, it's *not* a date, he reminded himself for the hundredth time. *Which is probably the reason it's going so well!"*

Unlike other women he'd dated, Maggie didn't try to hide her healthy appetite. And when the waitress brought the dessert menu, they agreed to split a slice of the restaurant's signature *Dulce de Leche* lava cake with a scoop of French vanilla ice cream.

"Mmmmmm," Maggie said, closing her eyes to savor her first bite of the powdered sugar-covered confection. The warm, gooey filling oozed out onto the plate, and she scooped up another dab of it, her pink tongue flicking out to lick it off the spoon.

Noah quickly took a bite to stop himself from staring and to hide the direction his mind was going, which had nothing to do with the delicious dessert.

He swallowed his bite and looked at her. The sun was now lower in the sky, casting the warm glow of twilight on her curling tendrils as they danced on the lake breezes. Her exposed skin looked warm and inviting, limned in the golden sunlight. And he couldn't believe how much he wanted to run his fingers over her smooth, bare shoulders peeking out from beneath the delicate straps of her dress.

Maggie looked up and noticed him watching her. "What? Is something on my face?"

Noah shook himself. "Um, actually, yeah, you've got a little..." He didn't finish the sentence but reached across the table with his napkin and scooped a bit of *Dulce de Leche* filling from the side of her rosebud lips.

For some reason he couldn't identify, this gesture felt strangely intimate. He saw her face redden, and he immediately dropped his hand, feeling a bit shocked at what he'd just done.

He quickly changed the subject. "So, you never answered my question from this afternoon."

"What question?"

"If you've had so much success with your matchmaking clients, why aren't you already matched up yourself, Miss Matches by Maggie?"

Maggie dropped the napkin she'd been using to dab at the remaining sauce on her lips, and she gazed steadily at him, as if she were contemplating how much to tell him. Then she lifted one shoulder. "I guess I've just been too busy to play matchmaker for myself. As a fellow entrepreneur, I'm sure you understand how hard it is to have a personal life—let alone a romantic one—while building your business. Right now, all my focus and energy is on helping my clients like you find true love."

Noah was about to reply when suddenly a voice came from beside their table. "Unbelievable. You're back again tonight?"

Noah looked up and felt his heart drop at the sight of the familiar elegant brunette standing next to them. She wore a chic black suit with a crisp white shirt beneath it. Her expression wasn't happy, and she tossed her long hair back over one shoulder, revealing a "Manager" badge on her lapel.

Uh-oh. "Well, hi there, Michelle! I didn't realize that..."

"That I worked here?"

"Well, actually, yes." He sounded lame, even to his own ears.

Michelle rolled her eyes. "I saw you yesterday and I chose not to say anything. But seriously? It was bad enough that you brought a date here last night, flaunting her in front of me. But two nights in a row? With *two* different women?" Here she looked pointedly at Maggie, who was looking confused.

"It's not what you think, Michelle. This is my friend, Maggie. She's helping me—"

Michelle cut him off, her words aimed at Maggie. "Listen, I'm going to give you some free advice. Stay as far away as possible from this one." She tilted her head in Noah's direction. "I know he looks good on the outside, but trust me, he's not worth it."

"I don't understand," Maggie said, her gaze flipping between the two of them. "You two know each other?"

"We went out once." Michelle tossed her hair again. "But once was more than enough."

"Please, Michelle, I explained—" Noah began.

But this time it was Maggie who cut him off, her focus on Michelle. "What happened on your date?"

"Let's see..." Michelle put a hand on one hip and began counting on her fingers with the other. "First, he was over an hour late picking me up."

"I told you that I took a couple of wrong turns coming to get you," Noah protested.

"Then," Michelle plowed on, holding up her second finger, "he conveniently forgot his wallet, so I had to pay for both of our meals, even though *he* asked me out."

"It was just a simple oversight!"

"And last but definitely not least," she continued, holding up her third finger, "after our lunch, he took me for a hike in the state park. And while we were standing on one of the open viewing platforms, he knocked me off it. I fell ten feet to the ground and sprained both of my ankles."

"I tripped!" Noah cried. "I didn't mean to knock you off!"

"I was housebound in a wheelchair for two weeks!" she finished, folding her arms across her ample chest.

"That must have been terrible!" Maggie said.

Noah knew there wasn't anything he could say to save the situation, so he mumbled, "I already told you multiple times how sorry I was, Michelle."

"Mhm." Her face was closed off.

"That sounds like an absolutely awful date, Michelle," Maggie said, her brows furrowed in sympathy. "I can't even imagine how frustrating and disappointing it must have been for you to experience all of that." Maggie shook her head. "And then to have him show up at your place of business with other women? That must really sting."

Michelle's expression softened in response to Maggie's obvious empathy.

Noah was exasperated and wanted to argue, but deep down, he knew there was truth in what Michelle was saying. So, he kept quiet as Maggie continued. "Have you ever considered that maybe that whole negative experience with Noah was actually a blessing in disguise?"

"What do you mean?" Michelle asked.

"Well, is it possible that the two of you just weren't a good fit for each other?"

"You know," Michelle tilted her head, looking speculative, "in the aftermath, I did sort of start thinking that. I mean, when we were together, he talked a lot about how much he loves the outdoors, mountain biking, camping, hiking. And I really hate all that stuff. I only agreed to the hike in the park because I was being polite. And his taste in music…" Michelle rolled her eyes.

Noah frowned and opened his mouth to protest this egregious insult, but a lightning-quick glance from Maggie quelled it, and he closed it again.

"It really sounds like you didn't have a lot in common with him. Definitely not what you're looking for in a long-term relationship, right?" Maggie said. "I'm sure there's a wonderful man out there for you who would be a much better fit."

"You know what? I bet you're right," Michelle said, then she smiled. "Thank you…was it Maggie?"

Maggie nodded with a smile.

"Well, thank you, Maggie. I feel much better about all of this now."

"I'm glad."

"Are you two finished?" Noah asked, feeling a bit miffed at the way they had been talking as if he wasn't even there.

Michelle turned to face him, her expression much softer now. "I think so. And now, the real reason I came over here is because my hostess mentioned that you wanted to talk with me about yesterday evening?"

"Yes," Noah said, relieved that they were finally moving on to the main topic of the evening. "Obviously, you've already mentioned that you saw me here last night with my, er, date."

Michelle nodded.

"I know this is going to sound strange, but can you recall any specifics about it?"

Michelle frowned. "Like what kind of specifics?"

"How was I acting? How was my date acting? How long were we here? And did we do or say anything that you overheard?"

Michelle frowned in confusion.

He sighed, wishing he didn't have to explain again. He decided not to tell her everything. "It's just that, for some reason, I'm experiencing selective amnesia. I have no memory of last night, and I...I'd like to remember exactly what happened."

"Wow, you don't remember anything? How strange." Michelle looked thoughtful. "Well, I did notice that your date was really into you. She kept touching you and giggling and feeding you bites of her food."

"Really," Noah said, feeling surprised.

"Yes," Michelle said with another toss of her hair. "You seemed to be enjoying it. But now that I think about it, you were acting a bit strange. You were talking and laughing kind of loud, almost like you were tipsy.

"And oh!" she added. "There's one more thing I almost forgot. Before all that, when you first arrived and got seated, there was a guy who came over to talk with your date. He seemed to know her. You all chatted together for a bit, then I saw you get up and leave the table. But your date and the guy kept talking. They never touched each other or anything, but there was a kind of intensity between them, almost like they were arguing about something. Then you came back a few minutes later and handed a sweater to your date, and the guy went to sit by himself up at the bar."

"A random guy, huh? What did he look like?" Noah asked.

"About six feet, dark hair, muscular, and *very* good looking." Michelle winked at Maggie with that last piece of information. "Probably in his late twenties or early thirties, I'd guess?"

Maggie gave Noah a questioning look, but he just shook his head. He couldn't recall any of it.

"Is there anything else you can remember?" Maggie asked. "Did they happen to mention where they were going next?"

"No, but I did see Noah ask the waitress to take their photograph with his cellphone before they left."

"Really?" Noah pulled out his phone and opened his photographs. He scrolled through to the most recent ones and his jaw fell open.

"What?" Maggie said, jumping up and coming around the table to peer at the images over his shoulder. Michelle joined them.

There was Noah with Valentina, her arms entwined around his neck and a seductive smile curving her full lips. Noah's smile looked extra wide and unnatural to him; his eyes were heavy-lidded and drowsy looking. There were several shots of them, the last one with Valentina kissing him on the cheek.

Michelle pointed at the screen. "That's the guy!"

Her finger indicated a man in the background of the shot. He was seated on a stool up at the bar. But he was turned in his seat, staring intently at Valentina with an angry scowl on his face.

"That doesn't look good," Maggie said.

"It looks like I took a few more pictures after these restaurant ones," Noah said. "Maybe we can figure out where Valentina and I went next." He continued scrolling through the images and cringed as a series of very bad selfies filled his phone screen. He was in a crowded room filled with low, colorful lighting. It looked like everyone around him was dancing. Noah, on the other hand, was striking some pretty strange poses.

"You look...interesting," Michelle said, clearly trying not to laugh.

Noah frowned, scrolling back to make a few of the images larger. He examined the background of several photos, and then suddenly his face cleared. "I know where these were taken!"

"Where?" Maggie asked.

"Can I interest you in joining me for a sunset cruise?"

Chapter 8

Maggie felt heat emanate through her body, originating at the point where Noah's hand lightly touched the small of her back as he escorted her up the gangplank to board the Lake Michigan Princess. Was it wrong that she felt excited about embarking on a romantic sunset cruise with Noah by her side? It was a secret dream come true for her.

She loved creating romantic experiences for her clients. But she'd never experienced any of them for herself. Neither of her previous boyfriends had understood the kind of romantic gestures that spoke to her soul. Nor had they probably even cared, if she was being totally honest.

She took a deep breath and pushed those negative thoughts from her mind as she felt the soft evening air wash over her. She was determined to enjoy as much of this night as she could, despite their true purpose for being here.

The eighty-foot vessel was a Victorian-style paddlewheel riverboat with two decks. There was an enclosed lower deck and an open-air upper deck covered with a crisp navy blue-and-white striped canopy. Both levels held comfortable seating and tables for the guests, but at the moment, nobody was sitting. Everyone stood around the perimeter of the boat to soak up the magical lake views. Maggie and Noah had been the last to board and immediately after they stepped onto the boat, the crew began lifting the gangplank and loosening the ropes that held the boat to the dock.

"May I see your hand, ma'am?" said a young man who was wearing the staff uniform of a navy blue polo shirt and white shorts.

Maggie extended it toward him and he placed a stamp on it. She looked at the dark blue rectangular boat shape with the words Lake Michigan Princess stamped inside it.

"Oh my gosh!" she said, extending it toward Noah. "Recognize this?"

"Riiiight," he said slowly, recognition dawning in his eyes as he looked at her hand. The fresh stamp was clearly similar to the smudged image that had been on the back of his own hand that morning, before he'd showered it off. "I knew it looked familiar, but I couldn't remember from where. Now we know."

Noah received a fresh stamp on his hand, and they moved into the ship. Now free from its mooring, the boat began drifting away from the dock, apple-red twin paddle wheels slowly churning the water beneath them.

Maggie took another deep breath, determined to get a grip on her emotions and keep focused on their goal. She turned toward Noah. "Where should we start?"

Noah looked down at her, a strange glint in his eyes. "I know this may make me sound terrible," he said. "But we're going to be on board for the next few hours. We have plenty of time to find out if anyone saw Valentina and me. But, right now, I think it would be nice to watch the sunset. It looks like it's going to be a beautiful one. Are you okay with that?"

Maggie's heart did a little happy dance in her chest. "I'd love that."

He took her hand as if they were an actual couple and led her toward the steps leading to the upper deck. The boat was full but not overly crowded, and they easily found a space along the rail.

They leaned against it side by side and looked out as the boat glided past the picturesque homes lining the shore.

The boat carried them along the edge of Pere Marquette Lake and onto its connecting river to enter Lake Michigan. Maggie looked down as the boat cut a swath through the rolling water below, the white foam tinged rose-gold by the lowering sun.

She thought about people's reactions upon first seeing one of the Great Lakes. The sheer size and immensity of the lakes always shocked them. Maggie had been to the shorelines of both the Atlantic and Pacific Oceans on vacations, and it was nearly impossible to tell the difference between those famed bodies of water and this one.

She glanced at Noah, who was looking toward the horizon. The wind off the water rippled over his dark curls, making her want to reach up and thread her fingers through them. He turned to her then, his light eyes reflecting the lake and sky. Looking into this man's eyes was like looking at a glittering gemstone, where every facet revealed something new to capture her attention. She could gaze into their depths forever. But instead, she dropped her own eyes, determined not to let her thoughts about Noah run away with her.

She faced back toward the water. "You know, I've arranged this as a first date option for my clients, but I've never actually taken this cruise before."

"Really?" Noah sounded surprised. "Why is that?"

She waved a hand to encompass the people around them who were all looking out at the view. "It's clearly more of a couple thing to do, isn't it?"

"I guess that's true." Noah angled toward her, leaning one arm against the rail. "I know you said you don't have much time to date, but I can't believe that not even one guy ever brought you here. It's one of the first ideas that would've popped into my head if I was taking you out." His voice trailed off as he spoke and she glanced at him, wondering if she imagined the warm flush suffusing his cheeks.

"Really? Why?"

He looked thoughtful, his eyes seeming to scan every inch of Maggie's face. "Because it offers the perfect recipe for romance. You've got the beautiful sunset and then dancing once we return to the dock." He leaned closer, his voice low. "And even without knowing what you do for a living, there's always been something about you, Maggie. Something that exudes pure romance. I suppose that's part of what makes you so good at your job."

Heat blossomed inside her as she struggled to maintain composure under his intense gaze. How did this man understand her deep craving for romance so easily when her previous boyfriends had been so hopelessly oblivious?

"Thank you," Maggie said softly. "That's...sweet. And you're right, I do love all things romance." She looked back out over the water. "I may not be in a place right now to experience romantic moments for myself, but it's satisfying to be able to create those moments for my clients. And at least now I can see for myself how this truly does make for a pretty dreamy date."

The glowing sun sank ever lower in a sky that was now painted in vibrant streaks of pink, purple, and fiery orange, their brilliance reflected in the undulating waves below. A crew member came past, offering glasses of champagne and sparkling water. They each took a sparkling water and clinked their glasses together before taking a sip.

Then they stood together in silence with the rest of the guests, soaking up the incredible panoramas as the boat made its way past the Whispering Pines lighthouse. The glimmering water reflected a path of liquid gold leading from the sun, and it felt like everyone watching held their breath until it slowly, finally slipped beneath the horizon. The crowd on both decks clapped and erupted in cheers, and conversation began flowing around them again. Eventually, the boat slowly turned to churn its way back toward the dock.

"So beautiful," Maggie breathed.

"Yes."

Something in his voice made her glance at him, and their gazes locked. The way he was looking at her caused little flashes of heat lightning to zing around her insides.

The boat reached the dock and the sound of dance music began drifting on the breeze around them as the boat's live band on the deck below started to play.

The music, the soft evening air, and being here with Noah were making for a very heady combination, and she felt like she was drifting along in a dream. With a monumental effort, she tore her gaze away from his. But then he spoke her name.

"Maggie?"

She looked back at him.

"Would you like to dance?"

She hesitated for a moment in surprise but then slowly nodded.

He took her hand again and led her back down to the lower deck. White plastic tables and chairs were arranged in a U-shape around a wooden dance floor. Several couples were already out on the floor.

"This song sounds different," Maggie said.

Noah grinned. "It's Ed Sheeran's 'Shape of You' in a salsa version." He took her glass from her and set it down next to his on a nearby table, then he took her hand and led her out onto the dance floor.

"Do you salsa?"

"No!" Maggie said, suddenly insecure as she attempted to pull her hand from his. She loved to dance, but she'd never learned any formal styles, let alone the salsa.

"I can teach you," Noah said with confidence. "Just follow my lead."

He swung her around to face him, placing her left hand on his shoulder and taking her right hand in his. He put his other hand at her waist, and she could feel the warmth of it through her dress.

Maggie had a moment to admire the expressive rhythm of the sultry music, and then they were moving. He taught her the basic steps, leading her forward as he stepped back and then back as he came forward. She caught on quickly, and with gentle pressure, he guided her, their hips swaying in sync with one another.

After a bit, with an impish grin, he began adding moves. She didn't always know what was coming next, but he guided her with surprising expertise.

To the beat of the music, he would pull her tantalizingly close, then away, close, then away, in an almost teasing motion. He lifted both her arms up over her head. Then he released one as he spun her out in a turn that had her skirt flaring between them, his free hand slipping lightly along her waist as she twirled, sending chills dancing up and down her spine.

The proximity of his body to hers, the way he touched her, the way they moved together, made her insides flame. When the song ended, he gave her a final twirl and a playful dip, making her laugh.

"That was fun!" She felt dizzy and exhilarated. "You can really move, Noah. Where did you learn to dance like that?"

The band had switched to a slower number, and Noah showed no interest in leaving the dance floor. He pulled her close and was now leading her in a gentle sway to the music.

"My Pops and Nana were great dancers," he said. "They taught my brothers and me some of the classic dances. But then for fun in college, I signed up for a Latin Dance class. I was one of the only guys in the class, so I got a lot of practice."

"I bet!" She laughed. "You're like every girl's dream." She felt her face grow red as she realized what she'd just said. She fumbled to recover. "I mean, a man who likes to dance. Where were you at all our high school dances?"

He led her into a slow spin before pulling her up tight against him again. His hard body pressed against hers, his hand firmer on her back now as the music enveloped them in its sensual embrace.

"At home," he sighed as the song came to an end. Then his eyes locked with hers in a way that made her heart flutter erratically. "Dreaming of—"

"Noah, my man! You're back again!" said a loud voice beside them.

They had been dancing at the edge of the dance floor and turned to face a smiling, mocha-skinned man with cropped corkscrew curls. He wore a cruise uniform and was now thumping Noah on the back. "How's your head?"

Noah's face registered confusion and surprise.

"Did I hear someone say Noah is back again?" The lead guitarist was squinting against the lights. Then a smile spread across his bearded face as his eyes landed on Noah. "Get up here, Riley, and do a number with us! Maybe something a bit less rowdy than last night, though!" The rest of the band guffawed with laughter, along with the man who was standing beside them.

Noah shot Maggie an apologetic look and made his way up to the front of the room. The band clearly knew him well, greeting him with man hugs and fist pumps. Maggie sat down at a nearby table, her mind whirling. Dreaming of... Dreaming of what? What had he been about to say? She focused on Noah now as he took the offered guitar and began strumming. The band soon had the crowd on the floor while Noah's clear voice sang the lead for Kenny Chesney's "Don't Happen Twice."

She was instantly transported back to high school, listening to him make music like he used to, and she couldn't wipe the smile from her face. The song was about running into a first love that he never forgot. He seemed to be looking right at her while he sang. And for just a moment, she let herself imagine what it would be like if he was singing that song to her.

Then she shut the thought down. She couldn't let herself go there. He was a friend and a client now. And that's where it ended.

When the song was over, Noah refused the band's insistence that he keep playing and he quickly returned to Maggie's side.

"Sorry!" he said. "I've played with these guys before. They're great."

"You were great!" she gushed. "I've missed hearing you sing, Noah."

He grinned at the compliment, looking almost bashful. Then he looked around. "Did you see where that guy went? The one that recognized me?"

"He's over there," Maggie said, pointing to the bar area. The man was talking with the bartender.

"C'mon!" He took her hand and pulled her up, leading her through the crowd to the bar.

"Excuse me," Noah said, leaning on the bar next to the man.

The man and the bartender both glanced at Noah. Then they broke into wide, matching grins.

"Hey, bro! We're so glad to see that you're all right," said the bartender.

"After last night, we were worried," said the man who'd originally spoken to them, and he stepped up to embrace a shocked Noah. Maggie watched Noah awkwardly thump the man's back.

"Yeah, so about last night," Noah said once the man released him. "I know this is going to sound strange, but I don't remember any of it. And I'm sorry to admit it, but I don't remember you guys either."

The bartender and the other man exchanged a glance, then looked back at Noah.

"Like, nothing?" said the man.

Noah shook his head.

"I'm not too surprised, bro," said the bartender. "You took a pretty hard punch."

"From who?" Noah asked, but Maggie laid a hand on his arm.

"Why don't we introduce ourselves first?" she said, and extended her hand. "I'm Maggie."

The two men shook her hand in turn and introduced themselves. The bartender was Eduardo and the other man introduced himself as Dante. Dante explained that he was in charge of social media for the cruise company.

"So, how did you meet Noah last night?" Maggie asked.

Dante broke into another of his wide grins. "He was on our cruise last night, and he was super friendly. Life of the party! He was dancing the night away with the entire crowd, including his date, who was one very smokin' hot, er..." He broke off and looked apologetically at Maggie.

She waved a hand, urging him to continue.

"Anyway, he danced a *lot*. And when he wasn't dancing, he was up making music with them." Dante indicated the band with a lift of his chin. "He had the whole place rockin'! I got some unbelievable photos and videos. We got so much action on Instagram and TikTok, my boss was singing my praises all morning. It was awesome!"

"So, where did the hard punch come in?" Noah asked.

"Yeah, so the punch," said Eduardo, who had just returned to them after serving drinks to several people. "It was literally the end of the night. These two rough-looking dudes showed up and started trying to manhandle your lady." Eduardo shook his head. "It was clear that she didn't want anything to do with them, and people all around you were starting to notice. Our bouncer was just moving toward you all when you suddenly stepped in front of your lady and shoved one of the guys back, telling him to keep his hands to himself."

"The way that guy looked at you?" Dante added with lifted brows and a shake of his head. "Man, if looks could kill..."

"What happened next?" Maggie asked.

"Pandemonium," said Eduardo.

Dante nodded his agreement.

"Pandemonium?" said Noah.

"Yeah," said Dante. "The guy you pushed hauled off and punched you in the face. You literally spun in a circle, man, and hit the floor like a dropped kettlebell. Your lady was screaming and swearing at the dudes. And the crowd, well, they went nuts. I mean, they loved you. You'd been making music for them and dancing with them all night, so they started attacking the dudes.

"Yeah, the crowd jumped them!" Eduardo added.

"But somehow, in the chaos, the two guys got away," Dante said.

"And me?" said Noah.

"You were really out of it, man. So, Eduardo called for an ambulance. It took you straight to the hospital, and your lady said she'd follow in the car."

"Wow," Noah said, plopping down onto a barstool. "I can't believe I don't remember any of this."

"Hey, I got pictures and video!" Dante said. "Lots of 'em. Maybe they'll jog your memory." He pulled out his phone and made a few taps on the screen, then opened the cruise line's Instagram feed and handed Noah his phone.

Maggie hopped onto the stool beside him, and together, they watched a series of short videos, including several of Noah doing some crazy dancing with Valentina.

"You've really got the moves, bro!" Dante interjected as he also peered over Noah's shoulder.

Another video showed Noah leading the crowd in a line dance. Then he was up on the stage belting out love songs and encouraging the crowd to sing along.

There were several still shots as well, and Noah scrolled through the images. Maggie lightly touched his arm again. "Wait, Noah. Did you see that? Go back!"

He went back a couple of images and stopped when Maggie pointed at the screen. "Look there!"

"What?"

"I think it's that man again!"

Noah expanded the image with his fingers to examine it and his brows shot up.

Now they could easily see that it was the same man from the restaurant photo. And the man's expression was identical to the one in the previous picture they'd seen. He looked angry. And his gaze was clearly directed at Valentina.

Noah angled the phone screen toward Dante. "Was this the guy that punched me?"

Dante squinted at it. "No, man. That's not him. But I did get some shots of the two guys. We didn't post them, of course, but I've still got them on my phone." He took the device back and, after a few more taps, handed it to Noah again. "These were the guys."

Maggie and Noah studied the images. The first shot showed Noah standing beside Valentina. They faced a man wearing black pants and a black button-front shirt with the sleeves rolled up. The ropy muscles of one forearm bulged as he gripped Valentina's wrist. His hair was distinctive, a textured buzz cut on top that blended into a fade with the shape of a dagger artfully shaved into the side of his hair. Part of an elaborate tattoo was visible on one side of his neck. If it weren't for the hate in his eyes, and the ugly sneer curling one corner of his thin lips, he might have been considered good looking.

He was a couple of inches shorter than Noah, but Maggie sensed a tangible underlying power there, like a panther about to strike. The man beside Dagger-head was even shorter, but he was built like a brick of solid muscle.

In the next image, Noah was between Valentina and Dagger-head. Valentina's wrist had been released, but her face looked furious. Her mouth was open as she shouted something at Dagger-head, her finger stabbing toward him aggressively.

In the third image, they could barely see Noah on the floor with Valentina squatting over him. The crowd was a mass of hands and bodies pulling at the two men.

"Wow," Maggie breathed, then murmured near Noah's ear, "I wonder if those were the same two guys from this morning?"

Noah gave a nod, then said to her, "I don't see that angry guy from the restaurant in any of the crowd shots, do you?"

Maggie slowly scanned all three photographs again. "Nope. But I feel like he's got to be involved somehow."

Noah agreed and handed the phone back to Dante. "So, you guys are saying after all this, the two guys got away, and Valentina and I went to the hospital?"

Dante and Eduardo both nodded.

"Okay then." He swiveled on the stool toward Maggie. "I guess we know where our next stop needs to be."

Maggie would have loved one more dance in Noah's arms. But she knew the more time that passed, the harder it might be to find Valentina. And possibly the more danger the woman might be in. So, even though the dancing didn't end until midnight, it was just after eleven o'clock when the two of them descended the gangplank.

They walked through the deserted parking lot, Maggie trailing a bit behind Noah as she re-scrolled through the images Dante had texted to Noah's phone just before they left.

"It's a little scary how much that punch affected me," Noah commented. "To think I not only don't recall it, but any of the stuff I did before I even got hit."

"It is scary," Maggie said, glancing up. "And I admit, I'm glad that our next stop is the hospital. You really should get checked out."

"Apparently, I already did," Noah said with a smirk.

"I'm talking about for your amnesia!" Maggie said, giving him a playful shove.

He pretended to trip and then turned it into a dance move, making Maggie laugh as he grabbed her free hand and gave her a twirl in the parking lot.

They were at the passenger side of the Porsche and Noah pulled out the key fob. But suddenly, a voice hissed out of the darkness behind them. "Don't move."

Maggie glanced at Noah and saw a glint of metal being shoved against his spine. Noah turned quickly toward Maggie, and she heard him suck in his breath as the owner of the weapon jabbed it harder into him. "I said, don't move!"

Maggie felt her hands grow cold as she recognized the voice. It belonged to one of the men from that morning.

The voice spoke again. "Check him."

A stocky man shrouded in dark clothing stepped forward to run his hands down each of Noah's pant legs and around his waistband.

"He's clean," the second man grunted. Maggie recognized his voice as well. He was clearly the other morning intruder.

"Now her purse."

Maggie gasped as her purse was yanked from her shoulder.

"Turn around, both of you," said the first voice.

Slowly, Noah and Maggie turned to face the two men they'd just been looking at photographs of. They looked even more menacing in real life. The man they'd nicknamed Dagger-head was lean and muscular. He exuded an intimidating sense of power that was unsettling. The stocky, shorter man had scabbed-over cuts on his face and a black eye that hadn't been visible in the photographs. He was pawing through Maggie's small purse. She could see the gleam of a gun at the waistband of his pants.

"Nothing." He threw the entire purse aside.

"All right." Dagger-head moved in closer and pressed the blade of the large knife he was holding up against Noah's throat. His eyes bore into Noah's, and his words fell like chips of ice. "Where is she?"

Chapter 9

Noah didn't move his head, but his eyes slid to Maggie. The other man now had a tight grip on her upper arm. Her eyes were wide with shock, and she was staring at the knife.

"Answer me!" Dagger-head said.

"I—I don't know."

The man's lips tightened, his eyes narrowing. "We know you were here with Valentina last night. And we saw you getting questioned at her place by the cops this morning. Now you're driving her car. Did you kill her?"

"What? No!"

"Then where. Is. She?"

Noah's mind was reeling. Who were these men? They'd apparently seen him and Maggie at Valentina's earlier. And now they were here. Had they been following them all day? And what was this about the Porsche being Valentina's car?

"He told you, we don't know," Maggie said. She now looked more angry than scared. She tried to shake off the other man's grip to no avail. "And it's not Valentina's car. It's Noah's.

Dagger-head frowned. "What are you talking about?"

"Go ahead," Maggie said with a lift of her chin. "Check the registration."

Noah wondered what Maggie could possibly be up to. How was this helping?

"Gimme the key," Dagger-head said.

Noah handed it to him and he tossed it to the other man, never removing the knife from Noah's throat. "Open it, Johnny."

Johnny did as commanded. Still keeping Maggie in a tight grip with one hand, with the other, he opened the car door and rifled through the glove box contents, pulling out the paperwork.

"She's telling the truth, Nick," he said a moment later. "It says the car is registered to a Noah Riley."

Nick's gaze slid from Noah, to Maggie, back to Noah again. His lip curled. "Just who exactly are you, Mr. Riley? And how did you come to be the owner of Valentina's car?"

Noah wasn't certain how to respond.

"You better start talking." Nick pressed the point of the blade into Noah's neck hard enough to draw a drop of blood. "Because if you don't, maybe I'll just slit your throat. After all, it's one of my favorite things to do." Nick's mouth curved into a humorless smile.

"If you do that, then you'll never know where she is," Maggie said quickly.

"So, you do know something," Nick said.

"Maybe they're cops," said Johnny.

"Now there's an idea," Nick said slowly, a light coming into his eyes. "Check their IDs, Johnny."

Johnny released Maggie's arm and retrieved her discarded purse from the ground. He squinted at the contents of her wallet, then shook his head. "Doesn't look like it."

"Check his," Nick said.

Johnny came around and pulled Noah's wallet from his back pocket. He searched through it, then shook his head again. "Just a regular ID."

"Well, Mr. Riley," Nick hissed. "If you're not a cop and you're—"

Just then the sound of wailing police sirens broke the stillness around them.

"That's right," Maggie said, looking smug now as she slipped Noah's cell phone out from the pocket of her dress. "I called 911. And the police will be here any second."

Nick and Johnny exchanged a quick look.

"Let's go," said Johnny, sounding worried.

Nick let out a stream of curses, but he didn't yet remove the blade from Noah's throat. "You have no idea who you're messing with, Mr. Riley. We will figure out exactly who both of you are and how you're involved in this."

As the sound of the sirens grew closer, Nick and Johnny turned away and vanished into the night.

Seconds later, the police car pulled into the parking lot.

"Over here!" Maggie called, waving her hands over her head.

Noah pulled Maggie close and looked down at her with concern. "Are you okay?"

"I'm okay," she said, leaning into him.

With his free hand, he pulled a handkerchief from his pocket to dab at the drip of blood trailing down his neck. "How did you call the police?"

"It's a trick I learned a couple of years ago," Maggie said. "If you press the power button fast five times in a row, it automatically dials 911 and they can see your location."

"Oh yeah," Noah said with a slow nod. "I completely forgot about that. Wade told me about that trick about a year ago. He even turned off the countdown beep in my settings for me so it wouldn't alert anyone if I did it." Then he smiled at her. "Thank God you think fast on your feet."

"And I had your phone in my hand," Maggie said, giving it back to him.

By now the police had parked beside them and two officers exited the vehicle. After taking their statement about what had happened, one officer searched the parking lot while the other put out an alert to the rest of the force to be on the lookout for Nick and Johnny.

"You've sure had a rough day, haven't you, Mr. Riley?" the officer said once he was off the radio. He'd introduced himself as Officer Bryan. Although Noah had met a couple of his brother Wade's co-workers since moving to town, Officer Bryan wasn't one of them.

Noah shook his head, feeling overwhelmed. "I definitely have," he said, then added, "Should I be worried about what they told me about this Porsche belonging to Valentina Romano? I already told the officers this morning about my memory loss. And I have no clue how it supposedly became mine. But all the paperwork says it belongs to me."

"Let me check on it," Officer Bryan said. He took the registration out and slid into his patrol car, tapping on the small computer keyboard inside it.

A moment later, he got out and handed it back to Noah. "It's definitely yours. And I don't see anyone else's name associated with this car."

"So weird," Noah said.

The officers left just as clusters of people began exiting the boat.

Noah glanced at the screen of his phone. It was now just after midnight. He looked at Maggie. All of her earlier bravado seemed to have disappeared.

She looked small and completely spent as she leaned back against the car with her eyes closed. He had an overwhelming urge to gather her in his arms and just hold her close. The urge was so palpable that it was actually painful to resist. So, he shoved his hands into his pockets and cleared his throat. She opened her eyes and looked up at him.

"I feel like we should wait until tomorrow to do our hospital visit," he said.

"I think you're right," Maggie said, stifling a yawn. "Why don't you drop me off at home and we can pick this back up in the morning."

"Yeah, um, I don't think I should take you home."

Maggie frowned. "Why not?"

"I hate to bring this up, but Johnny saw our IDs. That means they may know where we live."

Maggie stood up straight, instantly more awake. "I didn't even think of that!"

"I'd feel a lot better if I knew you were safe, Maggie. So, I have a suggestion."

"Yeah?"

"I think we should spend the night together."

Chapter 10

If Maggie had been wiped out a moment ago, that was no longer the case. Her heart thumped loud in her ears at Noah's words. She was positive he could hear it reverberating in her chest.

"S-s-spend the night together?"

Noah gave her a smoldering look. Then he winked and broke into a huge grin. "Maggie Milena, where is your mind going?" Then he put his hands over his heart. "I only have the most honorable intentions. I mean, I have my virtue to protect, after all."

Maggie couldn't resist smiling back at him. Despite the stress of their day, including this latest debacle, Noah had a way of lightening the mood and easing her worries. He made everything less scary.

"Okay, Mr. Honorable Intentions. How is this going to work?"

Noah looked around and then moved in close, bending to whisper in her ear. "This may be overly dramatic, but I have no idea if those guys have returned and could be nearby listening." His soft breath tickled her skin, making gooseflesh rise all over her body. "My brother Wade and his wife Cassie have a house in town with a state-of-the-art alarm system. They're gone right now on their honeymoon. So, I figured we could just sleep there tonight?"

"I guess that sounds like a good idea," Maggie said slowly, feeling a little strange but unable to argue against the logic of Noah's solution.

"Okay." Noah stepped back with a satisfied smile on his face. "Let's go."

Wade and Cassie's home was only ten minutes from the marina, but Noah drove a circuitous route to get there, making certain they weren't being followed.

As they pulled into the driveway, Maggie could see by the streetlights that the house was a charming little Cape Cod with a steeply pitched roof and dark clapboard siding. Two windows framed in white bordered each side of the entryway, and warm lights glowed from inside them, as well as from within the matching dormer windows above.

"Are you sure Wade and Cassie are still gone?" Maggie asked as Noah parked the Porsche behind the house in a space next to the detached garage.

"Yeah, they have their lights on a timer so it looks like someone is there at night," Noah explained.

Noah led her through the gate of the low, white picket fence surrounding the property and then up the steps to the front door. The small porch was flanked on either side by showy purple hydrangeas and blooming red rosebushes. Although their colors were muted in the darkness, their intoxicating perfume mingled with the fragrance of fresh basil and mint growing in pots beside the front door.

Maggie inhaled deeply, admiring the entire setup. "Wow, talk about a traditional American dream home!"

Noah focused on punching in a code on the front door keypad. "Yeah, having that classic homey feel was important to them, especially for my sister-in-law, Cassie. She grew up in the foster system and never really had a place to call home as a kid.

"I love the little porch herb garden here," Maggie said, bending over to rub her fingers on a mint leaf, releasing even more of the plant's scent.

"That's all Wade," Noah said as Maggie heard the sound of the lock release. "He uses them in his cooking. He's quite the chef."

He opened the front door and ushered Maggie inside.

The interior was just as cozy as Maggie imagined it would be. Polished wood flooring ran from the tiny living room into an equally tiny sitting room, separated by a couple of pony walls. And she could see the open French doors of the kitchen beyond. A painted white brick fireplace filled one wall of the living room, and to its left, a doorway stood open, revealing the start of a wooden staircase leading up to the loft area.

A thick, patterned area rug in a patchwork of greens and blues lay beneath a well-worn loveseat, coffee table, and two wing-backed chairs in the living room.

The sitting area beyond held a matching rug that sat under two chunky recliners facing a bookshelf-filled wall on the opposite side. Strategically placed lamps spilled pools of warm light around the space.

"What a sweet, little place," Maggie said, feeling instantly at home.

"Yeah, they've done a really good job," Noah said. He was now punching in another code on the interior wall unit of an elaborate alarm system. "This place was built in the 1920s. When Cassie and Wade bought it, it needed a lot of work. They did most of the renovating themselves, trying to keep as much original as possible. But they added some modern conveniences too, like this." He aimed his thumb at the alarm unit that had finally stopped blinking.

Maggie walked over to look at it more closely. "Whoa, they sure aren't messing around when it comes to home security systems."

"Nope, that's cops for ya," Noah said with a laugh. "Oh, and for extra security..." He pulled out his phone and, in a few taps, showed her views of the home exterior.

"Cameras!"

"Yup, I told you it was state of the art," he said with a look of satisfaction.

"You're right, I definitely feel safer here than I would at home," she said and stifled another yawn. But Noah noticed.

"I think we're both exhausted and need a good night's sleep. Let me get you something to wear."

"No, no!" Maggie protested. "I'll be fine. I can sleep in...this." She looked down at her dress and heels. She knew that she hadn't sounded convincing when Noah shook his head.

"I know neither Cassie nor Wade will mind sharing some of their clothes with us. I'll be right back."

He moved off to the right past the bathroom toward an open doorway to the left of it. He returned several moments later, holding a folded stack of clothes. He pulled some items off the top and handed the rest to her, including a T-shirt, sweatshirt, and a pair of soft, cotton boxer shorts.

"What about you?" Maggie asked, already dying to get into the comfy clothes.

"I already pulled out this stuff of Wade's." He indicated the rest of the clothes in his arms. "You can change in there." He indicated the bedroom he had just exited. "I'll change in the guest room across the hall. I also put a fresh towel and washcloth on the bed for you, in case you'd like to wash up."

"Thank you," Maggie said, feeling incredibly grateful.

She changed her clothes and then moved into the tiny bathroom to wash her face in the pedestal sink. She studied herself in the mirror. There were dark circles under her eyes and her curls were out of control. She pulled a hair clip from her purse and did damage control, clipping it up in back to create a more manageable cloud of curls on top of her head.

She wished she had a toothbrush, but rummaged in her purse again and pulled out a piece of gum to chew instead. She remembered how she'd offered a piece to Noah after he'd been sick. Had it really only been that morning?

She pinched her cheeks to give them some color and daubed on some lightly tinted lip balm, determined not to look like a total slouch despite the circumstances.

She exited the bathroom and found Noah in a gray Whispering Pines Police Department T-shirt and shorts. He was holding two steaming mugs.

"What is it?" she asked.

"I made us each a mug of chamomile tea," he said. "My Nana always used to drink it in the evenings, so it must be good for relaxing."

He handed her one of the mugs and she curled her fingers around it to take a small sip, feeling the warmth of it seep into her.

"Do you want to sit for a bit?"

"Sure," she said.

They walked over to the loveseat and sat down. Maggie attempted to sit on the far edge of one side, but it seemed that the springs at the center of it were broken, causing her and Noah to end up squished together in the middle.

She was hyper-aware of the skin-to-skin contact as their bare legs and arms bumped against each other. She thought about getting up and sitting in one of the wingback chairs instead. But she didn't want Noah to know how much this was affecting her. So, she remained where she was and attempted to play it cool, taking another sip of her tea.

"This is perfect, thank you, Noah," she said, cradling the mug in her hands.

"I thought we could use a little unwinding after the day we've had."

"I agree. That Nick and Johnny were seriously scary. I wonder who they are and how they're involved with Valentina?"

"I don't know," Noah said with a shake of his head. "Can you believe they thought we were cops?"

"Crazy, right?" Maggie agreed. "And it's clear from the way they said it that for them, being cops was not a good thing."

"Yeah. So, it's probably good that they sound no closer to finding Valentina than we are."

"I really pray nothing bad has happened to her," Maggie said.

Noah put his mug down on a coffee table coaster and ran a hand through his hair. "I just wish I could remember more from last night."

"Well, at least we know Valentina was still fine while you two were dancing the night away on the sunset cruise last night," Maggie said.

"Mhm, and according to the videos, I was clearly using some of my best dance moves." He grimaced.

Maggie giggled at the memory of the cell phone images and videos.

"You know, despite all the chaos of today, I really had a nice time with you tonight," he said. "It reminded me of how much fun we used to have when we hung out together in high school."

"Yeah, me too," she said, keeping her eyes focused on her mug and trying to keep her tone light. "Although I don't recall ever getting to dance with you before."

There was a breath of silence after she spoke. Then she heard his voice, soft beside her. "Well, I'm glad I got to remedy that tonight, Maggie."

She felt his eyes on her and lifted her gaze, her eyes snagged by his. "Me too."

There was another long pause. He was so close to her right now. Her body felt aflame everywhere their skin connected, and her insides fluttered like someone had just released a flock of butterflies. It was so late and she was feeling loopy, almost dreamlike.

Was it possible that he'd moved even closer? The two of them were now practically nose to nose, their faces inches apart. The electricity between them was tangible, sparking and igniting every nerve in her body. Her eyes drifted down to his tempting lips, and she couldn't tear her gaze away. The urge to kiss him consumed her thoughts. She wondered what it would feel like. She imagined the heat of his mouth on hers, the softness of his lips, the taste of him. Desire pulsed through her veins, urging her to lean in just a fraction more.

His voice was a heated whisper. "Maggie..."

She blinked. Then she set down her teacup with a clatter and stood up abruptly. "It's late. We'd better get some sleep."

Whatever magic spell had been holding them captive was instantly broken. She felt the absence of his warmth beside her like a splash of cold water on her overheated emotions. She needed to get away from him, now, before she said or did something stupid, like ruining everything by sharing her true feelings for him.

"I can sleep here on this little sofa or wherever," she said.

"Don't be silly," Noah said, rising. His voice held a hint of frustration. "There are two perfectly good bedrooms on this floor. I'll take the guest room across the hall and you can have the master bedroom. I already changed the sheets when I was in there earlier."

"Okay, well, great. Thanks." She was already moving toward the bedroom he'd indicated. "I guess...it's good night then."

And she was gone.

Chapter 11

Noah was almost grateful when his alarm went off at seven-thirty the next morning. He'd hardly slept, tossing and turning all night as he thought about the beautiful woman sleeping two doors away.

He knew he should have been thinking about Valentina and the dangerous men who seemed to be after all of them. But all he could think about was Maggie. How incredible and brave she was to be helping him like this. And how beautiful she'd looked last night in that little black dress. And later here, with her fresh face scrubbed clean of makeup, her soft rose-petal lips practically begging to be kissed. Not to mention what her curves did to that ordinary T-shirt and cotton boxers. It was criminal.

At first, he'd been frustrated that she'd ended their night together so abruptly. He'd wanted to spend more time with her in ways that didn't have anything to do with solving the mystery of Valentina's disappearance or running from a couple of dangerous thugs. But in retrospect, he realized it had been a blessing. He wasn't certain how much longer he could have resisted the overwhelming desire he'd had to pull her into his arms and kiss her last night.

He swung his legs over the side of the bed and rubbed his hands briskly over his face to wake up. He peeked out of his bedroom door, but he could see that Maggie's door was still shut. So, he padded into the bathroom, took a quick shower, and dressed in a pair of khaki shorts and a short-sleeved button-down shirt that he'd nabbed from Wade's closet along with the other items last night. He and his two brothers had the same tall, lean, athletic build, making it easy for them to share clothing.

He cleared out of the bathroom, then tapped lightly on Maggie's door. "Hey, you alive in there?"

He heard a soft moan, then a muffled "No."

He laughed. "Can I come in?"

"As long as you don't frighten easily; I can look pretty scary in the morning."

"I can handle it." He pushed the door open and stepped into the dark room.

Maggie reached over and turned on the bedside lamp. She sat up in the bed and rubbed her eyes while he soaked up a view of Maggie Milena in the morning. Far from scary, she looked lovelier than ever. Her sleep-warmed skin held a rosy golden color that made him long to caress it. And her hair was a tousled, curling cloud that cascaded about her shoulders.

"Is it late?" she asked, picking up her phone from the bedside table.

"It's eight." He sat down carefully on the foot of the bed, wanting to be near her but not wanting to make her uncomfortable. "How did you sleep?"

"Fine," she said. But he noticed a warm flush color her cheeks. "You?"

"Fine," he lied.

"So," she said, setting her phone down. "Is it still our plan to head to the hospital this morning?"

"Yes, but maybe not right away."

"Huh?" She frowned, looking confused. "I thought we agreed we'd go first thing."

"Wouldn't you like to grab some breakfast before we tackle any new challenges? After all, if yesterday was any indication of what we might encounter today, we're going to need all the sustenance we can get."

She smiled at him. "Very true."

"I texted my brother Jake to let him know about everything that's happened so far. He and Alex are going to meet us at a restaurant in town and give us Boon back."

Maggie yawned and stretched. Her shape was highlighted to perfection inside the soft T-shirt and Noah blinked as he attempted to keep his focus on her face.

"That sounds like a plan," she said. "You know, I kind of miss that crazy dog."

"I do, too." Noah smiled.

"Will I be too overdressed if I wear what I wore last night?"

"We're not in that much of a hurry. How about if I take you back to your place? I can stay there to make sure you're safe so that you can shower and change."

She smiled gratefully. "That would be wonderful."

Together they cleaned up the dishes from tea the night before, then stripped and remade the beds.

They gathered their things and Maggie told Noah they could wash all the dirty sheets, towels, and clothes at her place.

Just after ten o'clock, Noah parked on the street in front of Chef David's in downtown Whispering Pines. The village was a popular tourist spot because of its massive state park, golden sand dunes, and location on the shores of stunning Lake Michigan. Throughout the summer and fall, tourists flocked there, filling the local shops and restaurants. But Chef David's—which only served breakfast and lunch—was tucked away on a side street off the main drag, and as a result, it catered primarily to locals. And just like Lakeside Latté, the establishment was dog friendly.

The outdoor seating area was an inviting oasis, with its bright umbrellas shading the outdoor table and chairs. Noah instantly spotted Jake waving him over to a table at the edge of the exterior dining section. The entire outdoor area was bordered with large potted planters filled with flowers in a profusion of colors.

Noah and Maggie started weaving their way among the full tables, but Noah stopped short when he heard someone nearby say his name. He glanced down at the table next to them and groaned inwardly. *Not again. This is NOT happening.*

"Noah, I thought that was you," said a young woman with a spiked pixie haircut featuring all the colors of the rainbow.

"Heeeey there, Christina! Good to see you again," Noah said, and then attempted to continue their path toward Jake through the crowded tables. But Christina reached out to grasp his arm, halting their progress. "Aren't you going to introduce me?"

Christina's eyes were studying Maggie with interest.

"Uh, of course," he said. "Christina, this is my friend Maggie."

"Friend?" She tilted her head, one corner of her mouth lifting in a smirk. "Count yourself lucky," she said, directing her comment toward Maggie.

"What do you mean?" Maggie asked.

"Well, if you're only his friend, then you're most likely safe."

"Safe from what?"

"From dating him, of course."

"You dated him?"

"Once. But once was enough."

Noah interjected, "Maggie, we really need to—"

"Why was once enough?" Maggie asked, clearly ignoring him as she focused on Christina.

"Well, for starters, I arrived at the restaurant for our date and found him getting up close and personal with another woman," Christina said, her expression turning sour.

Noah sighed. "If you recall, I explained that I thought she was you."

Christina rolled her eyes. "Seriously, dude? She looked *nothing* like my online picture! I mean, have you ever seen anyone with hair like mine?" she asked, turning her attention back to Maggie. "Then, he insulted my profession."

"I apologized!" Noah said. "I didn't realize you were the artist of the piece in that shop!"

"Mhm," Christina said. "But the worst thing of all was that he completely forgot that I told him I had a food allergy. So, he invites me back to his place and serves me a homemade dessert with walnuts in it. I spent the rest of the night in the emergency room."

Christina looked quite satisfied at the impact she was having on Maggie, whose mouth was now hanging open. This was not good. Not good at all.

"Look, Christina, I told you before how sorry I was. My brother Wade made that dessert for me and I...just forgot about mentioning your food allergy to him. But I got you to the hospital quickly. And you're fine now, right? So, uh, as much as I'd love to stand here and relive even more of that disastrous night, Maggie and I really need to go." He firmly took hold of Maggie's hand and pulled her along to the table before she or Christina could say anything more.

When they reached the table, Noah saw that Jake and Alex weren't alone.

"Wow, the whole gang is here!" he said, scanning the crowded table before giving his brother Jake a one-armed hug and thump on the back in greeting.

"We went to an early church service and decided to meet y'all for a nice, big family breakfast," said an older man with a booming voice and handlebar mustache. He indicated the table of people with widespread arms before standing up to wrap Noah in a huge bear hug.

"Hi, Pops," Noah said, hugging him back. "Let me introduce my friend, Maggie."

Noah began working his way around the table. "This is my grandfather J.P., also known as Pops," he said of the older man. "And his wife Tilly." He indicated an elegant woman with a chic, snowy white bob and sparkling blue-gray eyes. "Of course, you remember Jake from high school." His brother gave a nod of acknowledgment. "And this lovely lady is his wife, Alex." The pretty, dark-haired woman sitting next to Jake smiled, her eyes were the same unique color as Tilly's.

"It's wonderful to meet you all!" Maggie said, then turned her attention to Alex. "You're the one who referred Noah to me, right? I haven't thanked you yet."

"It was my pleasure!" Alex said with a smile. "I had a friend who used your service and had a great result."

"That's nice to hear!" Maggie's face lit up.

"Hey, don't forget this old lady over here!" laughed a woman seated at the far end of the table. She had a distinctive Southern drawl and bright red hair teased into a fluffy mound on her head.

"You are not old, Rita," Noah said. "You're classic."

"Charmer! C'mere and gimme some sugars!" Rita rose to cradle Noah's face in her hands; her fingernails were tipped with bright pink fluorescent polish. She planted a loud kiss on his cheek.

Noah returned to Maggie's side. "Rita worked for my dad and Jake at Riley Development for years, but she's now semi-retired and working part-time for me, handling admin for my marketing business."

"It's a blast! A big change from construction and development," Rita said, then winked at Jake. "No offense, sugar."

"None taken." Jake grinned at her.

"Besides, Noah here is a lot less intense than your daddy," she said.

"I can believe that," Jake muttered. "Noah may have inherited Dad's entrepreneurial spirit, but at least he understands the importance of not letting his business consume his life the way Dad does."

"Okay, okay," Noah said. "Let's not overwhelm Maggie with all of our family drama right now."

Boon rose from where he'd been lying at Jake's feet to greet his old friends. He was closely followed by a friendly looking golden retriever and a small, fluffy white dog.

"Oops, forgot to introduce these guys! Maggie, this is Rex," Noah said, introducing the retriever. "And this little angel is Angel," he said, reaching down to pet the little white dog. "She belongs to our brother Wade and his wife. As you know they're off on their honeymoon, so Jake and Alex are dog sitting."

Maggie bent over to give the three dogs their due attention. "Hi there," she said, scratching Boon behind a flopped over ear with one hand, and Rex with the other, then she leaned further down to pat Angel on the head. The bigger dogs pressed against her in immense joy at the attention, and she started to stumble backward from their combined weight.

"Rex, *nien! Hier!* Jake commanded, and the retriever instantly backed away from Maggie and returned to his side.

"Wow, what a well-behaved dog," Maggie commented. "And…was that German?"

"Yeah!" Jake laughed. "He's a retired police dog, so I can't take the credit for his training."

"Have a seat! We haven't ordered yet," boomed J.P.

Noah held out an empty chair for Maggie and then sat down beside her.

They all looked over the menus. Then the waitress arrived with glasses of ice water and took their orders.

As soon as she left, Alex said, "Did I see you talking with Christina, Noah? She's an amazing artist. Works with metal. I didn't realize you were friends with her."

"It didn't exactly sound like they were friends," Maggie murmured, taking a small sip of her water.

"Oh no." Alex's face fell. "Not another one."

Maggie looked at Noah with suspicion. "Another one what?"

"Another one nothing. Can we talk about something else, please?" Noah said.

"Oh, but why would we want to talk about something else when your love life provides us all with such entertainment, bro," Jake said with a sly grin. "Plus, I'm sure your matchmaker here would love to know all about it if she doesn't already."

"Matchmaker!" Tilly said. "Is that what you do?"

"Yes, I'm a professional matchmaker," Maggie said.

"She's the one who fixed Noah up with the missing Valentina," Jake said.

"I thought everyone was doin' all that online now," J.P. said.

"A lot of people do, but online isn't always the best option for some people. An algorithm can't predict chemistry," Maggie said. "Or connect with you to create a more personalized experience. Plus, some people just don't like having their personal life out there for the entire world to see."

"I can understand that," Tilly said, looking thoughtful. "I suppose if I were dating, I'd prefer doing everything in real life."

"Dating?" J.P. laughed. "I sure hope you're not already bored of me after only a couple of years of marriage, darlin'!"

"Never," Tilly smiled, and J.P. dropped a kiss onto her cheek.

Noah loved seeing how happy Pops and Tilly were together. Pops had been so lonely after Nana died several years ago. She'd been the love of his life, and Noah and his brothers had assumed he'd remain a widower. But then he'd met Alex's grandmother Tilly when Alex and Jake had gotten involved a couple of years ago. He'd even figured out he wanted to marry Tilly before Jake ever realized he was in love with Alex.

So many happy couples. Noah sighed inwardly and glanced surreptitiously at the beautiful woman beside him. He wished there was some way she would see him as more than just a friend.

The waitress arrived with their meals, and Noah hoped that the distraction would shift the conversation from his love life to something else. But that hope was instantly dashed when Pops said, "So, Miss Maggie, you think you can help our boy here even with all the dating disasters he's had?"

Maggie put down her forkful of French toast and slid a glance toward Noah. "Well, J.P., I'm getting the feeling that Noah may have left some things out of the dating history profile he gave me."

Jake snorted. "You mean he didn't tell you about his epic pattern of FDFs?"

Maggie frowned. "FDFs?"

"First Date Fails," J.P. supplied.

"What exactly does that mean?" Maggie asked.

"It means that he's never gotten past the first date with a girl," Jake said bluntly.

"Ever?" Maggie looked shocked.

"Ever," Jake said.

Noah felt all the blood rushing to his head, along with the feeling that he was trapped on a runaway train with no way to escape. He could feel Maggie's eyes on him. But what could he say? It was all true.

"Now, let's be fair," Alex said. "It hasn't always been his fault."

God bless Alex!

"Yeah, but it usually is," Jake said without tact. "I mean, how many times did he mess up the day, time, or location of a date?" Jake said. "Too many to count! I wonder how many poor women he left sitting there wondering if he'd actually seen them but just ran away or something."

Noah narrowed his eyes at his brother. He was going to punch Jake at the next available opportunity.

"And don't forget all the freak accidents that seem to befall these poor women," J.P. added, shaking his head. "Remember when he had that poor girl trying to guide him out of a tough parking spot and he ran right over her toe."

"Oh yeah." Rita nodded.

"But what about that crazy woman?" said Alex. "The one who kept talking about how Hitler was the most misunderstood man in history? That wasn't Noah's fault."

"Oh, she was terrible!" Rita said. She took a sip of her coffee, then looked at Noah. "How'd you ever end up on a date with her anyway?"

"I don't know," Noah mumbled. "The online site I was using matched us up somehow."

"See!" Maggie said. "That's exactly what I'm talking about with algorithms. Also, with my vetting process, that woman wouldn't have even become one of my clients!"

Maggie returned her gaze to Noah. "This whole FDF thing doesn't make sense to me though, Noah. I mean, I know you dated in high school."

He nodded, but couldn't meet her eyes. "In college, too. Back then, they weren't 'dating disasters' as Pops called them." His gaze flicked to his grandfather. "What used to happen is that I never got past a first date simply because we didn't click. Or I just didn't feel enough of a connection with any woman to go out with her again. Sometimes we'd just become friends. But after college, things just seemed to get worse. That's why I initially turned to online dating in the first place. I thought if I couldn't choose well, maybe software could do it for me."

"Well, we all know that was a big, fat fail!" Jake supplied after swallowing a mouthful of omelet. "And I hate to say this, bro, but this has to be your worst FDF ever. I mean, your date is literally missing, and hopefully she's not—"

"Don't say it!" Alex said, laying a hand on Jake's arm.

Noah ground his teeth. He'd just opened his mouth to let his brother have it when a voice behind him said, "Hey, Maggie, is that you?"

Noah swiveled in his chair to see Maggie's best friend from high school standing next to their table. A distinguished-looking older gentleman stood beside her.

"Jaime! George!" Maggie jumped out of her chair to give them both a hug before introducing them to everyone at the table. It turned out that George was Jaime's father.

"I invited her to brunch for a little father-daughter bonding time," said George. "We just finished."

"Why not join us for a cuppa and some conversation!" J.P. said with a welcoming grin. "The more the merrier!"

"Sure," said Jaime, after a nod from her father.

Everyone shuffled chairs around and squeezed together, and the waitress returned to take George and Jaime's coffee orders.

"I didn't realize you and Jaime were still in touch," Noah said to Maggie.

"Of course we are," Jaime said. "BFFs since elementary school." She threw an arm around Maggie and gave her a squeeze. "I was thrilled when she decided to move here from Grand Rapids and join me in living the sweet, small town life. It's been a blessing for Dad, too."

Noah was confused. "How so?"

"George is my unofficial business manager," Maggie explained. "He used to be a CFO for an automotive supplier, and he's much more knowledgeable than me in the financial aspects of running a business."

"One of the hottest-looking business managers I've ever seen," said Rita, openly batting her eyes at George. Somehow she'd finagled her seat to be right next to his, their shoulders brushing. George's face turned bright red.

"We were in the middle of discussing Noah's love life," Jake said, his eyes bright with mirth. "And we're all hoping that Maggie here can help him."

"She absolutely can!" Jaime said. "Maggie has a rare gift. She's helped so many people find true love, including a happy ending for me and my hubby, Jack."

"Really," Tilly said. "Tell us about it."

Jaime shared how Maggie had been the first one to recognize the potential between her and Jack, even though she initially hadn't given him a second glance. She explained how Maggie had masterminded their "accidental encounters" in college.

"Jack was so shy that Maggie even secretly helped him by providing conversation starters for him to use with me," Jaime laughed. "Before I knew it, I was head over heels for him."

"What a wonderful story!" Tilly clapped her hands together, her eyes twinkling.

"She has lots more," Jaime said, taking a sip of her coffee. Then she added with a sideways glance at her friend, "And someday soon, I hope to hear her own story."

J.P. put down his coffee mug and leaned forward in his chair. "Do you have a good story on how you found your own true love, Miss Maggie?"

Noah truly felt for Maggie as he watched her blush. But he didn't try coming to her rescue because he was too happy to finally have the attention off himself.

"I actually haven't found my own true love yet, J.P.," Maggie said lightly.

"Really?" Rita said. Even though she was responding to Maggie, she was resting her chin on her hand and staring straight at George, who seemed deeply occupied with stirring cream into his coffee.

Noah narrowed his eyes at Rita. He was certain that her blouse had been buttoned up higher only a moment ago.

Rita continued, her gaze still on George, "So, you haven't just...stumbled upon the perfect man yet?"

"Not yet," Maggie said with a tilt of her head.

"Maggie has such great success with her clients," Jaime said. "But when it comes to her own love life, well...let's just say that sometimes I think the matchmaker could use her own matchmaker."

"Jaime, I don't need a matchmaker!" Maggie objected. "Right now, I get all the satisfaction I need by helping my clients find their happily ever after's. And when the time is right, I'm sure I'll be just as successful at finding my own."

"Sweetheart, I think you should stop harassing your friend," George said to his daughter.

"Okay, okay," Jaime said, lifting up her hands. Then Noah heard her mutter quietly under her breath, "I just wish those losers hadn't messed her up so much."

He knew Maggie had to have heard her, but she gave no indication. Noah wondered who the losers were that Jaime was referring to. Old boyfriends? He wished he knew more about Maggie's own romantic history.

"So, George," Rita said. "You're retired, eh? I'm semi-retired myself. What do you like to do in your free time?"

"Spend time with my daughter and granddaughter Emma," George responded promptly.

"He also golfs quite a bit," Jaime said.

"Oooh, golf!" Rita gushed. "I've been thinking about learning. Do you ever give lessons?"

"Well, I...uh," George said.

"What a great idea, Dad!" Jaime said, seemingly oblivious to her father's discomfort with Rita's blatant attention. "He taught me and my brother how to play years ago. He's great at it."

"I bet you are, George," Rita said; somehow she seemed to have moved even closer to him.

Suddenly, George jumped in his seat. Then he scooted his chair away from Rita just as Noah noticed that one of Rita's hands was out of view. He flashed her a stern look. And barely looking contrite, she placed it back on the table.

Suddenly Boon, who had been lying quietly at Maggie's feet, got up and went over to George. He jumped up and put his two large front paws on George's lap. Then he laid his head on top of them.

"Oh!" George leaned away in surprise.

"No, Boon!" Noah said, rising from his chair. "Down, boy."

Boon's soft brown eyes shifted to Noah, but he remained where he was.

"It's actually okay," George said as he stroked the dog's silky back. "He just caught me by surprise, that's all. He seems very good natured."

"What a sweetheart!" Rita said, reaching over to pat Boon's furry head. Due to the dog's position, this caused George to flush red all over again.

"Aside from a few strange behaviors, like this," Maggie said, waving a hand in Boon's direction, "he does seem to be pretty well-behaved." Then she sighed. "Along with our search to find Valentina, we need to find Boon's owner as well."

"Right," Alex said, looking concerned. "I'm so sorry all this happened to you, Noah. We've been teasing you about your love life when you have a truly serious issue on your hands. Do you have any clues as to where Valentina may be?"

"Not yet," Noah said. "But we're still retracing my steps from Friday night. Apparently, after attempting to defend Valentina on the sunset cruise, I ended up in the hospital. We're heading there now to see if we can get any leads from that."

"Based on what you told me about yesterday, please be careful, bro." All joking had left Jake's face, and he looked at his brother with concern. "You don't have Wade and Cassie here to back you up. So, if you need me for anything..."

Jake didn't need to finish the sentence. Despite all his messing around, Noah knew that no matter what, his brother would always have his back.

"Don't worry," Noah said. "We're being extra careful. And I'll keep you posted."

He and Maggie rose to leave, but they paused when Jaime said, "Hey! Before you take off, I want to invite you all to a beach party Jack and I are hosting this afternoon. We're being spontaneous! The weather is just so gorgeous today; we want to enjoy it with friends by the lake. Just show up at the Village Park any time after two o'clock and bring a dish to pass. We're grilling brats and burgers and we'd love to have you join us!"

Everyone at the table thanked Jaime and promised to come.

But Maggie shook her head. "I don't know, Jaime. We really need to find Valentina."

"Come on, Mags," she pleaded. "You know Jack always says that taking breaks actually helps your brain work better. I think you and Noah could both use a little break from all your intense detective work."

Maggie held up her hands in protest. "All right! Far be it from me to contradict your brainiac husband. We'll stop by."

Noah and Maggie left the rest of them all chatting together and, accompanied by Boon, they made their way back to the Porsche.

Once inside, Noah started the engine and glanced at Maggie who was studying him with an odd expression on her face.

"What?"

"FDFs, huh?

"Yeah, yeah, can we forget about that for now?"

"I suppose...for now."

Chapter 12

The drive to the hospital was less than fifteen minutes. Neither of them spoke much during it. Noah seemed to be in his own head, which was fine because hers was still reeling from what she'd learned about Noah's dating history.

This was Noah. The handsome, funny, kind, and caring man she'd secretly crushed on in high school. Actually, if she was being totally honest with herself, he was the man she'd fallen in love with in high school. The fact that he couldn't seem to make it past the first date with a woman defied all logic.

She couldn't resist stealing a glance at him as he pulled into a parking space. A slash of sunlight illuminated his tanned, muscular legs that were on full display in the khaki shorts he wore. Her gaze traced up his flat abs to his chiseled jawline and the thick, dark curls that brushed the collar of his shirt. She envisioned twining her fingers into those curls, their bodies pressed close, feeling the heat of his breath on her skin. And as their eyes locked in an intense gaze, she could see his gray eyes sparking with desire as they looked deeply into hers.

She instantly snapped out of her daydream when she realized his gray eyes actually *were* looking deeply into hers.

"You all right?" Noah asked, his features flickering with concern. "You look a little flushed."

She looked quickly away, certain if she maintained eye contact, he'd know exactly what she'd been thinking. "Nope, all good over here."

She gathered her purse from the floor and sat up just as Boon stuck his head between their seats.

"Oh, what should we do with Boon?" she said. "We can't leave him in the car."

"Right," Noah said with a slight frown, then looked around the parking lot.

"We can tie his leash to that bike rack over there," Maggie suggested, pointing to the far left of the hospital entrance. "There's some grass beside it and shade from the tree."

"Good idea!"

They walked over to the bike rack and Noah attached Boon's leash to its frame. "We'll be back in just a minute, bud," Noah said. Boon cocked his head, both of his ears pointing straight up now, as if at attention. "You can lay here if you want."

Maggie watched in amusement as Boon instantly folded himself into a surprisingly small ball on the ground and laid his head on his paws. As he relaxed, both of his ears flopped over at ninety-degree angles, reminding her of paper airplane wings. She'd never seen such expressive ears on a dog before. He looked adorable, his warm brown eyes watching them steadily.

"I swear he knows exactly what you just said!" Maggie marveled.

"He's a smart one, all right," Noah agreed.

They walked together to the hospital entrance. The automatic doors swished open, then closed behind them.

The hospital lobby was clean and bright with white floors and walls. The large semicircular desk in front of them was made of dark wood with a sign on the front that read "INFORMATION" in bold letters. Hallways shot off to the left and right, and behind the desk stood a wide set of double doors leading to another area. A few visitors headed toward the hallways while staff members wearing scrubs walked back and forth, some on their phones or carrying clipboards with papers.

A young woman sat at the information desk, speaking into a telephone as they approached. They waited patiently until she hung up and turned her attention to them.

"Excuse me," Maggie said when Noah didn't speak right away.

"No. Flipping. Way," said the young woman behind the desk. She was staring at Noah.

"Heeeey there, Nora," Noah said in that uncomfortable tone that was starting to become all too familiar to Maggie.

Maggie glanced at him and saw the equally familiar shade of red creeping into his cheeks.

"Seriously, Noah?" she said.

"Well, if it isn't Mr. Never Showed Up!" Nora said.

"Nora, I explained what happened," Noah said.

"Yeah, I know you did," she said with a toss of her mahogany curls. "It's just a little hard to believe that you went to the wrong restaurant...twice."

"It's the truth!"

"Uh-huh. Well, some may say that the third time's the charm. But in my book, two strikes and you're out, buddy."

"Excuse me," Maggie said. "Are you saying that he booked two *different* dates with you and didn't show up to either one because he...because he went to the wrong location *both* times?"

"You got it!" Nora replied.

Maggie turned to face Noah. "How is that even possible?"

"I'm gifted," Noah said. "Look, I think we're forgetting the real reason why we're here." He turned his attention back to Nora. "Can you please put your feelings about me aside for a moment and just check to see if I was here for treatment Friday night?"

Nora gave him a long look, then, with a huff, turned back to her computer and began tapping on the keyboard.

A moment later, she read from the screen. "Yes, you were in our Emergency Room, and you saw Dr. McCaughan. He was the on-call doc that night."

"Is there any way I can speak with him?"

"I'm not sure," Nora said. She did more tapping on her keyboard and then glanced up at them. "You're in luck. He's in the building right now."

Nora directed them through the double doors behind her. They went through them, then walked along a tangle of hallways, following signs to the Emergency Room on the other side of the building.

"Noah," Maggie said as they walked. "Maybe you should give me a list of all the women in town that you FDF-ed with so that I don't accidentally match you up with one of them. Although that might be a challenge since we seem to be running into them literally everywhere!"

Noah sighed. "Look, I know it *seems* like there have been a lot of women, but…" He ran a hand through his hair, making it stick up in that absolutely adorable way of his. "Oh, whatever! Maybe it has been a lot. But please, Mags, can we just focus on Valentina right now?"

"Okay, okay," she said with a small smile, feeling warmth flood through her upon hearing him use the nickname he'd had for her in high school.

Eventually they walked through another set of double doors to enter the Emergency Room lobby.

Where the main entrance had exuded a somewhat calm, quiet ambiance, this area was bustling with activity. Many of the chairs that ran around the perimeter of the room were filled with people, some reading books, some staring into space, some talking, while a few others were clearly in need of help and were waiting their turn.

Noah and Maggie stepped up to the small desk area. A sliding glass window allowed for communication between staff and visitors.

"Driver's license and insurance card, please," said the woman behind the glass, barely glancing up from the paperwork in front of her.

"I'm not here for an emergency," Noah said. "I was here Friday night, and I'd like to speak with the doctor I saw, Dr. McCaughan?"

The woman looked up then. She was middle-aged and plump with a slightly frazzled air. Dark-rimmed reading glasses were perched at the end of her nose.

"He's with a patient right now," she said. "I can let him know that you're here, but you'll have to wait a bit." She indicated the full waiting room with a wave of her arm.

"We understand," Noah said. "Whenever he's available. I promise not to take up much of his time."

Together, he and Maggie claimed two seats away from the other waiting patients.

"I'm sorry I harassed you about your FDFs," Maggie said, nudging one shoulder against Noah's. "And you know, despite all the teasing you endured at breakfast, it's clear that Jake, Alex, Rita, and your grandparents care a lot about you."

Noah leaned back in the hard plastic seat, his long legs extended straight out in front of him. "I know they do, and I love them. But that doesn't mean

I don't owe Jake a few good punches for messing with me like that in front of you."

Maggie smiled. "Isn't that what brothers do? Not that I have any brothers, but I feel like that's what most guys always do. They find some way to tease or insult one other, instead of coming right out and admitting they love each other."

Noah tipped his head, thoughtful. "Yeah, I guess that's kind of true."

Maggie turned serious. "Noah, can I ask you something?"

"Sure."

"Why didn't you come right out and tell me about your real dating history when I did my intake interview with you?"

Noah looked down at his hands that were folded in front of him. He slowly rubbed his thumbs together. He was quiet for so long that Maggie wondered if he'd heard her. But then he spoke. "I guess, I was just embarrassed."

"But why? Back in high school, we used to be comfortable talking about anything with each other," Maggie said.

He looked up at her and something unreadable glittered in the depths of his eyes. "We did. But high school was a long time ago."

Maggie thought she heard a hint of sadness in his voice. She dragged her eyes away from his and brushed some imaginary lint off her white shorts. "Let me ask you a different question then. Why do you think you keep choosing the wrong women and having FDFs?"

"Because the universe doesn't want me to be happy?" Noah said with a smirk.

"Be serious, Noah!"

He let out a deep sigh. "I don't know, Maggie. I'm just bad at it. I've always been bad at it. Like I said, even back in high school."

"I always thought you were this hot guy who just liked playing the field."

"You thought I was hot?" His smirk returned.

"Gimme a break, Noah. You know you are!" Maggie said, hoping the heat flooding her cheeks wasn't too obvious. "But that's not the point. Was I wrong about you being a bit of a player back in the day?"

"Dead wrong," Noah said. "That was more my brother Jake, not me. I actually just wanted..." He hesitated.

"Wanted what?"

His gaze was fixated on his hands once more. "I just wanted to find one special girl who I could truly care for," he admitted softly, then added, "But for some reason, I can't seem to find her."

"Noah Riley?" a woman in dark pink scrubs stood in the open doorway beside the reception desk. "Dr. McCaughan can see you now."

The woman led Noah and Maggie down a hallway lined with hospital beds separated into makeshift rooms by curtains. Some rooms were completely enclosed by the curtains, others were empty and open, and she led them into one of them. Maggie sat in the chair beside the bed while Noah paced anxiously in the small space.

A middle-aged man with short salt-and-pepper hair rolled a small cart into their room. He wore blue scrubs under a white coat.

"Hang on just a second," he said as he stood and typed quickly into the small laptop computer perched on top of the cart. Then he looked up at Noah and Maggie and smiled. "Sorry about that. Just trying to keep up with the paperwork. I'm Dr. McCaughan."

Noah nodded and introduced himself. "And this is my friend Maggie," he said, turning to look at her.

"Nice to meet you, Maggie," Dr. McCaughan said. "And nice to see you looking so much better than you did on Friday night, Noah. How's your cheekbone feeling?"

"Better, thanks."

"I understand you have some questions for me?" Dr. McCaughan said.

"Yes, uh..." Noah cleared his throat. "Dr. McCaughan, for some reason I have no memory of what happened to me on Friday night."

Dr. McCaughan frowned. "That's strange; let me pull up your chart." He began typing into his laptop, and his frown deepened. "That doesn't make any sense. My examination didn't reveal any damage to your head." He looked up at Noah. "Can you get on the bed here, please?"

Noah did as instructed and Maggie watched as the doctor performed an examination, flicking a small light between each of Noah's eyes and gently probing his head and neck area. "Any tenderness?"

"No," Noah responded.

Dr. McCaughan stood back looking puzzled. "Hmmm...let me check one more thing."

He moved back to his computer and began typing. Then his frown cleared. "Ah, I see what the problem might be."

"What is it?"

"We drew some blood for testing when you were here, and I have the results. We found a large amount of alprazolam in your system."

"Alpra-what?" Noah said.

The doctor looked up from the computer screen. "Alprazolam, it belongs to the class of medications called benzodiazepines, otherwise known as Xanax."

"Xanax!" Noah looked shocked. "But I've never taken Xanax in my life!"

"Apparently, you did on Friday night," Dr. McCaughan said. "And at the level you were at, I'm not surprised that you don't remember anything. But don't worry. Alprazolam is a short-acting medication, and overall, it's generally safe. However, overdose side effects can include drowsiness, poor coordination, confusion, slurred speech, and temporary amnesia."

"Noah!" Maggie cried. "This makes total sense! Remember how some of the people we spoke with thought you seemed drunk?

"But how could I have that drug in my system when I don't even own any?"

Dr. McCaughan rubbed this chin thoughtfully. "There's actually a liquid form of alprazolam. It's difficult to get, but it does exist. Is it possible you drank something on Friday that contained it?"

"I don't really see how," Noah said. "The only drinks I had were in my own home and then in public dining venues."

"Hmmm, well, the good news is that the effects are not lasting. You may not get your memory of Friday night back. But the level you had in your system won't do any permanent damage."

"At least there's that," Noah mumbled.

"Is that all? I have other patients I need to get to." Dr. McCaughan prepared to roll his mobile desk cart out of their room.

"Wait, Dr. McCaughan," Maggie said. "There's one more thing. Do you recall a young woman accompanying Noah?"

The doctor's brows shot up. "Oh, yes, I almost forgot about that! Just before we released you, there was an altercation going on in the waiting room. Two men were placed under arrest by the police. I heard that the young woman who accompanied you here was addressing them with some very colorful language as they were being escorted out of the building. She accused them of stalking her. They all put on quite a show for our staff and everyone else in the waiting room."

"Did you see the two men?" Maggie asked.

"I'm sorry, I didn't," he said. Just then, an older woman in blue scrubs walked passed their room and he called out to her. "Lara, you were here Friday night, weren't you?"

Lara turned and gave a nod. "I was."

"Did you see all the drama and the arrest in the waiting room?"

"I sure did," she said with a shake of her head.

"Noah," Maggie said. "Show her the picture of those two guys from the cruise that you have on your phone."

Noah pulled out his phone and quickly scrolled through the images. Then he held up one for Lara to see. "Was this them?"

She peered at the screen for a few seconds and then nodded. "I believe so."

Maggie and Noah exchanged a look. Then Noah turned back to the doctor. "I'm sorry, I just have one final question. Did I give you any indication where I was planning to go after I left here Friday night?"

The doctor shook his head. "I'm sorry, I don't recall."

"That's all right," Noah said. "Thanks for everything you did for me, and for this information. You've both been really helpful."

Back outside, Noah unhooked Boone's leash from the bike rack and he trotted beside them as they all walked back to the Porsche.

The day had grown warm, the sun shining bright in the cloudless blue sky. Noah grabbed a collapsible dog dish from the floor of the back seat and placed it on the ground in front of Boon. He took a water bottle out and poured the contents into the dish for the dog.

"Wow," Maggie said. "You're really prepared."

Noah acknowledged her comment with a small nod, but his expression remained serious.

"What's wrong?" Maggie asked.

"I'm just frustrated. We've hit a dead end and we're still no closer to finding Valentina."

"Maybe you should call your friend Hugo, and let him know that those two guys, Nick and Johnny, were arrested here Friday night," Maggie suggested. "Maybe he can find out some information about them that will help us."

"Good idea!"

Noah dialed Hugo's number and put him on speaker so that Maggie could hear. He updated him about the two men, the attack last night, and about the drug found in his system. Hugo promised to look into the arrest for him. Then he said, "I was actually about to call you, Noah. First of all, they rushed the preliminary toxicology report on that bottle of wine we found in Valentina's condo."

"What were the results?"

"They found arsenic in it."

"What?"

"Calm down, Noah. I admit it doesn't look good, but right now there's still no body and no hard evidence specifically linking you to her disappearance."

Maggie saw Noah go pale.

"One more thing," Hugo said. "The police found Valentina's cell phone."

Chapter 13

Maggie and Noah exchanged a shocked glance.

"Where?" Noah asked.

"There's an old guy who regularly goes through public trash bins downtown looking for stuff he can use or sell. He found it in the garbage can on Main Street, just outside the animal shelter. The battery was removed, so it's pretty clear that it was intentionally tossed there."

"How strange," Maggie said.

"The old guy posted it for sale on a local social media marketplace, and a young hacker bought it," Hugo continued. "She was messing around with it and accessed the photos on it. Because of the news story, she immediately recognized Valentina's image in several of the pictures."

"What news story?" Maggie and Noah said together.

"Uh..." Hugo hesitated. "I thought you guys would have seen it already. I hate to have to be the one to break this to you both, but somehow the story got out about Valentina missing and..."

"And what?" Noah cried.

"Look, there's no need to get worked up about that right now," Hugo said reassuringly. "It's just typical media trying to stir up drama. What I want you to know is that the hacker did the right thing and turned the phone over to the police. Their IT specialist was able to retrieve Valentina's call history and text logs, which showed she had been contacting one specific number frequently, but it wasn't yours. The police suspect that the messages are in some sort of code. I'll keep you updated as they gather more information."

Noah thanked Hugo and they disconnected. He leaned back against the side of the car, looking dazed. "Now what?"

Maggie thought for a moment. "Well, since we don't have any other leads right now, maybe we should visit the place where the phone was tossed out. It might help you jog your memory."

Noah agreed and they all climbed back into the car. Noah started the engine and Maggie hit a button on the center console. She clapped her hands with delight as the convertible top opened smoothly, folding into a secured slot at the back of the car.

"How did you know how to do that?" Noah asked.

She gave him a sidelong look. "I might have done a little Googling about Porsches after I went to bed last night."

Noah laughed, and Maggie thrilled at the sound of it. She was pleased that in the midst of all the stress they were under, she could make him smile.

They headed back downtown, and Maggie pointed out a parking spot right in front of the animal shelter entrance.

"I dunno," Noah said. "It looks a little tight!"

"Trust me," Maggie said. "Just pull up alongside that car in front of it."

Noah did as she instructed, then looked at her. "I still don't think—"

He stopped speaking when Maggie reached her hand forward and tapped a button on the touchscreen. The car instantly began rolling backward and then angled smoothly into the parallel parking spot.

Noah closed his gaping mouth and turned to give her a look. "Google?"

"Yeah!" Maggie gushed. "It has a parking-assist system. Isn't that so cool?"

Noah rolled his eyes, but she could tell he was suppressing another grin.

"Okay, there's the animal shelter," Maggie said, pointing her finger toward it. "And there's the garbage can. Does anything around here seem familiar?"

Noah glanced up and down the sidewalk, then shook his head.

Although Boon had been calm and quiet, lying in relative comfort in the cramped back seat, he sat up now, pushing his long nose between the seats. His brown eyes were alert, and he began to whine.

"What is it, boy?" Noah asked, reaching to pet the dog's head in an attempt to soothe him. "What do you see?"

Maggie and Noah looked around at the string of small, local businesses lining the street. Since it was Sunday, most of them were closed. And being a distance from the popular tourist shops, there were only a few pedestrians around, but none of them were near the car.

"Why don't we get out and just stand here for a minute," Maggie said. "See if it sparks anything." Then she looked at Boon. "I promise we won't be long, buddy," Maggie added her own scratches behind one of Boon's ears, both of which were now pointed straight up again. "You know," she added. "He could easily jump out of the car here with the top down like this."

"I could put it back up."

"No!" Maggie responded so fast it made Noah laugh again.

"Okay, okay. How about this," he said, carefully looping the dog's leash around the interior front door grip. "That should keep him secure."

With a final pat on Boon's head, they both got out of the car and started walking toward the animal shelter and the garbage can beside it.

Suddenly, Maggie halted in her tracks. "Oh. My. Gosh," she said, pointing.

"What?" Noah followed the direction of her finger and saw that she was pointing at the newspaper stand in front of the building.

"I know, right?" Noah grinned. "Where else would you even see a real newspaper stand like this anymore? My Pops still loves to read what he calls a 'real newspaper' every—"

"Not the stand," Maggie interrupted him. "The newspaper inside it!"

She fumbled in her purse and pulled out a credit card to swipe through the reader at the top, then opened the box to pull out a paper. She stepped several paces into the shadowed alley beside the building and unfolded it, quickly skimming the front page.

Noah came to stand behind her and looked over her shoulder.

The front page of the newspaper displayed a large photograph of Valentina beneath a bold headline, "Local Woman Missing After Date from Matches by Maggie."

"Oh no," Maggie groaned. She handed the newspaper to Noah and leaned back against the rough brick wall of the building, putting her hands over her face.

Noah began reading out loud. "One of Whispering Pines' newest local residents, Valentina Romano, is missing and presumed dead. She was last seen on a date with fellow Whispering Pines resident, Noah Riley. The date was arranged by local matchmaking service, Matches by Maggie." He looked up, sputtering. "What the heck! And where did they get these photographs of us!"

"What?" Maggie stepped away from the wall to look more closely at the article and saw small photographs of each of them included further down in the article. "I don't know. I feel sick."

Noah read on. "This is another huge issue for the startup dating service run by local resident Maggie Milena, who personally approves each of her clients. The company has lately been the subject of multiple negative reviews on social media." Noah looked up from the page. "Really?"

Maggie just lifted one shoulder in acknowledgment, trying not to cry.

He read on. "With regard to the missing woman, police found incriminating evidence in Ms. Romano's home, including a partially empty wine bottle laced with arsenic. So far, no charges have been brought against Mr. Riley, but the search for Ms. Romano's body is a top priority for the Whispering Pines Police Force."

Noah looked up again. "How did they get access to details about the crime scene? And seriously, why did they have to say 'body' and 'presumed dead' like that? They're literally trying to sensationalize it as a murder before anything has even been proven."

"And is it murder, Mr. Riley?" a low voice hissed.

Noah lowered the paper and they found themselves face to face with Nick and Johnny from the night before. The man named Nick stepped in close and pressed a long blade between Noah's ribs.

"I wouldn't do that if I were you, Ms. Milena," he said without looking at her. "I promise you, this time, I'll be much quicker with my knife than you are with your cell phone."

Maggie started to lower her cell phone just as the man named Johnny stepped forward and gripped her upper arm, just as he'd done the night before. He wasn't much taller than she was and she tried to shake him off, but his fingers were like an immovable vise, digging painfully into her flesh. There was a slight bulge beneath his shirt as he moved, letting Maggie know that he must still have the gun she'd noted at their last encounter.

She glanced quickly up and down the alley they were in. They were a decent distance from the sidewalk, and there were no passersby.

"Move!" Nick ordered, forcing Noah further back into the shadows of the alley.

Johnny dragged Maggie along with them. Maggie observed that Nick was still dressed in the same clothes from the night before. The collar of his shirt was open. She and Noah could more clearly see the tattoo on the side of his neck that they'd noticed in the photographs. It was a series of letters, "OMERTÀ," and she wondered what it meant.

"Answer my question, Mr. Riley," Nick said, his voice deceptively calm. "Is it murder?"

"No!" Noah said.

"Then where is Valentina?"

"Just like I told you last night. I don't know!" Noah said.

Maggie watched as Nick took a deep breath and then cocked his neck at a strange angle, making it crack, his cold blue eyes never wavering from Noah's face. "Who's paying you?"

"Nobody! What are you talking about?" Noah was clearly getting angry now.

"Did you really think you could mess with Papa Dom and get away with this?" Johnny asked, glaring at Noah.

"Who is Papa Dom?"

Nick continued to study Noah's face, saying nothing as several long moments ticked past. Then he smiled. But it was a smile that didn't touch his eyes. "You know what, Mr. Riley, I think I might actually believe you. I think it's possible that you really don't have any idea what I'm talking about."

"Good," Noah said. "Because I don't."

Nick raised his non-knife-wielding hand and Noah flinched. But Nick only slowly patted the side of Noah's face. "I'm even starting to think that you may just be an innocent bystander in all of this."

"Yes! That's me, an innocent bystander. So, can you please stop terrorizing us like this?"

This time Nick's smile did touch his eyes as he gave a short laugh. "A polite one, isn't he, Johnny?"

Johnny made a non-committal grunt.

"Unfortunately, after everything that's happened so far, letting you go free is not an option," Nick said in a light, casual tone, like he was discussing the weather. "You both know just a little too much now. And that's a risk the Partnership isn't willing to take." He shook his head. "We're going to have to remedy that."

Maggie saw Noah's Adam's apple bob as he swallowed.

"Hey!" came a sharp voice from the entrance to the alley. "What's going on there?"

Everyone looked to see two little old ladies marching toward them.

"Gretchen, please!" cried one of the women. She was trailing behind the first woman who strode purposefully toward the group. She stood barely five feet tall, but she was built like a small tank. Her short hair was dyed a flat brown color that had been teased and hair sprayed into an immovable helmet on her head.

"Pipe down, Margot," the woman called Gretchen snapped. She stopped a few feet from them. "What are you doing in this alley?"

"Nothing for you to concern yourself with, Grandma," Nick said. He'd already snatched the newspaper from Noah's hand to drape over his knife. "We're just having a friendly discussion."

Her small, dark eyes shifted from face to face and lingered on the way Johnny still held tightly to Maggie's arm.

"It don't look all that friendly to me," she remarked. "Why are you holding onto her arm like that?"

Gretchen and her friend, Margot, were now side by side. While Gretchen exuded a tougher vibe, Margot looked more like a classic grandmother. She wore a flowy, floral-print dress over her plump frame and carried an oversized handbag. Her silver hair was twisted into a soft bun at the nape of her neck. Nervous fingers played at the delicate lace collar of her dress as she surveyed the group with wide, pale blue eyes.

"She looks scared, Gretchen," Margot whispered, but it echoed clearly in the small alleyway.

"She does." Gretchen took a step closer to Nick and Noah, this time focusing her attention on Noah. "Aren't you one of them Riley boys?"

"Yes, ma'am," Noah said. "But we're fine here, really. I think that you and your friend should—"

"Whatcha got under that newspaper?" This time Gretchen addressed Nick, ignoring Noah's attempt to get rid of her.

Nick's nostrils flared, and a wave of fear washed over Maggie. As scared as she was, she didn't want anything to happen to these innocent ladies.

"He just told you we're fine here," Nick said. "Now, beat it!"

Gretchen advanced another step closer. She was right beside Nick now.

"What is that? A knife?" Gretchen asked, and Maggie could see the point of the blade was slightly exposed, glinting from beneath the edge of the newspaper.

Nick rolled his eyes and dropped the paper. "Yeah, you old bag, it's a knife. I was just showing my friend Noah here how sharp it is."

Gretchen's beady eyes narrowed, then she and Margot exchanged a look.

Gretchen turned to squarely face Nick. "Why don't you show me how sharp it is?"

Maggie was appalled. What was this crazy lady doing?

Nick gave a loud snort of frustration through his nose and turned toward Gretchen. Stepping forward, he grabbed a handful of fabric at the neckline of her shirt, and with his other hand, he thrust the blade at her throat. "Sure, old lady, take a good look."

As Maggie watched, everything seemed to happen in the blink of an eye.

In a lightning fast move that belied the woman's advanced age, she watched Gretchen angle her body away from the blade. She grabbed hold of Nick's knife arm with her left hand and delivered a powerful strike to his throat with her right. She followed it up with a forceful knee to his groin, causing him to double over in pain. With precision, Gretchen twisted his knife arm, lifting it up and forcing his wrist forward until he released his grip on the knife. She quickly snatched it from his hand before delivering a swift kick to his face.

Nick howled in pain and blood streamed from his nose as he rose back to a standing position. But by now Gretchen had leapt back, the blade securely in her hand.

Suddenly Margot was in the game, whacking Johnny with her oversized purse like it was a baseball bat. "You. Let. Her. Go. Right. Now!" she panted between blows as Johnny staggered back with each impact.

In the pandemonium, Maggie was vaguely aware that she could hear Boon barking.

Then she heard a voice call out, "Hey, what's going on here?"

"Call 911!" she heard another voice cry out. "Someone's trying to mug those old ladies!"

Suddenly Boon stood at the alley entrance, barking loudly.

The gathered crowd rushed toward them as one with Boon leading the way, his leash trailing behind him. Without another word, Nick and Johnny bolted in the opposite direction, racing down the alley away from them.

"Get those men!" another voice shouted as the crowd and dog rushed past, chasing after the fleeing men.

Within seconds, Maggie, Noah, and the two women were left alone in the alley.

"What just happened?" Noah said.

"I'm pretty sure these ladies just saved our lives," Maggie said. She turned to face them. "Thank you so much!"

"Sure thing," Gretchen said. Then she waggled the large knife at her friend. "I told you them Krav Maga lessons I took at the senior center would come in handy one day."

"Oh, for heaven's sake, Gretchen! Please don't point that thing at me," Margot said, taking a step back. "Do you realize you could have been killed?"

Gretchen gave a small shrug. "But I wasn't. And what about you, beating up that guy with your handbag?"

Margot blushed. "Well, I couldn't just stand here and do nothing! That man was clearly hurting this poor girl." She looked at Maggie. "Are you all right, dear?"

"I'm fine now." Maggie laughed. "Seriously, the two of you were amazing! By the way, I'm Maggie."

"We're grateful you were here," Noah said. "But now I think we should get out of this alley."

Together, they all walked back up onto the sidewalk.

"I'm curious," Noah said, looking at Gretchen. "How did you know I was a Riley?"

Gretchen snorted. "Seriously, kid? Everybody in town knows that you and your equally hot brothers are J.P.'s grandsons. And now that your brothers are both hitched, you're the most eligible bachelor in town, even considering the fact that you're probably a murderer."

"Gretchen!" Margot cried out, looking appalled.

"Well, that's what the top story is about!" Gretchen waved the newspaper she'd picked up after Nick had dropped it in the alley. "By the way, mind if I keep this. That's why we stopped. I wanted to get a newspaper."

"Sure," Maggie shrugged. "It's not any news I want to read right now." She looked at Noah. "What do you think we should do now?"

Noah's shoulders slumped. "I suppose we should start by letting the police know we were attacked," he sighed. "Again."

He pulled out his cell phone and made the call. Within minutes, two officers arrived at the scene. After getting a statement from each of them, and securing the knife in an evidence bag, the officers made certain everyone was all right and then left.

"All right, Margot," Gretchen said. "Shake a leg! We're going to be late for the party."

"Oh my goodness!" Margot said. "In all the excitement, I forgot."

Maggie and Noah thanked them again, standing side by side, waving as the two women climbed into an ancient blue Impala and drove off.

Together, they walked slowly back toward the Porsche, and Maggie could feel the worry emanating from Noah like it was a tangible entity.

She nudged him with one shoulder. "You okay?"

"Me!" he sputtered. "I feel awful for ever getting you involved in this."

They were at the car now and he turned to face her. "Of all my FDFs, this is the absolute worst ever."

Maggie smiled ruefully. "It's not your fault, you know."

"Then why does it feel so much like it is? We still haven't found Valentina, and if those guys find her first, who knows what might happen to her."

"Noah, those guys are clearly a couple of very dangerous men, and it's equally clear that they were already involved with Valentina somehow."

"I just..." He ran a hand through his hair. "I'm out of ideas. I still don't remember anything from Friday night and I just don't know what to do next."

Maggie couldn't resist. She reached up to smooth back the dark curls he'd just messed up. He looked surprised, but not displeased. And she let her hand linger there for a few seconds longer than necessary before dropping her hand. Then she said, "I know what we need to do next."

"What?"

"Have you ever heard of the Pomodoro technique?"

Noah looked at her quizzically. "No."

"Well, it's a productivity technique I use when I'm working on something that requires a lot of time and concentration," Maggie said. "It's one that Jaime's husband Jack recommended to me. It's based on the theory that taking regular breaks to relax your mind ultimately helps you work more efficiently and effectively."

"You think we should take a break?"

"I know that seems counterintuitive right now, but maybe relaxing for a little while will help you remember something. Besides, we did promise Jaime that we'd go to her beach party which is happening right now."

Noah studied her for a moment, then he nodded. "Okay, let's do it. It's not like we have any new leads to follow anyway."

"Okay then," Maggie said. "Let's beach party!"

They turned toward the car and Noah reached to open her door for her. They both spotted Boon's water dish on the floor of the back seat at the same time and exchanged a look.

"Oh man! On top of everything else, I can't believe we lost Boon, too." Noah said sadly.

Woof!

They both turned around in surprise to find Boon trotting toward them, his leash trailing on the ground beside him. His tail wagged happily as he came to a halt beside them and dropped a scrap of dark fabric from his mouth onto the ground.

"Uhhh," Maggie said. "Do you think that's from...?"

Noah grinned. "Definitely looks like the fabric from Nick's pants to me. I guess we'll need to drop off one more piece of evidence at the police station before we join the party."

Chapter 14

After dropping off the piece of fabric at the police station, Noah drove Maggie home and insisted on waiting while she changed for the beach. With Nick and Johnny still on the loose, he had no intention of leaving her alone for a single second.

Afterward, they drove together to his place so he could change. Then they were on their way.

"They're at the north end of the beach," Maggie said, looking up from Jaime's text on her phone.

After parking, Noah attached Boon's leash while Maggie gathered their small contribution to the party feast, a container of hummus and pita bread that she'd had on hand.

"I hope this isn't too lame of an offering," Maggie fretted.

"I'm sure Jaime will understand," Noah said with a wry smile as they all walked toward the water. "Especially considering how busy we've been playing detective and being attacked again and all."

"True." She smiled up at him, her honey-colored eyes twinkling, and his heart jumped in his chest. She looked beautiful in a lacy white beach cover-up over her turquoise bikini, her spiraling curls floating on the soft lake breeze. "It's not like we're having a typical run-of-the-mill weekend."

"We definitely are not." Noah laughed.

A swath of velvety green grass dotted with wooden picnic tables, charcoal grills, and tall shade trees formed Whispering Pines' small Village Park. It butted up against a stretch of soft, sandy Lake Michigan shoreline. Noah instantly spotted Jaime among a small cluster of people near one of the picnic tables and they made their way over. The tangy scent of the lake mingled with the aroma of food sizzling on the grill, and Noah's stomach growled. All the adrenaline of the past few hours must have depleted his energy reserves from breakfast.

"Hi, guys!" Jaime said as they drew near. "I'm so glad you could join us! Noah, this is my husband, Jack. And this is Emma," she said, referring to the golden-haired baby, who was bouncing up and down on chubby little legs while Jaime held onto her tiny hands.

Jack stopped grilling to reach over and shake Noah's hand. "Nice to meet you. And perfect timing. I'm almost done here and we're just about to eat. We've got brats and burgers on the menu, plus all of that." He waved his spatula toward a nearby picnic table filled with an array of side dishes.

"Sounds great!" Noah said.

He and Maggie walked over to add their hummus and pita bread to the mix, then Maggie introduced him to several of her and Jaime's friends who were standing nearby. However, she notably skipped one of the women standing in the cluster.

As the group chattered together, Maggie stood on tiptoe and whispered into his ear, "Sorry about that, but I don't know that other woman."

Jaime had just walked a waddling Emma over to them. So, Maggie gave a surreptitious tilt of her head toward the woman and asked quietly, "Who is that?"

Jaime glanced in the direction Maggie had indicated. "Oh, that's Amy Jude. She owns the Little Lakeside Bookshop here in town. She went to college with us."

Maggie frowned. "I don't remember her."

Jaime smirked. "That's because she didn't hang out in the same circle as us. She was in some brainiac club with Jack or something."

Almost as if the woman guessed they were discussing her, she looked up and stared directly at Maggie. She was thin and wiry, with dark hair pulled back into a low ponytail. Her round glasses made her eyes look slightly larger than they were.

Noah watched as Maggie smiled and lifted her hand in acknowledgment, but the woman's gaze was cold, almost hostile. She stared hard at Maggie for a long moment before pointedly turning her back.

That was weird, Noah thought.

"Hey," Jaime said, recapturing their attention. "We claimed some space on the beach over there if you want to lay out your blanket and towels and stuff."

Maggie thanked her. Then she and Noah trudged across the warm sand to spread out their large blanket next to the spot where Jake, Alex, and the rest of Noah's family sat, lounging in chairs and on blankets beneath colorful beach umbrellas. The fragrance of coconut sunscreen wafted on the breeze as people basked in the warm sun.

Rita McCay was there too, waggling her bright, lacquered fingers in a friendly hello. Noah noted that Rita would have been impossible to miss in the vibrantly colored cover-up she wore draped over her electric green tankini. Her bright red hair peeked out from beneath a large sun hat.

Rex and Angel trotted over to greet Boon, which involved a lot of sniffing and tail wagging.

"I thought dogs weren't allowed on the beach," Maggie said. "We were going to tie Boon up in the park area."

"As a retired police dog, Rex gets special dispensation," Jake grinned. "And I'm sure the Whispering Pines police force will make an exception for a couple of Rex's friends."

"Probably not when they know one of his friends is owned by a potential murderer," said a voice from beside J.P. and Tilly.

Noah looked over and spotted two familiar faces beneath a pair of matching, floppy sun hats.

"Margot and Gretchen!" he cried in surprise. "What are you doing here?"

Tilly looked confused. "How do you know my friends?"

"We met earlier this afternoon," Noah said. "After Maggie and I got threatened by those two thugs from last night again."

"What?" Alex cried.

Noah went on to recap everything that had happened earlier, including how the two little old ladies had come to their rescue.

"Pshaw!" Gretchen waved a hand. "No big deal. Just glad my training paid off."

"And really, Margot, again?" Tilly asked, giving the woman a playful nudge with her elbow.

"I don't know what you're referring to," Margot said primly, dusting some imaginary specks off her voluminous, pale pink caftan.

"Oh knock it off, Margot," Gretchen said, looking at her friend over the top of her sunglasses. "It's not the first time you've used that handbag as a weapon."

"Really?" Maggie asked.

"Oh, yeah, she once used it to beat up this old fart who was stirring up a lot of trouble for Jake and Alex a few years back. But Margot attacked him with that weaponized handbag and it took care of him."

"I was just...frustrated," Margot sniffed.

"Beware, folks! You don't want Margot frustrated with you when her handbag is anywhere nearby!" Gretchen said, then snorted with laughter at her own joke.

"Hello, everyone! May I join you?" All heads turned to see that Jaime's father George had arrived. He'd clearly already been swimming, his salt-and-pepper hair now dark with water and slicked back from his face, a damp towel hung over one tanned shoulder. "It's such a warm day, I couldn't resist jumping right in when I got here. The water feels great!"

"Oooh, I saved a spot for you right over here, Georgie!" Rita flashed him a brilliant smile and patted a spot on her blanket beside her.

"I'm sure I can just squeeze in over—"

"Don't be silly," Rita said, jumping up. She crossed the sand and hooked her arm through his, pulling him along to the space beside her. "Besides, your towel is wet now, so you can't sit on it!" She pulled a fresh, fluorescent-colored towel from an oversized beach bag and spread it out for him right next to her. Noah watched as George reluctantly sat down on it.

"You know somethin', sugar?" Rita said. "Your shoulders look a little red. Let me get some sunscreen on that."

"No, no!" George protested. "I'm fine. I already—"

But it was too late. Rita had already whipped a bottle of coconut-scented sunscreen from her bag and was massaging it slowly and generously over George's shoulders and back. His face was bright red and he was looking at Maggie helplessly.

Noah glanced at her and saw that she was biting her lip to stop herself from laughing. Noah cleared his throat and tried to signal Rita with his eyes to let her know that she was going overboard, but he was pretty sure that she was deliberately ignoring him.

"We saw the newspaper article about your missing date, Noah," Tilly said. "I'm so sorry they wrote it in such a sensationalistic style."

"Yeah, bro," Jake said, using both of his hands to stroke the two bigger dogs' heads as they now both lay on either side of him. "That article was way extra. I'm the only one who should be allowed to mess with you about your losing record of FDFs."

Noah shot his brother a withering look, then shook his head. "I get it. They want to sell their stupid papers. What I'm more annoyed about is the way they purposely cast Maggie's business in a bad light."

"Unfortunately, that part of the article wasn't inaccurate," Maggie said with a sigh. "I did set up the date. I do personally vet my clients. And I have been dealing with some bad reviews lately."

"But those reviews are not legitimate!" George said heatedly. "You are a consummate professional, Maggie." His eyes moved around the small group. "She is very proactive about seeking feedback from her clients. And even those who haven't yet found their perfect match have nothing but positive things to say about her and her business."

"Oooh, Georgie! You sound so...*formidable* when you talk like that," Rita said, letting her hand rest on the shoulder where she'd just been focusing her efforts. Then she leaned in close to his ear and whispered something.

It seemed impossible, but George's face went even redder than before. However, Noah noticed that he didn't remove Rita's hand.

"Thanks, George," Maggie said, giving him a small smile. "At least my trusty business manager is always here to encourage me."

"I'm only speaking the truth, Maggie," George said. And Noah could see in his eyes how much the older man cared for her.

"It's just so frustrating because I really do try to ensure that every client that I work with is satisfied. But to get hit with those reviews and then the news article, I'm afraid they're really going to do damage to my fledgling business."

"I'm so sorry this is happening to you, Maggie," Alex said with a sympathetic look.

"Soup's on!" Jack called from the grill.

"Woohoo!" J.P. shouted as he rose. He reached out a hand to help Tilly to her feet. "That's great, because I'm starved."

The partygoers headed into the park area, and after loading up their plates, everyone spread out among several of the picnic tables.

Noah and Maggie ended up seated with Tilly, J.P., Gretchen, Margot, Rita, and George. As they ate, the conversation picked up where it had left off.

"Have you tried to figure out who exactly the reviews are from?" J.P. asked after swallowing a mouthful of his burger.

Maggie nodded. "They've come from several different social media accounts. But whenever I try to find the bio of the reviewer, I can never find anything."

"Maybe I can help," Margot said.

"You?" Gretchen shot Margot a look of surprise, pausing in the midst of drizzling mustard over her Italian sausage.

"Yes," Margot sniffed and lifted her chin. "While you were busy learning Krav Maga, I took several online research classes offered by the public library. I'd be happy to look into it for you, Maggie."

"That would be wonderful," Maggie said.

"What would be wonderful?" Jaime asked, coming up to stand beside Maggie. She was holding Emma, but when the baby saw Maggie, she immediately put out her arms and Maggie placed her on her lap, cuddling her in a hug.

With her little halo of yellow curls, Noah could easily imagine her as Maggie's own baby, which sent his mind into a reverie, wondering what their babies would look like if they ever married. Then he instantly gave himself a mental slap. *What the heck is wrong with you, Riley?*

"Margot may be able to help me figure out who has been leaving those terrible reviews," Maggie said.

"Oh good!" Jaime said. "My Emma is a rock star, and she doesn't deserve that negative stuff they've been saying about her online!"

"Emma?" Tilly looked in confusion at the baby in Maggie's arms.

Maggie laughed. "Jaime has been calling me Emma ever since I started applying my matchmaking skills back when we were in college."

"Ah," Tilly said. "I'm guessing she named you after Jane Austen's heroine?"

"Yup," Jaime said with a grin. "Except that *my* Emma is *way* more successful than Jane's."

"Have I met this Jane person?" J.P. said, pausing mid-bite to give Tilly a sidelong glance.

"No, love," Tilly laughed. "She's a very famous romance author from the early nineteenth century."

"Oh," he grunted, and took the bite.

"I just love all of Jane Austen's books!" Margot said with a dreamy look.

"They're all right," Rita said. "Although, I prefer my romances with a lot more steam in 'em."

"Shocker," Gretchen muttered, jabbing a slice of sausage with her fork.

"Oh my goodness, sugar! You have a bit of ketchup on your shirt. Let me get that for you." Rita began daubing her paper napkin against George's chest, and Noah watched George's face go red for about the hundredth time.

Gretchen rolled her eyes. "Seriously, McCay, you're about as subtle as a brick."

Rita didn't seem the least bit phased by Gretchen's blunt comment. She simply turned a dazzling smile in George's direction and gave him a wink.

Now it was Noah's turn to press his lips together to stop himself from laughing out loud.

Suddenly Boon, who had been lying quietly beside him, got up and walked around the table. He reared up on his hind legs and put his two front paws on the picnic bench seat beside George, similar to what he'd done earlier that day. Then the dog gave George a big lick on the face and attempted to lay his large, upper body across George's lap.

"What's he doing?" George sputtered.

"Nothin' I haven't already thought about doin'," Rita murmured.

"I'm so sorry." Noah jumped to his feet. "No, boy! Boon, down!"

The dog looked at Noah with his gentle, brown eyes, but he didn't move until Noah came around the table and physically lifted the big dog off George's lap.

"There must be something about you that invites doggie cuddles, George," Tilly commented.

"It isn't just you, George," Maggie commented. "He did the same thing to me. Maybe once we find his owner, we'll figure out what's behind this weird behavior."

"It's all right," George said, reaching down to pat Boon's head since the dog still stood by his side gazing up at him. "I can tell he doesn't mean any harm. In fact, in the right circumstances, it might even be comforting."

"With McCay so obviously makin' the moves on you like that, you could probably use some comforting," Gretchen said, and everyone laughed.

Noah glanced up at Jaime, wondering how she was reacting to Rita's extremely forward behavior toward her father. He expected to see shock or annoyance. Instead, he noted the hint of a smile playing at her lips. Then she surprised him by saying, "I think it's kind of refreshing to see someone flirting with you like that, Dad."

"Jaime!" her father exclaimed.

"Seriously, Dad!" Jaime put her hands on her hips. "You've been alone for four years now. And I may as well confess, half the reason I wanted you to work with Maggie is because I knew if anyone could help you find someone special to bring into your life, it would be Maggie."

"No offense to your skills, Maggie," Rita said, throwing an arm around George and pressing against him. "But this sweet man won't need any kind of matchmaking service while I'm around!" Everyone at the table laughed again.

"Aside from my dad, there is one other person I would love to see get the benefit of Maggie's amazing matchmaking services," Jaime said lightly, taking baby Emma back into her arms.

"Who?" Maggie said, her attention suddenly sharp. "Did you give them my card?"

"I don't need to give them your card," Jaime said with a twinkle in her eye.

"Why not?"

"Because it's you!" And with that, she bade the group farewell and moved on to chat with the people at the next table.

Chapter 15

When the meal ended, everyone drifted back toward the beach. Noah and Maggie joined in an exhilarating game of beach volleyball. Amidst the flurry of volleys and dives, Boon bounded into the game with unrestrained enthusiasm. With a playful bark, he intercepted the volleyball mid-air, paws kicking up sand and tail wagging as he skidded to a stop in front of Noah.

Both teams exchanged looks, then broke into amused grins followed by peals of laughter as the volleyball game transformed more into a game of keep-away and fetch with the dog.

Once the game ended, Noah went to fill up Boon's water dish, and left him tied up at the base of a tree with the other two dogs, while he and Maggie went to splash in the white-crested Lake Michigan waves.

Maggie had initially tried to avoid swimming, telling Noah that she was fine standing on the warm, sugar-sand beach and occasionally letting the cool blue waves slide over her feet and ankles.

"C'mon, Mags," Noah insisted. "Swim with me!"

"I dunno. I think the water's too—" But the rest of what she'd been about to say got lost in a shriek as Noah suddenly picked her up, tossed her over his shoulder, and strode into the water.

"What. Are. You. Doing?" she puffed with each step.

"I'm taking you swimming."

"I love *looking* at Lake Michigan. But I only swim in well-heated pools!" she said, trying to wriggle free.

"Until now," he replied, giving her backside a couple of playful pats.

She shrieked again. "Noah Riley, you put me down right now!"

"As you wish." And with that, he pulled her off his shoulder, cradling her against his chest for one blissful second before tossing her high into the air—more shrieking—and letting her land in the water with a solid splash.

She came up sputtering, her curls now limp and plastered all over her face. She peeled the strands away and her toffee-colored eyes narrowed dangerously. "That was really not a wise thing to do."

"Why not?" Noah was still laughing.

"Because I'm really good at this."

Before he realized what she was doing, she executed a swift somersault, her legs sweeping his from under him, and he teetered off balance, water swirling over his head.

He popped back up to the surface, coughing.

"Guess you shouldn't have had your mouth open," she smirked.

"All right, Milena. It's game on!"

She laughed, deftly sidestepping his playful advance, and dove beneath him. He felt her fingers at his waist and then her legs wrapped around his, tipping him off balance and leaving him submerged once again.

They continued playing in the waves like a couple of kids until Maggie finally called it quits. "I'd like to get at least a little lounging on the beach before this day is over," she told him.

They trudged out of the water, throwing splashes at each other as they went. Jaime's and Noah's families, along with most of the partygoers, had already left. But back on the sandy shoreline, Noah and Maggie's towels and blankets still lay side by side where they'd left them. They first checked on Boon, who now lay sleeping comfortably in the shade of the giant oak. Then the two of them stretched out and let the golden rays of the late afternoon sunshine warm them up.

Maggie lay on her back, her sunglasses hiding her eyes. Noah started out lying on his stomach, but eventually rolled onto his side and propped his head up onto one hand. He took a moment to admire the lush curves of her sun-kissed body, accentuated by her vibrant bikini.

Maggie was such a fun, beautiful, intelligent woman. He marveled again at the fact that even after all these years of providing people with happy endings to their love stories, she still hadn't managed to find her own.

He considered her prone form thoughtfully. Then, sitting up, he said, "All right, Milena, what's your story?"

Maggie tipped her sunglasses down and looked up at him in confusion. "What are you talking about?"

"When we were in high school, you dated Joe, the most popular guy in school," he said. "But everyone knew he was a total loser and didn't deserve you at all. You're smart and beautiful, Mags. At any moment, you probably could have snapped your fingers and dated anyone else, because half the guys in our class were in love with you." *Me most of all.* But he could never say that last part out loud.

"Get outta here!" she said, replacing her sunglasses.

"I'm serious, Maggie!" Noah said, unwilling to be put off. He was determined to understand her better. "You now know all about my embarrassing dating history of FDFs. I know I'm your client and you have a right to know all that to help me. But we're also friends, right? So fair's fair. How have you remained single all this time? And what did Jaime mean at breakfast this morning when she said she wished those losers hadn't messed you up so much? What was she talking about?"

Maggie sighed and sat up as well. "You're not going to let this go, are you." It wasn't a question. And Noah continued looking at her expectantly.

The warm glow of the sun enveloped them and waves lapped along the shore, their foam gently shaped by the warm evening breeze.

Maggie took a deep breath and removed her sunglasses. Her eyes swept the horizon as if searching for the perfect words, then her golden gaze turned to his. "Like I mentioned before, in college, one of my majors was psychology. I find the subject fascinating, particularly with regard to interpersonal relationships. I've read loads of books on the topic, and over the years, I've come to psychoanalyze myself. I made the big mistake of sharing my theory about myself with Jaime a while back."

"Why was it a mistake?"

"Because Jaime is like a dog with a bone," Maggie said with exasperation, "and she just won't let it go now!"

"What's your theory?"

Maggie's eyes dropped to the sand and she drew her knees tight to her chest, as if building a protective barrier. "I already told you about how after growing up in a loving family environment, I was sent to live with my aunt and uncle after my parents died."

Noah nodded his acknowledgment. "You said that your aunt and uncle didn't have a great marriage and fought all the time. And that's what sparked your desire to bring romance and happy endings to other people in your life."

"Yes," Maggie agreed. "But there's more to my story than I originally told you."

Noah could see genuine sadness reflected in Maggie's eyes, and he could hear it in her voice.

She lifted her eyes to look out over the water again as a few nearby children shouted, playing tag with the waves. Seagulls wheeled on wind currents overhead, their bright white wings almost glowing in the fading light of early evening. "It wasn't just that my aunt and uncle didn't love each other, they...didn't love me either." Her voice broke a bit. "After I moved in, it was quickly clear that they didn't want me. Never wanted me. I was a burden to them, an obligation they felt they had to fulfill."

Noah frowned, but didn't speak, waiting for her to continue.

"For as long as I lived with them, I bent over backward trying to do anything and everything I could to earn their love and acceptance. I tried to be the perfect student, did chores around the home without even being asked, made myself as amiable as possible. But it didn't matter. Nothing I did was ever good enough."

Her gaze returned to his. "Over the past couple of years, I've come to recognize that their attitude toward me affected me in some specific ways."

Noah tilted his head. "Such as?"

She took another deep breath and let it out slowly before speaking. Her next words sounded almost as if she was reading from a textbook. "When a child has unresponsive caretakers, that can often trigger deep-seated feelings of being unworthy or not good enough. Children that lack self-worth often begin telling themselves that they're not loveable enough to have the relationships they want." She dropped her chin to rest against her knees. "And, well, basically, I've given myself a classic diagnosis of self-sabotage. I choose the wrong men and maintain unhealthy relationships because deep down, I just don't feel worthy of love."

Noah was stunned. Maggie was a literal gift to everyone who knew her, *to him most of all*. How could such an incredible woman feel this way?

"But if you know that's what you're doing, can't you just stop?" Noah asked, feeling confused.

Maggie smiled, but it didn't touch her eyes. "You'd think so, wouldn't you? But even though I know with my head that my belief is wrong—I mean, we're all worthy of love, right? Even though I intellectually understand this, on a subconscious level, I haven't yet been able to convince my heart. So, I keep choosing men who don't treat me well. Who don't value me. And I keep repeating the same destructive behavior of bending over backward to try and earn their love in order to make my relationships work."

Noah's mind flashed back to high school. Everyone in their class knew that Joe was sleeping around on Maggie, but she'd been completely loyal to him. He'd watched her fight to keep that worthless relationship going until it had all come to a head. Joe's cheating had finally become so blatant she just couldn't ignore it anymore.

"So, you're saying that even the guys you dated in college and afterward were as disrespectful to you as Joe was in high school?"

Maggie gave him a solemn nod, then added, "But there is a bright side."

"What?"

"Through the help of a really good counselor, I've finally come to realize that even though I've been on a self-destructive path, I am fixable."

Noah grinned. "I'm glad you realize that."

Maggie smiled back. "My counselor has helped me understand that my previous relationships didn't fail completely because of me. They failed because—to be blunt—the men I chose were narcissists who never truly loved anyone but themselves. And I understand now that those relationships were not worth saving anyway."

"That's a great step forward, Mags," Noah said, smiling at the lift of her chin and the determination he saw reflected in those heart-melting eyes.

Now that she'd shared all this with him, his heart began to lift. He understood now why she didn't have a special man in her life. His thoughts whirled. He'd been called many things in his life, but never a narcissist. Maybe he could finally have his shot with Maggie, ask her out, and move out of the friend zone where he'd been trapped for so long. And maybe, just maybe, he could finally confess the true feelings he'd harbored for her ever since she'd first tutored him in chemistry.

"Yes, it is," Maggie agreed, breaking into his daydream. "But now, in order to prevent my unhealthy pattern from continuing, I've stopped dating completely. No men, no relationships. Period."

The hopeful high Noah had begun riding only a few seconds ago deflated like a balloon inside him. He felt as if he'd just been sucker punched. "Oh. Uh...for how long?"

She gave a small shrug. "I don't know. Months? Years maybe? As long as it takes for me to feel confident that I'll get it right next time."

Noah fought to keep his expression neutral. This was her solution? Even if he was brave enough to finally ask her out—admittedly a dangerous proposition for her in itself—she'd clearly never agree to it now.

Noah had fallen in love with this woman when he was sixteen years old. And spending this time with her over the past few days had only solidified his feelings. He still loved her deeply. But now a feeling of sadness sank like a rock in the pit of his stomach, because she'd just made it clear that there was nothing he could do about it. He'd finally reconnected with her again, only to be forced into what? More waiting? He felt overwhelmed with the hopelessness of it all. Would their timing ever work out?

"Noah, are you feeling all right?" Maggie was looking at him with concern.

"Yeah, yeah," he said with a small shake of his head. "I'm just...processing."

"You know, all of this self-reflection right now is making me think more about you and your situation." She looked thoughtful.

"What do you mean?"

"Well, now that I understand the truth behind your dating history, the whole story about your FDFs..." She narrowed her eyes at him.

Noah grinned, not even embarrassed anymore.

"I'm starting to wonder if maybe you're doing some self-sabotaging yourself?"

He frowned. The idea that he could possibly have been self-sabotaging his first dates with women had never occurred to him. "But, I've never struggled with feeling unworthy of love," he said. "And with only a few exceptions, most of the women I ask out are...well, nice ladies. They're certainly not narcissists."

"True," she said, studying him. "And I didn't mean that you were doing it for the same reason I was, or even in the same way. But could you be self-sabotaging for another reason?"

"I don't know why I would," he said. "I mean, I see what my brothers have, what Pops has with Tilly. And I want that for myself. I want to find true love. I came to you for help because I just figured I'm really bad at trying to choose the right woman for me."

Maggie nodded slowly. "Maybe just think about this whole idea for a bit, whether there could be something that's holding you back from giving your all on these first dates?"

"I guess I can do that," Noah said. "But maybe to play it safe, after we find Valentina, I'll try the 'not dating thing' too for a while."

"Oh no! Did I just talk you out of being my client?" She laughed.

Just then, Noah's cell phone rang. He pulled it out of his duffel bag and tapped the screen before setting it down between them.

"Hey, Hugo! I'm with Maggie at the beach right now, and you're on speaker. What's up?"

"I could ask you the same question, *amigo*. Is there something you forgot to tell me?"

"What do you mean?"

"The police just found your car."

Chapter 16

Noah and Maggie exchanged wide-eyed looks.

"The Porsche?" Maggie said, immediately rising to scan the parking lot.

"Porsche?" Noah could hear the confusion in Hugo's voice. "No, his Trailblazer."

"Where?" Noah cried.

"Before I tell you, why didn't you mention it was missing when we spoke on Saturday morning?"

"I didn't realize it was gone until after you'd left. And then there was the whole thing with the Porsche."

"What whole thing with the Porsche?"

Noah launched into an explanation of finding the Porsche in Valentina's parking lot after Hugo and the police had left them and about how all the paperwork stated that the car was his.

"So, this Porsche is actually in your name?" Hugo sounded incredulous.

"Yes," Noah said. "The police have checked it out already, and everything seems to show that it really is mine. But, again, I have no memory of buying it, Hugo."

"Strange," Hugo said, sounding thoughtful. "Well, I have some other news to share with you besides the discovery of your car. Can you take the phone off speaker? I want to make certain passersby can't hear the rest of what I want to say."

Noah did as Hugo asked, and then scooted closer to Maggie so they could both lean in to hear. She smelled like warm vanilla and sunshine and he inhaled deeply, nearly forgetting he had the phone in his hand until Hugo began speaking again.

"I'm technically not allowed to share all of this with you, so what I'm about to tell you is officially off the record, okay?"

"Okay," Maggie and Noah said together.

"Needless to say, a potential murder in Whispering Pines is a big deal. So, naturally, the police are putting all hands on deck to get to the bottom of this missing woman. As a result, they're moving a lot faster than normal when it comes to getting back results from the lab, like the arsenic in the wine I told you about."

Noah sighed.

"But they've learned more. Even though the wine bottle had enough arsenic in it that just a few sips would have been enough to kill someone, there were no traces of it in either of the wine glasses that were on the table."

"That's good, right?" Noah said.

"Well, it certainly doesn't hurt," Hugo replied, then continued. "And about your car, Noah, they found it abandoned on a back road outside of town. The police have thoroughly examined it. Any fingerprints inside and out have been wiped clean, including yours, which is strange. And there was no evidence that anyone else may have driven it."

Noah shook his head, and Maggie placed a hand on his shoulder. But he couldn't even appreciate her gentle touch. "Please tell me there was no dead body in my trunk, Hugo?" he said in a low voice.

"No dead body," Hugo said. "And another positive for you is that they've uncovered new evidence that's leading them to consider other suspects in Valentina Romano's disappearance."

"Like what?"

"They were able to obtain a print from the knife your alleyway attacker used. The knife belongs to a man named Nicola Verilla, also known as 'Nick the Knife.'"

"Nick the...what?" Noah exclaimed.

"Apparently, Verilla is the number two man for the Detroit Partnership crime family," he paused for effect. "As in, the mafia."

Once again, Noah and Maggie exchanged shocked looks.

"But why would the...er," Noah looked around furtively to make certain nobody was nearby, but still whispered the next part of his question, *"family* be coming after me? Or Valentina?"

"They haven't figured out a connection yet, but they're working on it. I just knew you'd want to know."

"I do! Thank you, Hugo!"

"One more thing before I let you go," Hugo said. "They don't have any further reason to hold your car, so I pulled a few strings and they're releasing it. You can come pick it up."

Noah thanked Hugo again and disconnected.

Maggie threw herself back onto the blanket and Noah followed suit, both of them staring up at the twilight sky. It was painted in streaks of pale pink and blue as the sun sank closer to the waterline, making its way toward sunset.

"I can't believe this," Maggie said. "First it was just Valentina, then arsenic in the wine, and now the mafia?"

"And don't forget my erased memory," Noah said.

She turned her face toward him. "This is all so much bigger than we ever realized."

"It really is," Noah replied. He sat up then, his eyes fixed on the horizon. The weight of everything that had transpired hung heavy in the air between them.

A moment later, he felt Maggie lay her hand gently on top of his, a silent gesture of support. "We'll figure this out, Noah," she said. "Together."

Noah pulled his eyes from the waves and gazed down at her. He studied her face, the slight furrow between her brows, the expression of concern coloring her features, and the curve of her lips as she nibbled the bottom one with her teeth. Then his eyes skimmed over her, admiring how her skin glowed like warm honey from their afternoon in the sun. In spite of everything that was happening, everything they had just learned from Hugo and the anxiety it induced, all he wanted to do right now was wrap her in his arms and pull her close. He could almost feel the softness of her body against his, feel her inviting warmth as he breathed her in.

His eyes moved back to hers and found her looking back at him, heat flickering in the depths of her gaze. Their eyes remained locked on each other's for a heartbeat, then two, as the tension between them seemed to grow with each passing second. The air around them crackled with unspoken words, and Noah felt his pulse begin to accelerate. He reached out a tentative hand, his fingers tracing the line of her jaw, brushing against the soft curve of her cheek. She leaned into his touch, her eyes fluttering briefly, as she seemed to savor the sensation.

Then, without breaking eye contact, Noah leaned slowly toward her, testing. But she didn't move away. Instead, her lips parted. The swell of her breasts rose and fell as her breathing increased. In that moment, time seemed to stand still, and the world with all its chaos faded away, leaving just the two of them.

Maybe it was the confusing roller coaster of emotions he'd been riding all weekend. Maybe it was the safe port in the storm that she represented for him in the midst of this turmoil. But no. Even as these thoughts occurred, he dismissed them from his mind just as quickly. It wasn't any of those things. It was the fact that he was in love with Maggie Milena. He'd always been in love with Maggie Milena. And now, he wanted to kiss her.

His heart pounded in his chest as he closed the gap between them until their lips were only a breath apart.

"Noah?" her voice whispered against his skin.

Woof, woof! Boon's sudden barking caused them both to start. Noah automatically looked up and Maggie quickly scooted from beneath him, sitting back up a distance away. They both turned to look at where the dog sat beneath the tree, staring at them. Both of his expressive ears were now pointed upward at full attention. The spell was broken.

"The poor guy is probably bored," Maggie said.

Noah nodded, certain that the regret he was feeling showed clearly on his face.

"I...think we'd better go," she said.

They didn't talk much on the way to the vehicle impound lot. Maggie was grateful for Boon's intervention. Who knows what stupid thing she may have allowed to happen if she hadn't been saved by the bark? She knew without a doubt that Noah had been about to kiss her back there on the beach. And heaven help her, she'd wanted him to with every fiber of her being.

Oh yes, I'm not dating at all anymore. No, siree. I'm staying away from men completely. Big talk, Milena.

The more time they spent together, the more difficult it was getting for her to deny her true feelings for him. She thought their years apart would have erased her feelings for Noah, or at least softened them. But she was even more in love with him than she'd been in high school.

She knew that Noah was a wonderful man, and she even recognized that he was not the type who would be a bad choice for her. In fact, he was the opposite. He was the kindest, most thoughtful, most gentlemanly—and yes, she may as well admit it—the sexiest man she'd ever known. The problem was that up until now, they'd remained strictly and safely in the friend zone. And even though he'd been about to kiss her, she was certain that her feelings for him ran much deeper than his did for her.

And there was absolutely no way that she was going to let herself get involved with him in some sort of casual way. She was smart enough to recognize the pain such an involvement would cause her down the road if she let herself act on impulse now.

She took a deep breath and reminded herself that he was her client. It was her job to find him his happily ever after. And a casual romance with her was not it.

They pulled into the impound lot Hugo had directed them to. And after Noah signed a form, the officer in charge led him to his car and handed him the key.

"They found your car unlocked with the key under the mat," the officer said with a shrug.

Noah unlocked the car and looked around inside, then checked the glove box. "Everything seems to be here," he said.

"Is the car still in your name?" Maggie teased with a smirk.

"Looks like it," he said, holding up the small, white car registration form.

"So, what do you want to do now?" she asked.

"I don't know," he said. "I've gotta be honest, I've felt pretty weird driving around in that Porsche. I think I want to hold off on driving it anymore until we get to the bottom of this whole thing."

"Sooo...what are you going to do with it?"

"If you're okay with this, can you drive the Porsche and follow me back to Valentina's lot? We can leave it there for now." He ran a hand through his hair. "I would take you home after that, but I think we should sleep at my brother's again tonight. I know the police have made it a priority to look for Nick the Knife and his partner, but they're still out there somewhere."

Maggie hadn't really heard much of anything Noah said after he'd asked if she'd drive his Porsche. With a broad grin, she held out her hand. "Key, please!"

Noah rolled his eyes and pulled the sleek decorative key fob out of his pocket. Maggie reached for it, but he pulled his hand back, looking her squarely in the eye. "No speeding!"

"Yeah, yeah," she said, snatching the key and slipping into the driver's seat. "Come to Mama," she said as the engine purred to life.

Back at the condo parking lot, she pulled into a space and regretfully turned off the engine.

Noah parked in the empty space on her passenger side.

It was well past sunset now and a few clouds had gathered at the edges of the sky, hinting at the possibility of rain later. But now, a blanket of summer starlight glittered overhead and a warm breeze teased at the curls around her face as she walked around to Noah's car. His window was down and she could see the flash of his white teeth as he smiled in the darkness. "She'll be all right, Mags, I promise."

"I'm just really going to miss her," Maggie said, climbing into his passenger seat and giving a dramatic sniff.

A panting Boon stuck his head between the front seats to greet his old friend. He gazed at her, his soft eyes glowing with concern.

"Hey, buddy," she said, scratching him behind one flopped-over ear. She giggled as his pointed wet nose nuzzled her and then she leaned away as his pink tongue shot out in an attempt to lick her cheek. "No kisses right now, Boon!" she laughed.

Noah had his hand poised to put the Trailblazer in gear, but he didn't complete the action. Instead, he seemed lost in thought, staring out into the darkness for so long, she started to wonder if he'd fallen asleep with his eyes open.

"Hey...Noah? You okay?"

He surprised her by shutting off the engine. Then he twisted in his seat to angle toward her. There was only a single light pole in the center of the parking lot and it wasn't very close to them, so most of his face was hidden in shadow.

"I'm not sure."

"What is it, did you remember something?" She leaned closer, trying to discern his features.

"No, it's something you just said."

"What?" she was mystified.

He cleared his throat. "Maggie, when we were at the beach earlier, just after Hugo called...well, it kind of felt like we were having a moment."

Maggie was grateful for the darkness now so that Noah couldn't see the heated blush suddenly staining her cheeks. *A moment? Yes, we were having a moment! You were about to fulfill my teenage dreams by pressing your lips against mine.* But no way was she saying that out loud.

"I'm not certain what you mean," she lied.

He didn't respond and they sat together in silence as several interminable seconds ticked past. Although the night hid his face, she knew that he was studying her.

Finally, he spoke again. "I think you do, Maggie. I think you know that I wanted to kiss you. And...I still want to kiss you."

His voice was a low, husky whisper that washed over her, making every inch of her skin tingle and a delicious warmth blossom deep inside her. She could not believe that he'd just said that out loud. Her mind whirled.

"I—look, Noah," she said, struggling to keep her voice calm, cool, rational. "I think we've had a couple of very long days here. And maybe the stress of it all is wearing on us and bringing up feelings that we wouldn't normally—"

The rest of what she'd been about to say faded to breath as he slowly leaned toward her, just as he had on the beach. The light of a crescent moon illuminated his face, casting shadows and soft highlights across his features, and she could clearly see the desire in his smoky eyes. Their lips were now only an inch apart and he hovered there, as if waiting to see what she would do. But she'd lost the ability to speak, to think. Her own lips trembled in anticipation as they almost brushed against his. She could feel the tantalizing warmth of his breath, the heat emanating from his body, the intoxicating scent of him overwhelming her senses.

Then the tender touch of his lips pressed against hers, soft and sweet. He lingered there, sending shivers of pleasure dancing down her spine.

At first, his lips moved slowly against hers, almost questioning. But if he was worried about moving too fast, she quickly disabused him of that notion. She knew she wasn't thinking straight but for once she didn't care. She reached up with both of her hands to cradle his face and began kissing him back with an abandon that shocked her. A soft moan issued from deep in his throat as their lips danced together. She felt his hand thread into her hair as he pulled her even closer and their kiss deepened.

Her lips parted and the tip of his tongue flicked ever so lightly against the sensitive underside of her upper lip. Without conscious thought, she rose up out of her seat to somehow end up on his lap. Her insides swirled with a fluttering heat and she gasped as his lips forged a tantalizing trail across the underside of her jaw and down her neck. His tongue flicked against the hollow of her collarbone before he made his way back to her mouth, savoring it with a combination of gentleness and intensity that took her breath away.

The fevered passion between them slowly began to ease, and his lips brushed against hers one last time before he finally pulled away and leaned his forehead against her own.

She was on sensation overload but still managed to hear his whispered, "I've wanted to do that for a long, long, long time."

She tipped back to look at him. She couldn't believe what she was hearing. "You have?"

"Yes. And maybe I'm wrong, Maggie, but from the way you responded just now, I think you've wanted it to."

She nibbled at her bottom lip, afraid that if she gave an inch, she'd end up giving a mile. How could she confess that it wasn't only that she'd wanted to kiss him? She wanted *all* of him. The time they'd spent together over the past few days had only made her more certain than ever. She was deeply, passionately, hopelessly in love with this man. But how could she tell him this? It was just a kiss. An incredible kiss, but...

"I can't deny that I've thought about it," she said carefully.

"I knew it!" he exploded, his teeth flashing again as he grinned in the darkness.

Boon gave a soft grunt at the sudden sound. "Sorry, boy," Noah said, reaching to give the dog a pat on the head.

"Really, Noah, this is totally inappropriate," Maggie said, wriggling off his lap and back into her own seat. "I'm your professional matchmaker. I'm not supposed to be...to be..."

"Making out with me?" he said helpfully, his tone tinged with amusement.

"Seriously, Noah, this is just not—" Suddenly, a light danced in her peripheral vision, distracting her from finishing her thought. She squinted out into the darkness. "What was that?"

Noah looked in the direction she was pointing and sucked in his breath.

In the window of Valentina's condo, they could both see the beam of a flashlight moving around inside it.

"What should we do?" Maggie whispered.

"Call the police," Noah said, pulling out his cell phone.

"Wait!" Maggie reached out to lightly touch his arm. "Look!"

Noah glanced up. The light had disappeared, and a second later, they saw a figure dressed in black leap out of what would have been Valentina's bedroom window. Only then did Maggie notice the white-framed piece of window glass leaning up against the side of the condo. The black-shrouded figure lifted the window and popped it back into place, then walked quickly from the building toward the parking lot.

"Duck!" Noah said. And they both scooted down low in their seats, peeking over the dashboard as the figure passed beneath the lone parking lot light.

"It's him!" Maggie breathed.

It was the angry-looking man from the photographs. The one who had been following Valentina throughout the date on Friday night. The night she disappeared.

Chapter 17

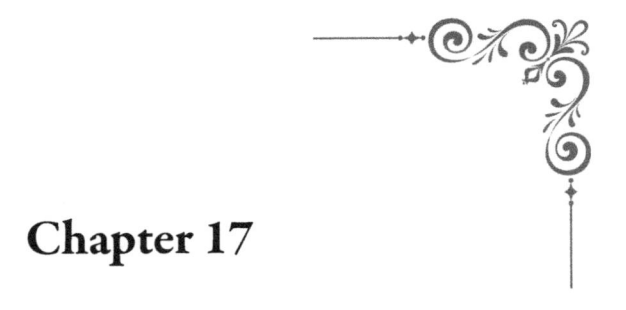

"Shhh, down, boy!" Noah whispered as the dog again poked his head between the seats, a low rumble issuing from his throat.

The man walked directly to a compact-size car and climbed inside. He started the engine and rolled slowly out of the lot.

A moment later, Noah started his engine.

"What are you doing?" Maggie gasped.

"We're going to follow him," Noah said, slowly easing out of his own parking space, but he kept his headlights off.

"Are you crazy?" Maggie said, sitting back up and buckling her seat belt.

"Maybe. But what if he leads us to Valentina? Or we find out where he lives? Either way, we'll likely have something more concrete to tell the police when we call."

"I don't think this is such a good idea," Maggie said, the dashboard lights highlighting her anxious expression.

"It will be fine," Noah reassured her. "And after everything we've been through, wouldn't it be great to finally find Valentina?"

"Well, yes," Maggie said reluctantly.

As they entered the road, Noah turned his headlights on and kept a discreet distance behind the other car.

They drove through town and then to the outskirts, passing an abandoned strip mall before watching the car pull into the driveway of a small motel, its ancient neon sign stating it was the Shoreline Inn. A red-lit vacancy sign with a few letters missing flashed on and off beneath it.

"You missed the driveway!" Maggie said as Noah sailed past the motel entrance.

"Avoiding suspicion," he said.

Maggie rolled her eyes. "I think you're getting a little carried away here, Sherlock," she said.

"Think about it," Noah gave her a sidelong look. "We've been attacked by mobsters two—actually make that three—times now. Do you really think that we can't be too careful?"

"Okay, okay. You're right," she agreed.

A moment later, Noah did a U-turn on the empty road and headed back toward the motel.

The unassuming, low-slung brick building had seen better days. Even in the dark lighting, it was clear that the doors and window casements were in desperate need of a paint job. The motel was small, offering only eight ground-level rooms, and there were only a couple of other cars in the parking lot. The one belonging to their target was in front of the room furthest away from the office.

Noah parked his car on the opposite side of the lot, near the closed office door, and shut off his engine.

"Should we call the police now?" Maggie asked.

"We don't know anything yet," Noah said, his eyes focused on the door of the last guest room. "I think I'm going to go listen at the door to see if I hear anything."

"I dunno..." Maggie hesitated.

"What if he's holding Valentina hostage in there or something? I need to know, Maggie."

She sighed audibly, then unbuckled her seat belt. "Fine, but you're not going alone. We're coming with you."

"We?" he frowned.

"Me and Boon," Maggie said. "He's a big dog, Noah. We know he attacked Nick the Knife, so he'll likely offer us at least some protection."

"Okay," he said reluctantly.

He and Maggie got out of his car and he attached the leash to Boon's collar before letting him jump out, too. Then he looked at Maggie. "Ready?"

She nodded, and they began moving silently along the sidewalk in front of the building. The wind had picked up. It sent litter skittering across the parking lot. And there was a rumble of thunder in the distance. Every room was dark, but a sliver of light shone down on the pavement in front of the last room at the end of the motel.

When they were almost in front of it, Noah turned and leaned close to whisper in Maggie's ear. "There's a slight opening in the curtains. Let's duck down low and try to get a look inside."

Maggie nodded her understanding and they both bent over low to move just beneath the guest room window. Then they squatted down. There was no sound coming from within.

Noah exchanged a nod with Maggie and they both lifted their heads to peer in through the small gap in the curtains.

They could see the ends of two twin-size beds lit by the soft glow of the guest room's small night table lamp. The man stood at the end of one bed, his back to the window. Noah noted that he held his head at an odd angle. As they watched, a pair of hands—very feminine hands—suddenly slipped around his waist and slid up his back. The man's body turned slightly, revealing the fact that he was kissing a tall, slender woman with long dark hair.

"Valentina!" Maggie whispered.

Noah could feel anger, confusion, and frustration over everything they'd endured the past few days roiling around inside him. He couldn't believe it. There she was. Alive and well and…kissing her captor?

He stood up. "This is unbelievable," he said. "I'm going to find out what the heck is going on here."

Maggie watched wide-eyed as Noah stepped to the door, pulling Boon with him, and began banging on it. "Pizza delivery!" he called.

They heard a muffled cry from inside and stumbling footsteps. Then the man's voice from inside. "You've got the wrong room, buddy. We didn't order any pizza."

"It's right here on the slip, room 108," Noah persisted, reading the room number off the door. "C'mon, man! I need to get paid."

There was a very long pause that caused Noah to doubt his idea would work. He was just wondering how difficult it would be to break down the door when it swung wide. The man stood holding the door. His eye immediately went to Boon with a look of surprise.

Valentina stood a pace behind him, looking beautiful, perfectly healthy, and holding a gun aimed directly at Noah's chest.

"Get inside. Now!" she hissed, her gaze fixed on Noah.

Noah, Maggie, and Boon instantly obeyed. They all stepped into the room and the man immediately shut the door.

"Sit down." She waved the gun barrel in the direction of one of the beds.

The man stepped to the window and stood for a long moment, peering through the gap in the curtains. Finally, he said, "I don't see anything." And he closed the drapes to eliminate the gap.

"How did you find us?" Valentina said, the gun still leveled at Noah.

"We followed him," Noah said, indicating the man.

The man's face reddened and Valentina sighed deeply. "I don't understand why you don't take the precautions seriously, Eric."

"I do!" Eric protested. "It's just that I'm not used to all of this, Tina."

"I should have never let you go back to get the ring," she said, glancing down at the simple diamond ring that glittered on her left hand. "What if it had been Nick, or even Papa Dom following you? Do you realize what could have happened?"

Looking completely exhausted, Eric ran a hand over his face and sagged down on top of the chipped and peeling fake wood dresser that sat beneath the window.

"Are you referring to Nick the Knife?" Maggie asked.

Valentina's eyes shot to Maggie's face and her eyes narrowed. "What do you know about Nick?"

"We know that he's looking for you," Noah said.

"Unbutton your shirt," Valentina said abruptly to Noah, stepping closer to them.

"What?" Noah said, confused.

"I want to see if you're wearing a wire."

"Tina, c'mon," Eric protested. "They're just—"

"Unbutton it," she said, ignoring Eric. Her dark eyes were inscrutable.

Noah did as he was directed. Valentina then made him stand up and turn around. When he was facing her again, she gave a nod, and he put his shirt back on.

"You're clear," she said to Maggie, her eyes sweeping over the crocheted beach cover-up she still wore over the top of her bikini.

"Gee, thanks," Maggie said drily and crossed her arms. "Now, will you please tell us what's going on here? We thought you were dead, Valentina."

Noah was surprised at how calm Maggie sounded considering the fact that Valentina was holding a gun on them.

"I am," Valentina said. "Or at least, I'm going to be."

Maggie frowned. "I don't understand?"

Valentina sighed. "You don't need to understand. And the less you know, the better."

"I don't know anything!" Noah exploded. "I have no memory of our date on Friday night. The only thing I do know is that we're being harassed daily by your pal Nick and his buddy. And that I'm under suspicion for your murder."

Noah noted how Eric's face paled at his outburst. But Valentina's icy expression never changed. "That was the goal," she said. "Until you and Miss Matchmaker here had to mess everything up."

"Mess what up?" Maggie said. "Valentina, we need to let the police know that you're alive so Noah doesn't end up in jail."

"Absolutely not." Valentina's tone was very matter-of-fact.

"Well, I'm going to tell them anyway," Maggie said, starting to rise from the bed.

"No. You won't." Valentina's hand shot out and she shoved Maggie hard back down onto the bed, causing her to bounce into Noah.

"It's unfortunate that you found us," Valentina said. "This wasn't the original plan. Nobody was supposed to die."

"Die? Who said anything about dying?" Noah said. "What, you're going to kill us?"

Eric now rose from his perch on the dresser, his formerly exhausted expression was gone. He stepped up beside Valentina, his eyes focused on her face. "No," he said calmly. "She's not going to kill you.

"Tina," Eric continued, his voice soft. "You know how I've felt about this from the beginning. I didn't even want to frame this innocent man for your murder." He waved a hand in Noah's direction. "So, we certainly can't commit actual murder. We just can't. That's not who I am, Tina. And I know it's not who you are either."

Noah and Maggie watched in astonishment as Eric reached out and carefully removed the gun from Valentina's hand. Then, the woman who had been an emotionless machine only moments before seemed to melt before their eyes. Valentina stared into Eric's eyes and then threw herself into his arms, a sob escaping from her lips.

"It's all right, love," he cooed, his free hand stroking her hair as she clung to him. "It will be all right."

"No, it won't, Eric," she cried against his chest. "It's all over." And then to Noah's shock, Valentina began to really weep, her body shaking with spasms of grief. Eric eased her down onto the end of the second bed and held her close.

Although the gun was no longer aimed at him, Noah was glued to his seat. He glanced at Maggie to find her looking on the scene in equal shock.

Boon, in contrast to the day he'd chased after Nick the Knife, had done zero in terms of performing any watchdog skills. Instead, when Noah and Maggie had been ordered to sit on the bed, the dog had simply lain at his feet.

Now, however, Boon rose and went over to Valentina. He laid his large black-and-gold head on her lap, causing her to start in surprise, and she pulled her tear-stained face away from Eric's shoulder. She looked down at the dog whose liquid brown eyes gazed up at her with concern. He whined softly and thumped his tail against the carpet, giving her hand a lick.

"What a sweet dog," she said, stroking his head. "Oh!" She was taken by surprise again as Boon leaped onto the bed and knocked Valentina back by laying half of his body across her lap. She struggled to sit up, looking over at Noah and Maggie in confusion.

"Yeah," Maggie said. "He does that sometimes."

Noah got up and lifted the big dog off Valentina while Eric pulled a tissue from the pocket of his black joggers and handed it to her. She dabbed at her eyes and then blew her nose. "I can't believe you still have that dog."

"What do you mean you can't believe I still have the dog?" Noah asked. "Where did he come from?"

"I'm actually not sure," Valentina said. "You just turned up with him after..." She sighed. "It's a long story."

"I'm really sorry about all of this," Eric said, looking over at Maggie and Noah. "We never should have involved you."

"But there was no other way," Valentina said defiantly. "You know there wasn't, Eric."

Eric looked tenderly at Valentina and gave her lips a soft kiss. "There's always another way, Tina."

"You're just too good, Eric," she said. "You don't understand how it is."

"I know when something feels right and when it feels wrong, love," he said. "And this has felt wrong from the beginning."

"I thought you loved me," Valentina cried, her face looking dangerously close to crumbling into tears again. "You said that you wanted to marry me."

"I do, but..." Eric cradled her face. "Do you trust me?"

"Always," she said.

"Then I think we need to tell them the truth." He angled his head in the direction of Noah and Maggie.

"How much of it?" Valentina asked.

"All of it," Eric replied.

Chapter 18

A crack of thunder sounded close, followed by a flash of lightning that briefly transformed the dark motel room curtains into a mottled gray. Noah and Maggie moved to the side of the bed to face Eric and Valentina on the opposite one. And Boon once again curled up at Noah's feet.

Loud raindrops began to spatter against the glass of the window as Eric took a deep breath and began talking. "Valentina is basically mafia royalty. Her name is not really Valentina Romano. It's Valentina Gianola and she's the daughter of the Detroit mafia boss known as Papa Dom Gianola."

"Mafia? Are you talking about the Detroit Partnership?" Maggie said.

Valentina lifted her head from Eric's shoulder with a look of suspicion. "You've heard of the Partnership?"

"Not really." Maggie blushed under Valentina's sharp scrutiny. "We actually just learned about it after our encounter with Nick the Knife."

Valentina made a sound of disgust. "He gave himself that stupid nickname."

"Well, whatever his name is, he's very, very determined to find you," Noah said.

"Of course he is," Valentina spat out. "God forbid he would ever disappoint my father in anything. His loyalty is pathetic. He probably still thinks there's hope for him in all of this."

"What do you mean?" Maggie asked.

Valentina sighed. "I'm an only child. And from my earliest memories, Papa Dom trained me to take over the *family business*." She emphasized the last two words. "In the world of crime families, he's actually considered progressive," she added with a humorless laugh.

"The Detroit Partnership is one of the original twenty-four Mafia families that make up La Cosa Nostra in America, or the mafia as you call it.

The reins of control in a family always pass to the oldest son of a boss or to an underboss in the absence of any sons. In our case, that would have been Nick.

"However, my father wanted me to follow in the footsteps of Maria Licciardi, who became the first female mafia boss in 1993. He wanted me to become *La Madrina*, the Godmother of the Partnership, when he stepped down.

"Nick knew all of this years ago, so he began pressuring Papa Dom to let him marry me. Nick figured that as my husband he'd have more power than he would remaining a mere underboss. My father was on the verge of agreeing to this when something happened to change everything."

"What changed?" Maggie asked, leaning forward, clearly captivated by Valentina's story.

"That's actually another long story," Valentina sighed. "Twelve years ago, the Gianolas partnered with Vitale Salvatore's family to defeat the Adamo group that was taking control of the Detroit market. It was a bloody battle, but we won. And our two families worked in harmony after that. Until a few years ago, that is, when one of my father's highest-ranking capos accused Vitale's oldest son of cheating on the proceeds from one of our bakery businesses."

"I'm guessing that caused a big problem?" Noah said.

Valentina shifted on the bed, looking uncomfortable, and Eric put an arm around her shoulders, pulling her up against him. "It did," she said. "Things escalated and it was war all over again, even bloodier than the last one. The Partnership split into West and East factions, both seeking total control. Everything came to a head several months ago when my Uncle Francesco was killed in a drive-by. It was a big deal because my uncle was my father's consigliere, and there's an unwritten rule that no matter how bad things get, consiglieres are off limits."

"A consigliere is a type of advisor to the boss," Eric said, noting the confused expressions on Noah and Maggie's faces.

"Right," Valentina nodded. "Anyway, before he fell, my uncle managed to get off a few shots at the car, and he killed Vitale's oldest son. Now there we were with major losses on both sides. On top of this, both my father and Vitale want to retire. So, they ended up meeting and negotiating a truce. And part of their agreement to ensure lasting peace between our families was that I would be forced to marry Vitale's remaining eighteen-year-old son. He would take over for the Salvatore family and we would co-rule together."

"That's terrible!" Maggie cried. "Being forced into marriage doesn't sound very progressive to me."

"True," Valentina said with a grim smile. "But it's a common practice within La Costa Nostra. Most members are related by blood or marriage. It's just like the days of medieval royalty. They use it as a tool for peacekeeping and empire building. For them, it's never about love and marriage, it's all about profit and loss." The disgust in Valentina's voice was clear. "Arranged marriages, plus the code of *omertà,* are what make it so hard for outsiders, especially law enforcement, to get any information about what goes on within the organization."

"*Omertà?*" Noah said. "We saw that word tattooed on Nick's neck."

"Of course you did," Valentina said with a roll of her eyes. "He's so intense. *Omertà* is a vow of absolute silence about our business and complete loyalty to the family that everyone must make in order to become 'made,' as in an official soldier of the organization. A broken vow means death."

"Have you taken the vow of *omertà?*" Noah asked.

Valentina's eyes dropped. "I did," she admitted. "Not willingly, but it came to a point where I had no choice. Any member of the organization wouldn't hesitate to kill their own mother in cold blood just to honor this stupid century-old fraternity." Then her eyes lifted again, their dark depths glinting with fire. "But years before I took that vow, I'd already made a vow to myself and I will not break it."

"What kind of vow?" Maggie asked, curiously.

"A vow that I would escape from this life, escape from my father's control. And that I would live free," she said fiercely.

"*We* will live free," Eric said, gently turning her chin toward him and planting another soft kiss on her lips. "We're in this together now."

"Yes," she sighed, threading her fingers through his, her expression softening as she gazed at him.

"So, is this a Romeo and Juliet thing?" Maggie asked, leaning forward again. "Are you from another rival family, Eric?" Noah suppressed a grin as he watched Maggie. Her desire for a romantic story was almost palpable.

Eric burst into laughter and Valentina's face held amusement. "Romeo and Juliet, I like it," Eric said, nodding slowly. "But, no. I'm just an ordinary guy who fell in love with a princess."

"There's nothing ordinary about you, *amore mio*," Valentina said, raising their clasped hands to her lips to kiss his.

Noah cleared his throat, drawing their attention away from each other. "Well, what's the story then? How did you guys get together?"

"It's kind of a fluke," Eric said.

"More like fate," Valentina said.

"I'm a physical therapist," Eric said. "I treated Valentina last winter after she got injured on a ski trip in the Swiss Alps. My Valentina is a bit of an adrenaline junkie," he added, giving her an indulgent sidelong look. "She went heli-skiing off the snow-capped peak of the Matterhorn."

"It's an incredible experience," Valentina said, her eyes dreamy.

"Anyway, she wiped out part way down and tore her medial collateral ligament. She was lucky in that she didn't need surgery, but she did need PT."

"Best accident that ever could have happened to me," Valentina said with a smile. "And God bless my father for one thing, he always has to have the best. And Eric is the best." She gazed at him adoringly.

"I don't know about that," Eric said modestly.

"You are!" Valentina exclaimed. "My father searched his entire network for the best physical therapist to treat my injury and I ended up with you."

"Anyway," Eric pressed on. "We began working together several times a week for a couple of months. I actually stretched out her treatment program longer than necessary because..." He turned to look at her again. "I'd fallen in love with her, and I didn't want our sessions to end."

Valentina glowed as Eric continued. "When I couldn't extend her treatment any longer, I bolstered up my courage to tell her how I felt about her, and I asked her to dinner. Then she crushed me by turning me down."

"But I explained why!" Valentina cried.

"Not at first, you didn't," Eric said with a gentle smile. "She was very mysterious. All she did was admit that she had feelings for me, too, but that she wasn't free to date. I had no idea what that meant. But the facility where I work is also connected to a gym. So, once her treatment ended, Valentina kept coming back in to work out, and we would talk."

"Over time, she told me the truth about her background. I couldn't believe it. She told me about the plans she'd already made to...disappear. She even tried to say goodbye to me. But by this time, we'd both confessed our love for each other. And I couldn't imagine my life without her in it. So, I told her I was coming with her."

"At first I refused," Valentina said, picking up the story. "I couldn't ask Eric to endanger his life for me."

"But she quickly found out that I could be just as stubborn as she is," Eric interjected.

"Hey!" Valentina punched him playfully in the arm, and he laughed.

Noah observed how Valentina's tough façade seemed to melt away when she interacted with Eric.

"There was no way I was going to let you go," he said. "I was all in."

"Until you learned all the details of my plan, that is," Valentina said.

Eric's lips tightened. "That's true," he said. "Honestly, I thought Tina was being overly dramatic about the lengths she was going to in order to escape. She comes from a world that I don't understand. And her plan sounded more like the plot of a movie than anything anyone would do in real life." He looked directly at Noah. "When she told me about framing you for her murder, I balked."

"But there is no other way," Valentina said.

"Uh, I can think of another way," Noah said. "How about just disappearing without involving me at all!"

"Unless my father thinks I'm truly dead, he will never stop looking for me," Valentina said.

"Couldn't you just go to the police," Maggie said. "Tell them about your father's illegal activities and go into witness protection?"

"Right!" Valentina scoffed, rising quickly to her feet, the venom in her voice clear. "I will never go to the police about any of this!"

"Why not?" Noah asked with a frown. "Because of *omertà*?"

"No," Valentina crossed her arms. "Because I've seen what police protection looks like, and I can do a better job myself."

Valentina pressed her lips tightly together and turned her back on the room.

Eric watched her for a long moment, then turned to Noah and Maggie. "I tried so hard to convince her to do just as you suggested. To go to the police and turn in her father and other key members of the Partnership. But no matter what I said, she refused. I couldn't sway her because of what happened to her mother."

Noah felt the tension in the room thicken. He'd seen the pain in Valentina's eyes as she'd turned away and had a sinking feeling he knew what was behind her reluctance to go to the authorities. He glanced at Maggie who seemed equally concerned.

After a moment of heavy silence, Eric continued. "Valentina's mother tried to escape the Partnership with Valentina when she was ten years old. Her mother went to the authorities, hoping for protection and a chance at a new life. But they couldn't keep her safe."

"My father found us," Valentina hissed, once again turning to face them. "He persuaded my mother that he'd forgiven her and wanted to make peace. But he lied." Unshed tears glittered in her midnight eyes. "He planned a family holiday for us in Paris to celebrate. We spent a week sightseeing around the city and having dinner as a family every night.

"But then, on the last night of our trip, I heard strange sounds in the middle of the night. I peeked out of my bedroom door and saw several of my father's men dragging my mother out of the penthouse where we were staying. She was trying to fight them, but they were too strong for her. I just watched it all, terrified and frozen in my hiding spot. You can't imagine the guilt I have over that to this day," she said, dropping her eyes.

"You were only a child, Tina," Eric said gently.

"I know that," she said, her chin shooting up, sparks flashing in her eyes. "But it doesn't stop me from feeling somehow responsible. Like maybe I could have stopped it if I'd only been brave enough.

"The next morning, my father tried to play it off as if my mother had run away again. But I know what I saw. And I have no doubt my father had her killed."

Fresh tears rolled down Valentina's cheeks, and Eric instantly rose to wrap her in his arms.

Noah couldn't help but feel a pang of sympathy for Valentina as he watched her break down once again in Eric's embrace. Her vulnerability was raw, her pain unmistakable.

Maggie rose from the bed and moved to gently place a hand on Valentina's back. "I'm so sorry, Valentina," she said softly, her voice filled with genuine empathy. "No one should have to go through something like that."

Valentina turned to look at Maggie, a mix of appreciation and determination reflected in her tear-stained face. "Thank you," she murmured. "In the end, I was forced to go back and live with my father. He told me to never mention my mother's name again. I had to act as if nothing had happened. But I promised myself that one day I would succeed where she had failed. I would find a way to live the life she'd dreamed for me."

"The only question now, is how?" Noah said. "What's another way we can make sure your father believes you're dead? Because I'm really not a fan of your original plan to frame me for your murder."

Chapter 19

"What was your plan going to be if we hadn't found you?" Maggie asked as she sat back down beside Noah.

"We were just waiting for the paperwork we need to start our new lives together," Eric said.

"I originally thought we'd have more time to execute our plan to frame Noah," Valentina said. "To make my murder more believable, my original plan was to go on several dates with Noah first, to build up our relationship."

"Little does she know how badly that part of the plan would have worked out," Maggie murmured, making Noah snort with laughter.

"What was that?" Valentina frowned.

"Nothing," Maggie said. "Please go on."

"I knew we had a big problem when a few days before our first date, I spotted Nick and Johnny spying on me. I didn't let on that I saw them, but I realized that my father must have sent them.

"The fact that they were here meant Eric and I needed to accelerate our plan. So, I used a discreet connection and got ahold of a liquid form of alprazolam, which I used to drug Noah's coffee on our date. Eric was waiting not far away so that as soon as Noah got woozy, we could take him back to my place. Once he passed out, my plan was to leave him there with the evidence of my murder."

"Oooh," Noah said. "That's why you got so angry when I spilled the coffee?"

"Yes," Valentina smiled grimly. "Thanks to you spilling it all over the shop floor, my perfect plan took an even bigger twist. While you and that coffee shop lady were mopping up the mess, I called Eric and made arrangements for him to get more of the drug. That's why I suggested we extend our date into dinner."

"Ah," Maggie said. "So, when Eric showed up at the restaurant, he passed you the drug?"

"Right," Eric said, looking embarrassed. "I slipped it to Tina, and she slipped it into his drink when he went out to get her sweater."

"Well, at least now I know how the drug got into my system," Noah said.

"So, all the stuff you did after the coffee shop...going to dinner, the sunset cruise, you were really just waiting for the drug to take full effect, waiting for Noah to pass out?" Maggie said.

"Yes," Valentina said, then added with a shake of her head, "He lasted much longer than I ever thought he would."

Valentina and Eric sat back down, and he put his arm back around her, pulling her close again.

"The sunset cruise almost blew it for us," she said, glancing at Eric. "I never expected Nick and Johnny to make such an overt move like that. I thought I'd been convincing about my plans. But apparently, my father either figured out I was lying about my extended bachelorette getaway party, or he wasn't going to take any chances that I might mess up his precious peace treaty."

Something connected in Maggie's mind, and she snapped her fingers. "The bachelorette party!"

Valentina tilted her head. "What about it?"

"We heard Nick mention something about someone named Clarissa and how you'd lied about the bachelorette getaway."

Eric shook his head. "That must have been it, Tina. Your father would have known that there was no way you'd have celebrated without Clarissa there."

"But I couldn't risk letting anyone in on our plan," Valentina said, and took a deep sigh. "What a mess."

"So, when Nick and Johnny confronted you on the sunset cruise, they were trying to force you to go back with them to your father right then?" Maggie said.

"Yes," Valentina said. "It was sheer dumb luck that the crowd happened to be super fans of Noah's." For the first time that night, she aimed a legitimate smile in Noah's direction. "They created the perfect diversion. But Nick knew we'd be at the hospital. So, while Noah was getting examined, I saw Nick's stupid black SUV pull into the parking lot. That's when I got the brilliant idea to call the cops. The two fools came into the waiting room and tried to start up with me again in front of witnesses. And they were still at it when the cops arrived."

Eric grinned. "They got hauled away just before Noah was released. So, Valentina was able to get Noah into her car. She drove a bit up the road and then parked to call me."

"I realized they were likely tracking my phone," Valentina said. "So, I called Eric to let him know and that I was going to ditch my phone in a nearby garbage can. I told him to meet me back at the condo so we could grab our burner phones, go-bags, and get everything set up for my disappearance.

"While I was talking with Eric," Valentina said, with a glance toward Noah, "I didn't even notice that you'd gotten out of the car. But when I hung up, I saw that you suddenly had this furry guy with you." Valentina reached down to scratch Boon's head. He nuzzled her hand, and Maggie noticed how Valentina's expression softened almost as much as it did when she was looking at Eric.

"You were getting even more loopy, and you insisted on putting the dog into the back seat of the car. I didn't want to waste time arguing with you, so I just gave in and drove you both back to my condo. Eric and I got you and the dog inside where you finally passed out. We set up all the evidence for the murder, locked the dog in the closet, and left."

"In my car?" Noah asked with an arch of his brow.

"Yeah, about that," Valentina smiled again. "Once Maggie told me she was arranging my date with you, I put another part of my plan in motion. I used a hacker I know to discover your full name and address. He altered the electronic records and databases to put the Porsche to your name. He created all the necessary documentation, too. I figured you suddenly owning an expensive Porsche might help implicate you in my disappearance. Besides, Eric and I knew from the start that we couldn't travel in it once I officially disappeared. It was too obvious.

"Anyway, I took your key and had Eric drive us in his car back to the coffee shop to get your car. I drove it and he followed me until we were outside of town, where we dumped it.

"Wow," Noah said drily. "You really thought of everything."

"Clearly not everything," Valentina said. "I didn't expect my father's men to come looking for me like this. And I certainly didn't expect you two to find me alive. My perfect plan has fallen to pieces."

"Okay, well, we've got to come up with a new plan," Maggie said. She rose and began to pace in the tiny room for several moments, thinking. Finally, she stopped moving. "Valentina, I'm sorry, but I just don't see any way around this. You've got to go to the police."

"No," Valentina said.

"But Noah could go to jail!" Maggie cried.

"That's unfortunate," Valentina said. "And I am sorry, Noah. But this is too important. I can't have Nick and Johnny thinking that I'm alive."

Valentina once again picked up the gun that was lying on the bed. "Look," she said. "I won't kill you. But we have to prevent you from talking to the police or anyone else before we're safely gone." She looked at Eric. "We can tie them up and force them to stay here until we get the paperwork. Then we leave their cell phones here and drop them off way outside of town on our way out of here." She glanced back at Noah. "I doubt the police will believe the man accused of my murder when he says that he saw me alive."

Valentina's face once again held no emotion. But Eric looked miserable.

"Wait, wait," Maggie said, whirling to face Valentina directly. "How about this? What if you let us go? Then Noah and I tell the police what you've told us. Noah has friends on the police force who I'm sure will help us. We get them to pretend that Valentina's dead body has been found, and they arrest Noah for your murder."

"What?" Noah cried.

"Hang on!" Maggie said, lifting a hand to forestall him. "If we do this, Nick will believe that Valentina really is dead and that you are the murderer. He and Johnny will report all this back to Valentina's father, and they'll leave Whispering Pines. Once they're gone, we bring you both out of hiding and you tell the police and the F.B.I. everything, about your father, the Partnership, everything. And this time, before you do it, we get them all to provide guarantees that witness protection will work for you."

Valentina was already shaking her head, but she stopped when Eric laid his hand over her free one.

"Tina," he said gently. "You know it's the right thing to do. We can't start our new life together in good conscience knowing that we potentially sent an innocent man to jail. That makes us no better than your father or anyone else in the Partnership."

Valentina gazed at him without speaking for what felt like an eternity. Eventually, she lowered her head and the gun, revealing her vulnerability yet again as she whispered, "Eric, I'm afraid."

"I am, too," Eric admitted. And for the second time that night, he eased the gun from her fingers. Then he wrapped her in his arms.

After a long moment, he looked at Noah and Maggie over the top of Valentina's head. "Before we do all of this, can I ask a favor?"

"What is it?" Noah asked.

"Would you give us a bit of time to just be alone together before...everything changes? I promise we won't run off."

Maggie could sense the sincerity in the young man's eyes, but Valentina's face remained hidden against Eric's shoulder.

"What about you, Valentina?" Maggie whispered.

Valentina took a deep breath and lifted her head, turning to face them. "I—I promise, too. I swear on my mother's grave, we won't run."

Maggie and Noah exchanged a look, an unspoken agreement passed between them.

"All right," Noah said. "We can do that. How much time do you need?"

Now it was Eric and Valentina who exchanged a look. Then Valentina said, "Just a day."

"How about if we contact you tomorrow evening at some point, as soon as we're ready to put your plan in motion?" Eric said.

"That works," Noah said.

Noah and Eric exchanged cell phone numbers, then Noah, Maggie, and Boon got ready to leave.

"I really am sorry about all of this, Noah," Valentina said; her gaze was now steady, her expression determined. "You have to understand that I grew up in a very different world from the rest of you. But with this man at my side," here she nudged Eric with her shoulder and gave him a small smile, "maybe there's hope that he can make a good woman of me yet."

Eric looked down at her, smiling tenderly. Then he lifted her left hand and kissed the spot just beneath where the ring glittered on her third finger. "You're already a good woman, Tina," he said. "You just needed me to remind you of that."

Chapter 20

In the pouring rain, Noah and Maggie dashed back to the car with Boon. They all clambered inside and Noah started the engine, but he didn't put it in gear. He pulled a handkerchief out of his pocket and handed it to her. She smiled at the old-fashioned gesture, but gratefully mopped off her wet face and then used it to squeeze the rain out of her dripping hair. Afterward, Maggie rested back in her seat, her eyes closed, mind whirling.

She was so happy to know that Valentina was alive that she wanted to dance. She knew the path before them was not going to be an easy one, but now, at least, Noah was going to be safe. There would be no murder charge against him, and it was a relief to have a solid plan in place.

But now that they were alone again, some of the underlying peace she'd just experienced dissipated as her thoughts flipped back to earlier that evening.

She and Noah had kissed. A really, really good kiss.

The thrill of that memory swept over her like a Lake Michigan wave, making her heart race. But coming right along in its wake was a feeling of dread. The love she had for Noah Riley that had begun blossoming in high school was now in full bloom. But she felt her throat grow tight as she thought about the fact that he didn't feel the same way about her, and she swallowed past the hard lump that had formed there. How could she possibly go back to trying to find the perfect match for Noah in light of her feelings toward him? The answer was, she couldn't.

Noah's voice broke into the turmoil of her thoughts. "Can you believe all this?"

She opened her eyes and sat up, pressing her hands to her forehead to stop the onflow of thoughts, trying to focus on his words. Then she slowly shook her head. "No, it's so much to take in."

Boon's snuffling nose poked between the seats at the sound of their voices. He whined softly and placed one furry paw onto Maggie's arm. She turned to meet his gentle brown gaze that seemed to radiate concern and couldn't help smiling at him. "It's okay, bud," she said softly, patting his head. "We're just overwhelmed."

"And then some," Noah said, stroking the side of Boon's neck. "It's just like Eric said, it feels more like something out of a movie than real life."

Maggie nodded, then turned in her seat to face him. "What about you, how are you feeling about all of this?"

"Me?"

"Yeah, I mean you've gone through a lot of abuse in their quest to escape mob life," she said. "You were drugged, lost your memory, endured the stress of potentially being accused of murder." She shook her head. "And all because...because I matched you up with a mafia princess." She covered her face with her hands, her voice muffled as she spoke through them. "I'm so sorry, Noah."

He gently grasped her wrists and guided them away from her face. His fingers trailed down to claim both of her hands. His touch was like the comfort of a warm blanket enveloping her. "Cut it out," he said softly. "There's no way you could have known any of this. Nobody could have known any of this!"

He dropped his gaze and they sat in silence for a long moment, but he still kept ahold of her hands. Rain droplets covered the car windows, forming blurred patterns of the outside that resembled the brushstrokes of an impressionist painting. When he finally spoke again, his voice held a strange note. "You really want to know how I'm feeling? Here it is. I'm glad Valentina is alive. I'm glad we didn't just die in there." Then he looked up and met her gaze, causing her heart to skip a beat. "But as crazy as this sounds, Maggie, I wouldn't have changed one single thing about the past couple of days. Except," his teeth gleamed as he flashed a grin in the darkness, "maybe the part where we were attacked by mobsters. But I will never regret one single second that I got to spend with you, Maggie, renewing our...relationship."

She noted how he stumbled over that last word, and it only strengthened her resolve in enacting the decision she'd just made.

"About that," she said, gently disentangling her fingers from his. "I agree, renewing our friendship has been great. Really great. But we need to talk about what happened earlier tonight, Noah."

He looked confused.

She rolled her eyes. "The kiss?"

"Aaahh." A slow smile curved Noah's lips. "You mean this?" And before she could react, he'd leaned in and was kissing her again. This time there was no hesitancy in it. His lips moved against hers with an intensity that took her breath away and sent a surge of desire coursing through her body. Maggie's head spun as she lost herself in the taste and touch of him. And for one blissful moment, she let her heart soar as she melted into the kiss. Her hands found their way to his broad shoulders, and he tunneled a hand through her hair, cradling the back of her head and angling her to deepen the kiss. His tongue teased at her lips, and when she opened to him, he explored her mouth with a hunger that matched her own.

But then the reality of their situation began to creep back into her consciousness. Something niggled at the back of her mind...something she was supposed to do. Or say. His lips trailed a tingling path along her jaw to her ear where he nibbled at her earlobe, the heat between them sizzling like a live wire.

"I need to...I want to..." She was losing her train of thought.

"Yes?" he whispered against her skin, sending fresh waves of sensation rocketing around her insides.

With Herculean strength, she fought for focus and lifted her hands, placing both palms flat against his broad chest and gently pushing him back. The moment his lips left hers, she felt the loss like a physical ache.

Her heart pounded in her chest as she tried to catch her breath. Then she took a deep fortifying inhale and let it out. "Noah, I need to say something."

He pulled back and studied her, his eyes held a mixture of desire and confusion. "What is it?"

"I'm dropping you as a client." The words came out more bluntly than she'd intended.

Even in the darkness, she could sense his surprise. Noah frowned, his brow furrowing. "Okay," he said slowly. "That makes sense in light of—"

"We can't do this," Maggie interrupted him. "Now that we know that Valentina is all right, and we have this great plan in place, it's time to get back to reality. The fact is, I should never have kissed you. I've not only compromised my business ethics, but I've messed up the entire process for you. I've distracted you from your goal of finding the right woman to share your life with."

"But—"

She held up a hand and he hesitated.

"We both know that woman isn't me, Noah." She shook her head and scooted back farther into her seat, putting even more distance between them. "Over the past few days, you've made it clear how much you value our friendship, and I don't want to jeopardize that just because our emotions are heightened due to the stress we've been under. We got caught up in the moment. And if we took this any further, you'd be doing what you always do: picking the wrong woman."

"But—"

"No buts, Noah. My mind is made up," she said firmly. She turned to face forward and reached for her seatbelt. "Tomorrow, I'll refer you to another matchmaker I know in Grand Rapids. With your permission, I'll share your file with her so that you're not starting at ground zero. I'll also refund your money, so you won't be out anything when you switch."

Noah was silent for so long, she wondered if he was going to say anything at all. The car suddenly felt small and suffocating, the dampness of the rain seeming to seep through the glass.

Boon whined and poked his head through the seats again, this time his focus was on Noah. "Sounds like you thought of everything." His voice was hoarse, scraping against the raw emotion she struggled to contain. She kept her hands tightly folded together in her lap, when all she really wanted to do was wrap them around him, hold him impossibly close, and kiss him again.

Without another word, he put the car in gear and pulled out of the parking space. She could feel the tension radiating from him like a palpable force. She knew that she'd hurt him. But better to hurt him a little bit now than to cause them both a lot of grief later.

They drove in silence, and as they approached Whispering Pines' downtown, Maggie glanced at the car clock. It was after three in the morning. Ugh. And it was Monday, so they'd both have work today. She had a lot to do in order to switch him over to the new matchmaker. But first, she had to get some sleep. After all the events of tonight, she was physically and emotionally exhausted.

Suddenly, she was aware that he'd made an unexpected turn. "Where are you going?" she asked, breaking the silence. "My apartment is the other way."

"I'm not driving to your apartment. I'm driving us back to my brother Wade's house," he said stiffly.

She shook her head. "Uh-uh, no way. Please, just take me home, Noah."

His face flashed in anger. "No."

"What do you mean, no?" she said.

He immediately pulled over and stopped the car on the side of the empty road. "I mean no, Maggie. Despite everything that happened tonight, Nick and Johnny are still out there. It only makes sense to stay someplace safe until we know they're gone."

Maggie shook her head. "I—I'm not comfortable with that, Noah. Please, just take me home, I'll be fine."

He pressed his lips into a thin line. "Well, we have a problem then, Maggie," he said, his tone firm. "Because I'm not comfortable with *that*."

They sat in a strained, angry silence just staring at each other while outside lightning flashed and thunder rumbled through the dark sky. The tension between them was heavy, each of them refusing to back down.

Finally, Noah broke the silence. "If you insist on me taking you home, you're not staying there alone. I'll sleep on the floor if I have to. But I will not leave you unprotected tonight."

"It's morning," she said, aware that she was just being contrary now.

"Morning, whatever. You've got two choices. We go to my brother's place again, or to your place. But either way, I'm not leaving you alone."

She took in the stubborn set of his jaw and realized she wasn't going to move him on this. "All right, fine, but it will be my place. And you don't have to sleep on the floor; I have a sofa."

"Great." He didn't sound like it was great, but he put the car back into gear and made a U-turn.

Inside her apartment, she disappeared for a moment and returned with a washcloth, towel, and blanket for him, along with an extra pillow, carrying them to where he sat on the small sofa.

Boon had already made himself at home on the rug beside it. He'd curled his long, lean body into a deceptively small ball of tawny and black fur. His head rested on his paws, and his dark eyes studied her solemnly. It was a little disconcerting.

"Do you need anything else?" she asked.

"Yes," he said. "But apparently it's not something you can give me right now."

She frowned in confusion.

"Never mind," he sighed. "No, I don't need anything else."

"Okay, well then, goodnight." She turned and walked back down the hallway to her bedroom.

He turned off the living room lamp just as she reached her door.

"Goodnight." His words were a whispered caress in the dark.

Chapter 21

Noah's alarm went off at seven-thirty and he groaned. He threw the blanket aside and sat up stiffly. He should have thought to turn the alarm off the night before, but he hadn't exactly been thinking straight. Besides, Maggie was clearly already awake. He could hear her moving around in the bathroom. He could see Boon in the kitchen, munching on his breakfast and vigorously lapping up water from the dog dishes he'd brought in from the car last night. The pet supplies and dog food his brother Jake had given him had certainly come in handy with all the running around they'd been doing with Boon in tow.

Noah stood up and groaned again. He felt like he'd been through a battle. The stress of their encounter with Valentina combined with tossing and turning all night long on Maggie's sagging sofa had left his muscles sore and his head was fuzzy. On top of that, Maggie's sudden declaration last night had devastated him. But his hours of self-reflection during the night had led him to some definite conclusions. And one thought was now crystal clear. He was about the lose the only woman he'd ever truly loved, for the second time in his life.

And he was not going to let that happen.

Why was she so convinced that she was the wrong woman for him? Both times they'd kissed, he was convinced that her passion had answered his own. It had been genuine. He was sure of it. But why couldn't she see it? Why was she in such denial?

He ran his hands over his face and sank back down onto the sofa. Apparently, he'd promoted the friendship angle a bit too much in his attempts not to push her too hard. But he was determined that this was not going to be a repeat of their freshman year of college. He wasn't about to let her just disappear this time. Not without a fight. He had to find a way to let her know he was in love with her—had been in love with her since high school. Convince her that his feelings for her were real. But how?

He was deep in thought, folding up the blankets he'd used when she emerged from the bathroom. She looked adorable, all wrapped up in a thick, fluffy yellow robe that reached to the floor, her damp curls framing her face. He looked closer and could see dark shadows beneath her amber eyes, which looked swollen and pink at the rims. Had she been crying?

"The bathroom is all yours," she said with clearly forced cheeriness, then turned and padded back to her room before he could respond.

In the bathroom, Noah breathed in the subtle vanilla and floral fragrance of Maggie's shampoo and soap, making him feel a pang of longing. He splashed his face with cool water and wet his hair, borrowing her comb to slick it back from his face. He ran a hand over the dark stubble that covered his chin and jaw and stared at his reflection in the mirror. The storm had ended. And now, in the bright morning light that poured through the bathroom window, he felt exposed. His emotions were raw and clearly visible on his face.

For all his thoughts about not losing her again, he wondered if he was just clinging to a fantasy. And he was suddenly terrified by the possibility that maybe she was just trying to spare his feelings by insisting on being "just friends." The thought sent a sharp pain through his chest. Then he shook his head, determined to push those doubts aside. He couldn't let fear dictate his actions. He had to fight for Maggie and show her that his love for her was real. If she truly didn't reciprocate his feelings, then that would be the end of it. But one way or the other, he had to know.

He opened the bathroom door and heard a groan come from her kitchen. He walked across the main room and poked his head around the corner. "What is it?"

Her golden curls were almost dry and she was dressed in a yellow sundress sprinkled with tiny daisies. She held an empty coffee can in her hands. "I completely forgot that I was out of coffee," she moaned. "And if there was ever a day when we needed coffee, it's today."

"That's true," he said, stepping into the kitchen to examine the empty can over her shoulder. The intoxicating fragrance of warm vanilla and Maggie wafted up to him again. He sighed inwardly but kept his voice light. "How about we pay a visit to the coffee shop before we start our day? I can drive you there and drop you back off here before I head home to change."

Her face filled with gratitude. "That would be wonderful," she said.

Noah drove the short distance to Lakeside Latté. It was busy with the morning rush. Noah put Boon on his leash and they all headed toward the entrance. Just as they approached, the door swung wide and a small group of chattering teenagers bustled out.

"Hey, Mr. R!" said one of the boys in the group, smiling at Noah. "Nice dog," he added, giving Boon a welcome pat on the head.

"Oh, hey, Ben!" Noah said, taking the boy's proffered hand and performing a complex series of handshakes, elbow knocks, and fist pumps.

"Are you coming tonight?" Ben asked.

Noah's caffeine-and-sleep-deprived mind moved sluggishly through his memory banks, then cleared. "Right! It's open mic night here, isn't it?"

"Yeah," Ben gushed. "I was just double-checking our time slot. A group of us are gonna be performing a few songs."

"That's great, Ben," Noah smiled. "I wouldn't miss it! By the way, this is my, er, friend, Ms. Milena."

"Nice to meet you," Ben said politely. "You should come, too! We're going to be performing some of our original pieces. It's guaranteed to be a good time!"

"Oh, um..." Maggie looked surprised. "Sure, that sounds fun."

Ben gave Boon one more pat on the head and then moved away to join his friends.

Maggie turned a confused look toward Noah. "Who was that?"

Noah was still smiling as he opened the coffee shop door. "That was Ben Newcastle. He's one of the students I tutor at JAMZ."

Maggie's expression cleared. "Oh, right, that's the music education charity program for low-income kids that you told me about before, right?"

"Right," Noah said, leading her to join the line-up for coffee.

"I didn't realize that the kids actually learned to write music in that program," Maggie said.

"Not all of them get that far," Noah remarked, gazing down at her. "But Ben and a couple of the other kids we work with have a natural talent for it. Along with music lessons, our program also provides the kids with musical instruments for free, which is so great. I just strongly believe that musical training shouldn't be limited to only those who can afford expensive private lessons."

Maggie was looking up at him with an unreadable expression in her eyes. There was something about the way she looked at him that made his heart flutter with hope.

Then an idea began forming in his mind.

"Look, Maggie," he said as they surged a step forward with the line. "I know you're ending our professional relationship. And you've made it clear that you're not interested in anything romantic with me, so what I'm about to ask you is not a date. But I'd really love it if you'd come with me tonight. Some of these kids are really gifted and I think you'll be impressed."

He studied her closely as she nibbled at her bottom lip for several interminable seconds.

He pressed on. "Think of it as a reward. We've definitely earned it! Now that we know Valentina is okay, and we have a plan in place to help her break free from her situation, we should celebrate. Just as friends." It pained him physically to add that last bit, but he kept his expression neutral.

"I...guess that would be okay." She finally nodded her agreement.

"Awesome!" he said, and clenched his fists to help him fight the overwhelming urge to wrap her in his arms and lift her off her feet.

"You're already awesome and you haven't even placed your order yet?" Olivia joked as they reached the front of the line. "What can you possibly be so happy about?"

"Getting to see your smiling, beautiful face," Noah said, giving her a wink.

"Pshawww! Get outta here!" Olivia laughed with a wave of her hand.

Noah continued grinning as they placed their orders and then moved to the other end of the long counter to wait for them.

"You really do seem ridiculously happy about just getting a cup of coffee," Maggie observed, taking a sip of her caramel delight latté—with extra caramel, of course.

"Just enjoying the company," he said as he took a sip of his own café Americano.

They were quiet as he drove her back to her apartment. When they stopped, he said, "Can I ask you a favor?"

She'd opened her door, but paused to look back at him with a questioning look.

"Could you keep Boon with you just until we meet again tonight? I haven't figured out what to do with him yet now that we know he's not Valentina's. I have some errands I need to run that would be difficult if he was with me. And besides, I'd feel better knowing you have a watchdog protecting you while we're both at work."

"I'm sure I'll be fine," she said. "But I admit I'd love his company. Are you okay with that, Boon?" The dog poked his head through the seats and gave her an answering lick on the cheek, making her laugh. He looked particularly adorable, with both of his long ears flopped over at cockeyed angles the way they sometimes did.

Maggie and Boon exited the car, and Noah watched them walk away, his plan solidifying in his mind. He grinned to himself again. He'd come up with the perfect way to share the true depth of his feelings for her. It was risky, but he knew in his heart that it would be the perfect grand gesture for a romantic like Maggie.

He'd reached the point of stay safe or risk it all. And he was ready to risk it all.

After tonight, either Maggie Milena would become the woman of his dreams or leave him broken-hearted forever.

Chapter 22

"I feel sick inside." Maggie slumped on Jaime's couch with a pillow covering her face. She'd finished everything required to transition Noah over to the Grand Rapids matchmaker, then she and Boon had headed over to Jaime's so she could debrief.

"I have no sympathy for you," Jaime said, cuddling sleepy Emma in her arms.

Afternoon sunshine slanted across the room, creating a warm and cozy ambiance that didn't match Maggie's mood at all.

"That's way harsh, Jaime," Maggie said, peeking at her friend from behind the pillow.

"Well, it's the truth," Jaime said. "I don't understand you at all. You've been in love with this guy forever. He's fun. He's hot. And he's into you. He even kissed you. Twice! And you think it's somehow wrong to pursue a relationship with him?" Jaime shook her head in disbelief. "Maggie, you're still sabotaging your own happiness."

Maggie sat up and tossed the pillow aside. "I already explained—"

"Yeah, yeah," Jaime said, cutting her off. "You're in love with him but he doesn't see you the same way. He's always only thought of you as a friend. Blah, blah, blah. Well, feelings can grow, Maggie, if you would just give them a chance. Besides, in my experience, friends don't make out."

"We didn't make out!" Maggie exclaimed, feeling heat burn her cheeks. "It was just a couple of kisses." *A couple of hot, toe-curling, heart-melting kisses that she would never be able to get out of her mind as long as she lived.* "I told you, we both just got caught up in the tension of the situation we were in, and then the relief of finding Valentina. And remember," Maggie added quickly, "you can't say anything about that to anyone until she comes forward."

"I understand," Jaime said, settling her sleeping baby into the nearby pack-n-play. Then she came to sit beside Maggie on the sofa, angling to face her friend. "I still can't believe all of that. I mean, the mafia, seriously?"

"Right?" Maggie said. "I can hardly believe it myself. To grow up with a father like that, a life like that."

Jaime shook her head. "And the police still haven't found those two guys that are after you all?"

"Nope," Maggie said. "Hugo promised to call Noah the minute the police had them."

"I think it's so sweet that despite your attempts to blow him off, Noah wouldn't leave you unprotected last night," Jaime said, clasping her hands over her heart like she was watching a romance movie.

Maggie would never have admitted it out loud to Noah, but she'd actually been deeply touched by his concern for her. He'd slept on her uncomfortable, lumpy sofa for goodness sake. She sighed inwardly. Just one more reason to love the guy.

"Tell me more about this date you're going on with him tonight," Jaime said.

"*Non*-date," Maggie emphasized. "It's an open mic night at Lakeside Latté. It sounds like Olivia holds them on occasional weeknights throughout the summer. Noah volunteers with a music education program for kids and some of his students are going to be performing."

"Oooh, that sounds fun!" Jaime said. "You know, I think Jack and I would enjoy that. And we could use a date night ourselves. Maybe I can rope Grandpa into babysitting Emma. What time is it?"

"He's picking me up at seven so we can get a good table," Maggie said.

"Seven, hmm? Should we go over your wardrobe choices again?" Jaime asked as she sent a text to her father. "You know how good I am at this. Let me help you put together a great look for your date."

"It's not a date!" Maggie said more loudly than she intended, making baby Emma squirm in her sleep. "And don't even think about it!" she hissed at Boon, who had risen to his feet, clearly preparing to perform one of his infamous leaps onto her lap. Instead, he sat down and cocked his head, studying her with suspicion.

"I'm fine," she said, returning his gaze.

"No, she's not, Boon," Jaime said, reaching down to pat the dog's head. "She's really, really not."

Back at her apartment, Maggie sat on her bed and puffed in frustration. Most of the contents of her closet and dresser drawers were strewn across the bed and floor. Boon had already attempted several of his doggie hugs—as she now thought of them—but he had finally given up and was lying on the bed beside her, regarding the disarray.

"Don't judge me!" she said, meeting his watchful brown gaze. "I need to find something that's nice but not too nice. Comfortable yet classy. Something that says non-date, but...date?"

"Whatever!" she said, and made her choice. "Just because it's not a date doesn't mean I can't feel pretty." She picked up a white, pleated skort off the floor and paired it with a clingy black top with a flattering sweetheart neckline. In the bathroom, she touched up the spiraling curls that bounced around her shoulders and freshened up her makeup. She studied her reflection in the mirror. Her cheeks were flushed, and her eyes were bright.

"You know what?" she said to the dog who had trailed in behind her. "If this is my last night with him, at least I can play my part with class," she said with a lift of her chin.

Just then, there was a rhythmic tapping at her door.

Boon gave a bark and followed her as she hurried to peer through her front door peephole. It was Noah, right on time.

She swung the door wide, and Boon danced around in happy circles, jumping up on Noah in greeting. "Down, boy," he laughed. Maggie noted that Noah's smoky gray eyes were brighter than usual as he looked at her.

"You look really pretty, Maggie," he said.

"Thank you," she said, hoping that there was no way he could hear how much faster her heart beat at the compliment.

Noah looked gorgeous as always. The bruises on his fine-cut jawline and handsome face had faded a bit over the past few days. And she loved the way his milk chocolate curls always broke free from his attempts to tame them, swirling on top of his head and behind his ears. As he led the way out of her apartment, she noted how his pale blue polo shirt accentuated the sun-kissed tan of his skin, and how the black jeans he wore nicely followed the long lines of his muscular thighs to the curve of his... She jerked her eyes to the back of his head. *We're just friends. Get a grip, Milena.*

There was a strange energy about him tonight, she observed as they got into his car. She wondered if he was picking up on her own nervousness. "Tell me about your students that will be performing tonight," she said, partly to distract herself and partly because she wanted to know more about this side of him.

"Well, there's Ben, who you met this morning. He's fifteen and he's participated in the JAMZ program for about five years," Noah said, pulling out onto the road. "He's being raised by a single mom, his father is in prison. His mom has told us over and over again what a lifesaver this program has been for him. Sometimes, even when these kids are only elementary school age, they can start getting into real trouble. And Ben was headed down that path. His mom likes to say that music saved him."

He shared stories about several of his other students, many of whom shared a similar story in that they came from single parent households.

Maggie was touched by the passion she saw in Noah as described them all to her.

"It's clear how much you really care for these kids," she said.

"I do," Noah admitted, pulling into the coffee shop parking lot. "It's always gratifying to discover kids with talent like Ben's. But it's more than that. I want to be a part of shifting the perception that making music is only for musicians. It's for everyone."

"I like that," Maggie said, smiling at him.

He got out of the car and ran around to open her door for her, before letting Boon out. *Always the gentlemen.*

Her gaze swept the crowded parking lot. "Wow, I wonder if we'll still be able to get a good table like you planned. It's so crowded already!"

The corner of his mouth lifted and there was an inexplicable glimmer in his eyes. "I think we'll be all right."

It was a warm summer evening, with just the hint of a breeze. The sun was on its downward trajectory toward the horizon and the overhead sky was a vibrant blend of oranges and fuchsia pink. A small platform was set up with a stool and microphone, and Maggie could see a sound system set up behind it. On the outside patio, Olivia had arranged tables in a loose semi-circle around the platform with tiny candles flickering on each of them. Twinkly lights were draped around the perimeter, adding to the magic of the scene.

Most of the tables were already taken and small clusters of people stood chatting together. As they approached the patio, Noah was immediately swarmed by a group of teens. He made so many introductions that Maggie's head was spinning with names and smiling faces.

"And last but not least, this is Ani, Hugo's daughter," Noah said after hugging a beautiful dark-haired Latina girl.

"Hi!" the girl greeted Maggie with a bright smile, then she was distracted by Boon who was sitting quietly by Maggie's side.

"Oooh! I love your dog, Mr. R.! Have I met him before? There's something familiar about him." She ran her hands over the silky fur of the dog's gold-and-black head. Then she leaned over to give his back a thorough two-handed scratch, which caused Boon to lean against her in appreciation.

"Nope, I just found him a few days ago," Noah said.

"Hmmm, I feel like I know him from somewhere. I'm sure I'll think of it," she said. Then she stood back up she returned her attention to Maggie. "So, are you Mr. R.'s girlfriend?"

Maggie laughed awkwardly. "No, no, we're just friends."

"Too bad," Ani said with a toss of her dark hair. "He could really use a nice lady in his life."

"Ani!" Noah cried.

"I'm just saying what I've heard my dad say," she shot back at him with a mischievous grin.

"Go play with your friends," he said, turning her around and giving her a gentle push away from them.

She laughed and immediately disappeared into a group of chattering girls.

"Maggie!"

Maggie looked around at the sound of her name and spotted Jaime and Jack looking cozy, seated at a small table near the center of the patio. She waved and was about to walk over to say hello when Ben approached. "Hey, Mr. R.! I saved a table for you and your lady up front."

Maggie saw the empty table for two with a handmade cardboard "RESERVED" sign sitting on it.

"That's great! Thanks, Ben." Noah led her to the table and then offered to get them drinks from inside. "Caramel latte?" he grinned down at her.

"Of course, but decaf this time." She smiled back. "And extra whipped cream, please, since it's my dessert."

As he walked away, she considered how the energy she had observed in him earlier seemed to be growing more intense. She decided it was probably excitement over the upcoming performances of his students.

He returned to the table with their drinks and sat down. "I'm assuming you haven't gotten a text or phone call from our friend yet?" Maggie asked in a low voice, taking a sip of her sweet, creamy drink.

"Not yet." Noah looked worried. "You don't think she'll back out, do you?"

Maggie considered the idea, then said, "I don't think so. I mean, maybe if it was totally up to her. But there's no way Eric would go for it. And I think she values him and his ethics too much to go against him on this."

"Good evening, everyone!"

They turned their attention to the platform where Olivia stood. "I want to thank you all so much for coming out for another one of our Summer Open Mic Nights. We've got some real fine talent lined up for you tonight along with plenty of coffees, teas, and baked treats to sustain you."

A couple of young people whooped from the back of the crowd.

Olivia smiled and glanced down at the notes on her cell phone. "To start off the performances, we have Ben Newcastle. Take it away, Ben!"

There was enthusiastic applause as Ben took the stage. He performed a fun Hawaiian song using a ukulele, a folk song cover, and then a mellow ballad on guitar that he'd written.

Maggie couldn't help but smile at the way Noah beamed with pride as the young man took his bow.

Following Ben were a guitarist and harmonica duo playing some rhythmic blues tunes, then a keyboardist, a jazz saxophone player, and an acapella rapper.

Noah had been right, Maggie was impressed with the level of talent on display. As the last performer left the stage, she turned to comment on this fact but found Noah holding his head in his hands. One of his legs was bouncing out a rapid staccato beneath the table. "Are you okay?" she asked.

His head shot up and his face held a guilty expression. "I'm fine, I'm fine, just…thinking," he said.

"Please don't worry about Valentina," she said, assuming that was the problem. She lay a hand on his arm and he jerked slightly but didn't pull away. "I'm sure she'll do the right thing and it will all work out. In the meantime, we should do just as you suggested and make this a celebration. C'mon," she lifted her mug of coffee as if to make a toast, "we solved the mystery!"

"We did." He lifted his mug and clinked it against hers with a grin. But his smile faded when Ben once again took to the stage.

"Okay, everyone, we're in for a special treat tonight. We have one final performer. And it's our own Mr. R.!" Ben said, glancing down at Noah. "He has a special song he wants to perform to close us out for the night." Ben began gesturing with his arms, encouraging the audience to clap. "Let's hear it for Mr. R.!"

Maggie looked at Noah in surprise as the patio erupted with enthusiastic applause and shouts of praise.

"All right, Mr. R.!"

"Woohoo!"

"I didn't realize you were going to perform!" Maggie said to him as he rose to his feet.

Noah didn't reply but walked slowly forward and stepped up onto the platform. Ben handed him a guitar and Maggie watched as he climbed up onto the stool.

The sun had set, and now the sky was a backdrop of deep navy blue for the softly glowing crescent moon and prickles of emerging starlight. The perfume of night-blooming jasmine in pots around the patio floated on the air, adding a touch of enchantment to the ambiance.

Noah sat with one foot braced against the rung of the stool, the other on the platform, and Maggie sighed inwardly. He looked so incredibly handsome with his dark head bent over the instrument while he tuned it. *Enjoy this moment while you can, Milena.*

She glanced back at Jaime, who smiled softly and lifted her mug in a silent salute, clearly in tune with the thoughts running through Maggie's mind. Maggie settled more comfortably in her seat, and rested her chin in her hands, ready to soak up every precious second of his performance.

"We've heard some great talent tonight, haven't we?" he started out, and waited for the enthusiastic applause to die down. "I'm grateful that we have JAMZ to bring music education to the young people of Whispering Pines. JAMZ wasn't around when I was a kid, but I was blessed to get an introduction to music from my Nana. She's no longer with me, but I feel like I share a piece of her legacy every time I play. I'm feeling it, especially tonight...because I know she would encourage me in this."

He cleared his throat and Maggie thought she saw his hands trembling.

"I wrote this song many, many years ago when I was eighteen years old. I've actually never performed it before. But I did practice it earlier today. So hopefully, I don't mess it up too much."

"You ROCK, Mr. R.!" came an encouraging call from the back.

"Thank you," he smiled, and began strumming lightly on the guitar. "This song is called *Dream Girl*."

The crowd quieted down under the spell of his music and Maggie was completely focused on Noah, the way the light struck the planes of his handsome face, and the feeling of warmth that washed over her as she watched his fingers dance over the strings. The melody was soft, slow, and sweet as it filled the night.

Then Noah lifted his eyes from the guitar, locked his gaze with hers, and began to sing.

All through our days at school
Dreams of you sparkle like a jewel.
The sunrise of your smile starts my day,
The warmth of your laughter like a sunbeam's ray.
Golden curls frame an angel's face,
You're a slice of heaven in my embrace.
I'm in love with you and I don't wanna wake up,
'cause you're my dream girl, livin' in my dream world.
I'm in love with you and I don't wanna wake up,
'cause you're my dream girl, livin' in my dream world.

Dreams of you fill my head,
every time I go to bed.
Hand-in-hand within my dreams,
we stroll together by starlit streams.
Your touch, your look, ignite my heart,
And in my dreams we never part.

As Noah began to sing the chorus again, Maggie felt all the blood rush to her head. Was...was this song about her?

I close my eyes and you're by my side.
I open them and my dreams collide,
With reality where we're still just friends,
But my love is yours and it never ends.
When the time is right I'll tell you what's true,
My days are richer when they're spent with you.
For now I'll wait and let things be,
Till your love is mine and you set my dreams free.
I'm in love with you and I don't wanna wake up,
'cause you're my dream girl, livin' in my dream world.
I'm in love with you and I don't wanna wake up,
'cause you're my dream girl, livin' in my dream world.

With a final strum, the last note slowly faded to silence. Then the patio exploded with cheers and wild applause.

Maggie couldn't see clearly anymore because tears had filled her eyes. She was aware of Noah stepping down from the stage. Aware that he was surrounded again by a flock of students who shook his hand and thumped him on the back. And finally, aware that he had returned to sit beside her once again. But she couldn't look at him, couldn't breathe, couldn't believe what was happening.

The crowd of people chattered and milled around them. Finally, she lifted her eyes to meet his and everything else melted away. It was as if the two of them were alone in a room.

She was incredulous, her voice barely a whisper. "You wrote that song..."

He took her hands in his. "About you. Yes, Maggie, I did."

Her heart swelled with a mixture of joy and disbelief as she tried to process what Noah had just revealed.

Noah continued. "Yesterday, after you told me you were dumping me as a client because you didn't want to jeopardize our *friendship*, I was...devastated. I've wanted to be more than just friends with you ever since we met, Maggie. But I want to thank you for what you did. Because it gave me the kick in the butt I needed to do what you suggested.

"Last night I did a full analysis of myself regarding my FDFs. And when I did that, I discovered that you were right. I have been subconsciously sabotaging my dates, making certain that those relationships never led anywhere. And I finally understood why."

"Why?" she breathed.

"Because," he said, reaching to cup her face with one hand, "I've only been in love with one woman in my life. But I never told her. And she left me. So, over the years, I've unsuccessfully tried to find another woman who can fill that void. But I never can. Because there's only one woman who can fill that void, Maggie. And that woman is you."

Her mind was whirling. "Are you telling me..." Her voice broke.

He took a deep breath. "I'm telling you that I love you, Maggie Milena. That I've been in love with you since we were in high school together. That you are a woman who is incredibly worthy of love. And if you're willing to give me a chance—"

"I love you too, Noah," she whispered, cutting him off. Her eyes were completely blurry with tears again. But she felt like she was seeing clearly for the first time in her life. "I always have."

Noah closed his eyes, as if savoring the weight of her words. Then he slowly opened them and looked deep into Maggie's tear-filled gaze.

"I knew it!" he whispered, giving her one of his heart-wrenching lopsided grins. "But why didn't you ever say anything?"

"Why didn't you?" she exclaimed.

"I asked you first."

She smiled and shook her head. "Because you always had a girlfriend hanging on your arm."

"That was only because I knew there was no hope for me while you were dating the loser," Noah said. "When you finally broke up with Joe, I thought I would have a chance. But it seemed like you were intent on confining me to the friend zone."

"No, you did that!"

"Man," he shook his head. "Were we a couple of insecure teenagers or what?"

She laughed.

"You know," she said, playing with their intertwined fingers. "I did plan to confess my feelings to you once when we were in high school."

Noah's face registered surprise. "When?"

"It was just before graduation, when you had that performance with your band."

His face cleared, his eyes taking on a strange light. "I remember seeing you there. But then you were suddenly gone. What happened?"

"I thought my idea was ridiculous when I saw that girl smothering you with kisses on stage," Maggie said, looking down at their hands. "I figured you two must've been involved."

Noah frowned. "I remember that. I was so angry when she did that. I wasn't expecting it, and I didn't invite it. I got away from her as fast as I could without humiliating her in front of the crowd. But apparently not fast enough, because by the time I looked for you again, you were gone." His gaze was intent. "Do you want to hear something even more ironic?"

"What?"

"I was planning to confess my feelings for you that same night."

"You were?" She lifted her eyes to his once again.

"Yeah, I had a whole plan in place." One corner of his mouth lifted. "Actually, it was the plan you just witnessed tonight. I was going to openly dedicate that song to you and sing it. I envisioned...well, I envisioned exactly what just happened tonight—that you would hear it, you would hear the truth in my words, and finally make my dreams a reality.

"But I never got to sing it to you. Then I left to spend summer here with my grandparents and you seemed to be avoiding me. When you stopped responding to my texts and phone messages, I just assumed you didn't feel the same way about me and had moved on with your life."

"Oh my gosh," Maggie said, her grip on his hands tightening. "We've lost so much time to miscommunication, our own insecurities, and..."

"Bad timing?"

She laughed. "And bad timing."

"But we can make up for it now," Noah said softly. "Now that we know how we feel about each other, I have a question for you." To Maggie's shock, Noah got out of his chair and down on one knee. "Maggie Milena, will you..."

"Noah, what are you doing? Get up!" She looked around wildly, hoping nobody was watching. They'd just revealed their feelings for each other, but this was a far cry from that. "Noah, please! We're definitely not ready for—"

"...go out on a real first date with me?"

Her mouth fell open and then she threw back her head and laughed.

He gave her a mischievous grin. "I realize it's possible you could be taking your life in your hands, but—"

"Yes, yes, and yes!" she cried, throwing her arms around his neck and kissing him.

"Whoa! Check out Mr. R. and his lady!" Ben called out.

Maggie vaguely heard another person whistle. But she was oblivious, lost in the pure, unadulterated bliss of finally being held in Noah's embrace, their bodies intertwining in a perfect fit. All the years of longing and missed opportunities melted away as their kiss deepened. She focused on the feel of his arms around her, the touch of his lips on hers, each tender movement sending sparks through her body. Time stood still as they poured all their pent-up longing and love into that one kiss.

That is, until she felt a soft tap on her shoulder. Reluctantly, she broke away and turned to see Jaime and Jack standing there smiling at them. "So, what exactly are we witnessing here?" Jaime said with a playful tilt of her head.

"He just asked me out. And I said yes!" Maggie cried.

Jaime and Jack looked at each other and then back at the two of them, broad grins on their faces. "Finally!" they said in unison.

The four of them stood chatting as the few lingering members of the crowd cleared out from the patio. Noah refused to let go of her hand and Maggie felt as if she might never stop smiling.

Suddenly Noah's phone that was sitting on the table lit up with an incoming call. She and Noah both looked down, saw the number, and exchanged a glance.

"Excuse me, I've got to take this," Noah said. He quickly picked it up and stepped away to answer it.

While Jaime hugged and congratulated her on this exciting new change in her relationship with Noah, Maggie was only half listening. Instead, she was straining to catch anything regarding the conversation Noah was having right now. Were Valentina and Eric finally ready to put their plan in motion?

Noah hung up and rejoined them all at the table. He gave Jaime and Jack an easy smile. "If it's okay with you guys, I'm going to steal my girl here for a bit."

"Of course, of course," Jack said. "C'mon, babe, let's go relieve your dad and give them some privacy."

As the couple moved away from the table, Noah pulled her close into another embrace and whispered in her ear. "That was Eric. Valentina is rethinking her plan to go to the police and he wants us to come back to the hotel to encourage her. He knows it's late, but he wants us to come now so they can get this over with tonight and move forward in their relationship."

Maggie grinned, planting a soft kiss beside his ear. "I'm all about moving forward in relationships. Let's go encourage them."

They pulled into the motel parking lot, and this time Noah parked the car directly in front of Valentina and Eric's door. He twisted in his seat to see Boon sleeping comfortably in the back seat. "Should we leave him here this time?"

"I think so," Maggie agreed. "But let's drop the windows so he gets fresh air."

They got out of the car and walked hand-in-hand to the motel room door. Noah stopped before knocking and pulled her close, placing a soft kiss on her lips. He released her and sighed.

"When we're done here, we have a lot more catching up to do in that area," he teased. "In some ways, I feel like this is all still a dream," he said, gazing down at her.

"A dream come true," she said, rising on her toes to kiss his cheek before he tapped lightly on the door.

"Who is it?" a voice hissed from inside.

"It's Noah and Maggie," Noah said.

The door opened to a narrow slit, and a single eye peeked out.

"Hi," Noah said, then frowned. "Why do you guys have all the lights off?"

"Come join the party and you'll see," said a gruff voice as the door swung open and Noah saw the glint of a gun aimed at his chest.

He rolled his eyes and only had time to groan, "Not again," before he and Maggie were yanked into the room.

Chapter 23

The door was shut and locked behind them before a lamp was turned on. Maggie gasped and Noah stared in confused shock as their gazes swept over the room. There was blood on the rumpled bedspread of one of the beds where Eric now lay. His hands were bound with duct tape and his chest was bare. His face was a bruised and bloodied mess, with one eye swollen completely shut. Fresh cuts on his chest and arms were still oozing blood.

Valentina sat on the opposite bed across from him. She was unbound, but her eyes were red rimmed and there was a trickle of blood coming from a small gash on her lip. Aside from this, she appeared unharmed.

Johnny was holding the gun; his swarthy face held a sneer as he looked Noah and Maggie up and down.

Nick the Knife stood between the two beds. Nick stared at Noah, metal glinting off the slim knife that he was expertly flipping around in his hand in a way that almost seemed like an art form. There was a clear bite wound on the arm of his knife-wielding hand, and Noah wondered if it was from when Boon had attacked the man yesterday.

"So glad you could join us," Nick said with a sarcastic twist to his lips; he tilted his head in mock welcome. "Have a seat." His white scalp gleamed in the lamplight where the shape of the knife was shaved into the hair on the side of his head.

When they didn't move, Nick stepped forward and roughly shoved Noah, causing him to stumble. "I said, sit down. On the floor. Both of you."

Barely containing his anger, Noah sank to the floor of the hotel room, and Maggie followed suit. Noah moved his body slightly in front of hers, uncertain of what Nick intended to do next.

"Now that the gang's all here, we can finally put an end to all of this," Nick said. "And I'll finally get what's rightfully mine."

"Rightfully yours?" Valentina spat out. "You'll never get away with—" The rest of what she'd been about to say was lost as Nick violently backhanded her across the face. She fell across the bed and Eric moaned, struggling to rise.

"Don't even think about it," Johnny said, flicking the gun in his direction before returning it to point at Noah.

Noah doubted Eric could do anything if he tried. He was in bad shape. In addition to the cuts and bruising covering his body, it looked as if one of his arms was broken.

"What do you mean, get what's rightfully yours?" Maggie said.

Nick's eyes flicked down to her. "Exactly what I said."

"Prison time?"

Oh man, Maggie. Don't push him. Nick's eyes narrowed and Noah tensed in preparation to jump him if he made a move toward Maggie, but Nick stayed put.

"No, Matches by Maggie," Nick drawled. "I mean getting what Papa Dom originally promised me, before everything got all screwed up."

"And what exactly is that?" Noah asked, although he already knew the answer from their previous conversation with Valentina and Eric. But he wanted to stall for time in order to try and figure a way out of this.

There was a crazed light in Nick's ice-blue eyes, making him seem even more dangerous than he had in any of their other encounters. And there was something unsettling about the way he moved, one minute twitchy and the next like a prowling wildcat trapped in a cage. Noah wondered if he was on something.

"Even before I was a made man, I always gave Papa Dom my unfailing loyalty. I've done whatever he asked of me without question. And in reward for that loyalty, I was promised her." Here he flicked the knife in Valentina's direction. "Along with the promise that she and I would co-rule the Partnership together when the time came."

"But then," Nick's face twisted in fury, "Papa Dom changed the plan. 'It's for the good of the organization, Nick,'" he said, his tone turning petulant.

"'There's been too much bloodshed in the family, Nick. We all have to make sacrifices, Nick.'"

Nick swore and in a lightning move, threw the knife hard against the motel room wall. It stuck there, the shaft vibrating with the impact. He walked slowly over to it and pulled it out. His eyes fixated on the sharp blade, seemingly entranced for a moment before he began to flip it back and forth again while he spoke.

"I could tell the old man was getting soft in his old age. But like a fool, I agreed to go along with his plan. Because loyalty is everything to me."

Valentina snorted at this, and he took a menacing step toward her. Noah marveled at the woman's audacity as she stared him down, certain she was pushing him too far. But this time Nick held back and instead began pacing about the tiny room.

"But then, I find out what a liar she is." Nick jabbed the knife toward Valentina again. "The daughter of the boss, the one he's chosen to take his place, has no concept of loyalty. She lied to him about her supposed bachelorette party. So, I do like Papa Dom asks. I track her car here, determined to bring her back to do her duty. But instead, I find her partying and hanging all over you." This time he points the blade in Noah's direction.

Then Nick tapped the flat of his blade against his temple. "So, now I'm thinkin'...Who is this guy? Is he from a rival gang? A professional assassin? I admit it. For a while, you had me. Our sources couldn't find out anything about either of you beyond your cover stories. Nothing made any sense."

Nick stared hard at Noah. But Noah said nothing, his mind working furiously. He thought he could successfully sweep Nick off his feet from his seated position, but that still left Johnny holding the gun.

"I still can't believe that you called the cops on us at the hospital," Nick said, glancing at Valentina again.

"You're welcome," Valentina said with a cold smile.

Nick stared at her hard for a long moment, then gave a small shrug, a satisfied smile curving his lips. "In the end, it doesn't matter. Because after trailing these idiots all weekend," here he indicated Noah and Maggie, "we finally got lucky. Thanks so very much for leading us here, by the way." His tone was mocking. "Honestly, I'm not sure we would have ever found Valentina without you two, don't you agree, Johnny?"

Johnny gave an affirmative grunt from his post by the door, his small eyes glittering.

"Once you two left here this morning, we paid our own visit to these two lovebirds," Nick continued, his expression hard. "Surprisingly, they didn't want to talk at first. But after quite a bit of...er, persuasion, we finally got the whole story.

"It wasn't just that the bachelorette party was a lie. But everything Valentina's done has been a lie. And she was about to commit the ultimate betrayal." Nick shook his head, clearly incredulous.

Noah could sense Maggie inch slightly closer to him. She placed a trembling hand against his back. He wished he could comfort her, but he knew that any sudden movements might set Nick off.

"But guess what, princess? It's all over." Nick turned to stand over Valentina. "Because I've decided that Papa Dom's got it all wrong. And now it's up to me to make it right for the good of the organization. I mean, here's me, loyal without question. And her," he grabs a handful of Valentina's hair and yanks it, getting close to her face, "a disloyal liar who I've now discovered was planning to break the sacred law of *omertà*," he hissed. He placed his knife at Valentina's throat, and she sucked in her breath. "And all just to run away with this *sfigato*." He kicked at Eric, who moaned in pain. Eric's eyes fluttered and Noah thought he looked like he was about to pass out.

"She's not worthy to run the Partnership," Nick spat. "So, I've decided I'll be doing Papa Dom a favor by getting rid of her."

"Get rid of her how?" Maggie asked.

"Do I really need to spell it out for you?" Nick said sarcastically, then sighed. "I suppose I do, little Matches by Maggie. It's pretty simple. Valentina here needs to die, along with her boy toy. And of course, the two of you."

Noah watched the color drain from Valentina's face, and he felt a knot form in his stomach. Despite the wave of dread washing over him, and the fact that they had no weapons of their own, there was no way he was going down without a fight. If nothing else, he would protect Maggie with his last breath.

Nick's grin widened at Valentina's expression. "That's right, princess. Did you really think that after all of this, I'd just take you back home to Daddy?"

The smile fell from his lips as he stared at her. "You're not worthy to lead the Partnership. The only one who is worthy to rule in Papa Dom's place, is me."

"She's still his daughter," Maggie said, scooting even closer to Noah. "So, I doubt he'll see it that way." As she spoke, Noah felt her hand lift from his back, and then he fought the urge to jump when he felt it slip slowly into the back pocket of his jeans. What the devil was she doing?

Nick smiled down at Valentina, but it didn't touch his eyes. "Oh, but he will. See, I've come up with a new plan. The perfect plan."

Noah felt Maggie's fingertips sliding over his phone and suddenly realized what she was up to. *Resourceful genius!* he silently praised her, shifting his body slightly to provide her with better coverage and easier access. He felt her press the power button five times before she slipped her hand back out again.

Nick shook his head in mock sadness. "Unfortunately, none of you will be around for the final scene. But let me share my creative vision." He waved his blade in Noah's direction. "Noah here is just as I suspected, a private assassin who is going to murder Valentina." Nick gasped in surprise, as if startled by this fake revelation. "Of course, I arrive too late to save her but still in time to avenge her murder for Papa Dom by killing Noah. And since we can't have any loose ends, Eric and Miss Matches by Maggie here are simply going to have to disappear."

"That sounds like a lot of murders you're going to need to cover up," Noah said.

Nick grinned down at him, and this time it looked genuine. "Don't you worry about that. I've had plenty of practice in that area."

"Enough chit-chat," Johnny spoke up from the door. "Let's get this done, Nick. How do you want to work it?"

Nick's gaze scanned the group. "Let's see..." He tapped the flat side of the knife blade against his lips. "We'll make it look like Noah shot Tina here. Then, of course, I'll slit his throat in my signature style. Man, I wish I'd killed that old bag who took my favorite knife." He frowned at the blade in his hand, then cocked his head, making it crack loudly before he continued.

His eyes moved between Maggie and Eric. "I think having these two here will be too messy and difficult to explain. So, we'll just take them to a different location and get rid of their bodies with an acid bath."

Noah felt a chill pass through him at the matter-of-fact way Nick discussed their deaths.

"Sounds good," Johnny grunted, pulling a silencer out of his pocket and screwing it onto the end of his weapon. "What about the blood on the bedspread?"

"It's fine. We'll need to call in the Cleaners to remove any evidence pointing to us after it's all done anyway," Nick said dismissively.

"Okay. Let's put these two in the trunk first then," Johnny indicated Maggie and Eric, "before we off the other two. That way we can take off right after it's done."

Nick gave an affirmative nod and Noah felt his hope for rescue beginning to slip away. He couldn't look at his phone now to confirm it, but if Maggie had successfully pulled the same trick she had during their first encounter with these men, then the police should already be on their way. But the motel was on the outskirts of town. What if the police arrived too late to stop his and Valentina's murders? And with his phone still in his pocket, there was no protection for Maggie if they drove off somewhere else with her afterward. Was he about to lose the love of his life when he'd only just found her?

"Okay." Johnny tossed a roll of duct tape toward Nick.

"You, stay right where you are, princess," Nick ordered Valentina. "The rest of you, get up."

Noah and Maggie rose slowly from the floor, and Nick proceeded to tape Maggie's wrists together in front of her. She exchanged a worried glance with Noah, who watched helplessly. Even if he managed to successfully jump Nick, he'd never be able to get to Johnny before he got a shot off.

Nick was about to tape Noah's wrists, when he realized Eric was still struggling unsuccessfully to rise from the bed.

"You. Help him," Nick ordered, looking at Noah.

Noah moved forward and attempted to lift Eric, who gave a sharp cry of pain.

"I'm sorry," Noah murmured as he struggled to support the wounded man. His mind raced, heart pounding against his ribcage. He needed to stall somehow, to hopefully give the police enough time to arrive. Adrenaline coursed through him and every muscle in his body tensed as he plotted his next move. He and Eric hobbled together toward the door, and he decided that when he was close enough he'd have to just let go of Eric in order to overpower Johnny and get that gun.

Suddenly, he heard something. A soft scraping sound at the motel room door.

"Quiet," Johnny hissed at the group, then frowned at the door. "What's that?"

The scraping came again, louder, and this time accompanied by a high-pitched sound.

Johnny lifted the gun and with his other hand, yanked open the door.

A giant, growling ball of sharp white teeth and black-and-gold fur shot into the room.

Noah blinked as the normally mild-mannered Boon knocked Johnny to the floor, barking ferociously before biting down hard on his gun-wielding hand.

Johnny screamed in pain as the gun fell from his nerveless fingers. Maggie wasted no time in scooping it up with her bound hands and trained it on Johnny.

In the same instant, Valentina rose to face Nick. With a lightening move, she gripped the back of his head with one hand, and with the other, slashed the flat side of her palm along his jawline in a single fluid motion. Nick dropped like a stone. Without hesitating, Valentina snatched the knife from his hand and turned to Noah. "Bind him," she ordered, indicating the duct tape.

"What did you do?" Maggie asked, her mouth gaping.

"Pressure point," Valentina said. "Doesn't take much strength, but it's very effective."

Valentina switched places with Noah, assisting Eric back down onto the bed, while Noah wrapped the unconscious Nick's wrists and ankles with copious amounts of tape.

Next, he stepped over to Johnny, who was unable to move as Boon kept him pinned to the ground. The dog continued to growl right in the man's face, his teeth bared.

"Get him off me!" Johnny whined. "He's gonna kill me."

Noah shook his head at the irony of the man's words as he bound Johnny's ankles.

"It's okay now, boy," Noah said to Boon. The German Shepherd immediately removed his paws from Johnny's chest and went to sit down next to Maggie, panting, while Noah tightly bound Johnny's wrists.

Valentina handed Noah the knife, which he used to remove the tape from Maggie's wrists. He had just pulled out his phone, when to his relief, he could hear sirens in the distance, growing louder.

"Woohoo!" Maggie cheered as she exchanged a look with Noah. "She shoots, she scores again!"

"What?" Valentina frowned in confusion.

"It's a very helpful trick Maggie knows." Noah grinned. "Suffice it to say, the cavalry is coming."

There was a groan from the floor as Nick regained consciousness, his eyes fluttering open. He struggled to sit up, pulling against the bonds holding his hands behind his back. "What happened?"

Noah had already moved to the open doorway and was waving his arms at the police car pulling into the lot.

He glanced back at the two trussed up men sprawled on the floor. "Let's just say, there was an unexpected 'boon' that put a big kink in your sick plan."

Boon thumped his tail on the floor at the mention of his name.

"Oh, you are just hilarious," Maggie said with a shake of her head, but she couldn't suppress a smile.

"I know, right?"

Chapter 24

"Okay, wait, I missed what you started to say about what happened after the police arrested Nick and Johnny," Ani said.

She was trailing behind Hugo as he carried a large plastic platter laden with an assortment of lunch meats and cheeses. He set it on the beachside picnic table and sat down across from Noah and Maggie. He'd invited them for a picnic lunch to celebrate the fact that Noah was no longer a suspect in the disappearance of Valentina. Noah could hardly believe it had only been forty-eight hours since they'd been held at gunpoint in that seedy motel room, afraid for their lives.

Next to the platter, Ani set down the condiment containers and loaf of sliced French bread that she'd been carrying. Then she plopped onto the bench next to Boon, who instantly rested his chin on her lap while she stroked the soft fur of his head. "I'm going to figure out where I know you from, you adorable pup," she said, then waved her hand airily at the group. "Okay, you may continue!"

Everyone began building their sandwiches, while Hugo picked up where he'd left off. "So, after everyone was taken to the station, the FBI was called in."

"Because of all the mafia stuff?" Ani said, spreading a layer of mayonnaise on one slice of bread.

Hugo smiled at her. "Yeah, because of all the mafia stuff."

"So, where are Nick and Johnny now?" Maggie asked, squeezing mustard on top of the meat of her sandwich.

"Nick 'the Knife' Verilla and Johnny LaRocca are being held for kidnapping, assault and battery, and attempted murder for starters," Hugo replied. "But it won't be long before they'll be dealing with a lot more charges than that."

"Why?" Ani asked.

"Because the FBI was able to convince Valentina to testify against her father and the Detroit Partnership."

"They can probably thank Eric for that. Getting her to agree was a hard sell after what happened with her mother," Noah said, after swallowing a bite.

"What do you mean?" Ani asked, looking around the table. "What happened to Valentina's mom?"

Hugo looked at his daughter. Noah could see that he was considering how much to tell her. "Valentina's mom tried to escape from the Partnership with Valentina when she was a young girl," Hugo said. "She was going to do exactly what Valentina plans to do, testify against them. But Valentina's father, the head of the Detroit mafia, found them and brought them back. Her mother disappeared shortly afterward, and Valentina firmly believes she was killed on her father's orders for what she tried to do."

"Oh my gosh!" Ani said, her hand freezing mid-pet on top of Boon's head. "That's...awful!"

"It is," Maggie agreed, pouring herself a cup of iced tea from the pitcher on the table. "After experiencing that, it's completely understandable that she would be afraid to try the same thing."

"But she is," Hugo said, and popped a potato chip into his mouth. "She's a brave woman. One of the FBI agents told me that over the past decade, criminal prosecutions of the Detroit Partnership have had little impact on their overall activity. But now, Valentina's testimony is going to decimate the organization. Based on her evidence, they're putting together seven prosecutions involving thirty-one individuals and multiple deaths."

"Whoa!" Noah said, pausing before taking another bite.

Hugo gave a nod and began ticking off on his fingers. "They're going to be indicted by federal authorities on charges including murder, conspiracy to commit murder, extortion, labor racketeering, mail fraud, taking bribes, obstruction of justice, violating the IRS code, and more. With Valentina's evidence, they anticipate they'll have an airtight case against the organization. Her father and many key players are going to be put away for good."

"But after what you just said about her mom, isn't there a risk that just like her mom, Valentina won't be safe either?" Ani asked.

"That's what she originally thought." Maggie nodded. "That's why she planned to simply fake her own death and toss Noah to the wolves." Maggie looked at Noah and clasped his hand that was resting on the table beside her. He gave her a reassuring squeeze.

"There were some specific issues that occurred with regard to Valentina's mom," Hugo said. "The FBI agents were able to explain everything to Valentina, to help her understand what went wrong with her mom, and to make certain she could avoid making the same mistakes."

"Like what?" Noah asked, taking a small cluster of grapes from the bowl on the table and tossing one into his mouth.

"Well, for one thing, even though her mother wasn't supposed to stay in touch with anyone in the family, she made the fatal error of trusting one sister-in-law and maintaining communication with her. She thought the woman was a true friend. But it was easy enough for Valentina's father to eventually track them down because of that connection.

"Valentina understands how crucial it is to avoid contact with anyone from her former life. She and Eric will be entered into the witness protection program where they'll be given new identities and moved to a new location to start their lives over. Valentina is committed to doing this. She feels that she's truly honoring her mother's memory by not only breaking free from that life, but also making certain that her father and the Partnership pay for their crimes."

"Wow," Ani said with a shake of her head. "She's really sacrificing a lot to do the right thing. I can't imagine losing all of my friends—people I love—in one single instant like that."

"It would be incredibly difficult," Noah agreed.

"I'm just so glad this whole thing is over," Maggie sighed, snuggling up against Noah's shoulder. He savored the feel of her soft body against his.

"Okay," Hugo said, brushing the crumbs from his fingers. "Who's ready for a game of two-on-two beach volleyball? Me and Ani against the two of you."

"Is that really going to be fair, old man?" Noah laughed as they all rose from the table and began cleaning up. "Our incredible athleticism against an old man and a kid?"

"You must not have experienced my dad's mad volleyball skills yet," Ani said, tossing a balled-up napkin at Noah's head. "Otherwise, you'd never be talking smack like that to us. You'd be afraid. Very afraid."

"Ha!" Noah said with a smirk, snatching the napkin out of the air. "Oooh, look at those reflexes."

"Oh yeah," Ani taunted, pressing the lid onto the bowl of grapes. "Try and catch this one." And she threw the bowl at him.

"Ani, no!" Hugo cried as the container flew through the air.

Noah made a dive for the bowl and caught it, but then tripped over a nearby grill, jamming his toe. "Ow, ow, ow!" he howled, hopping around for a few seconds before landing hard on the ground.

Boon was by his side in an instant, licking his face. Then in his now familiar style, he clambered onto Noah's prone body and tried to lay down on him.

"Boon, get off me!" Noah cried, pushing at the dog's massive body.

"Finally," Maggie laughed. "It's your turn!"

"Oh my gosh!" Ani cried.

Everyone looked at her. But she was staring at Noah and pointing at the dog with her mouth hanging open.

"What?" Noah said, still struggling to get out from underneath Boon.

"I just remembered where I've seen Boon before!" she said.

Noah parked and turned off the engine. They were on Main Street in the center of downtown Whispering Pines, only steps from where they'd been assaulted by Nick and Johnny in the alleyway beside the trash can where Valentina had tossed out her cell phone.

"I still can't believe I didn't recognize this place when we were here before," Noah said.

"Well, as we now know, too much alprazolam can do that to you," Maggie said from the passenger seat. Then she sighed deeply. "I'm glad Ani remembered meeting Boon here when she and her friends volunteered a few weeks ago. But I sure wish we didn't have to do this."

As if sensing that they were talking about him, Boon poked his nose in between the two front seats. He was panting softly and his ears were flopped over in that uniquely adorable way of his.

"It'll be all right, boy," Noah said, scratching the top of his furry head. "But we sure are gonna miss you."

Maggie buried her face in the ruff of his neck and Boon whined softly, giving her a lick. "Let's get it over with," she said with a sigh.

Noah attached the original blue leash to Boon's collar and they all climbed out of the vehicle.

Together, they walked toward the door of the Mitten Mutts Dog Rescue. Maggie opened it and Boon pulled them through, straining at his leash.

As they approached the counter, a massive Great Dane suddenly peered over the top of it.

"Well, hello there," Maggie said with a grin. "Are you the official greeter?"

The dog tilted his head as if in inquiry at the sound of her voice.

Just then, a young man came around the corner from a room behind the counter. "Oh hey! Sorry about that. Down, Mack!" he said.

And the dog obediently sat down, but continued to gaze at them.

"Can I help you?" he asked. Noah guessed him to be about sixteen or seventeen years old. His sandy brown hair was long, flopped low over his forehead, and he kept flipping his head to one side to get it out of his eyes.

"Yes," Noah said. "I believe he belongs here." He lifted his leash hand above the counter and the boy stepped forward to peer over the top of it. Then his eyes grew wide.

"Boon-doggle? No way! Where've you been, buddy?" The young man came out from behind the counter, and Boon's tail instantly started wagging.

The boy squatted down beside Boon who began nuzzling and licking his face.

"Easy, boy. Easy." He chuckled, standing back up.

The boy's gaze shifted between Maggie and Noah, but settled on Noah who was still holding Boon's leash. "Sorry, it's just that he's been missing for days. I somehow lost him when I stopped in here late Friday night to check on one of our newest arrivals. My parents were super ticked off at me. They own this place. My mom's working in the back with the dogs right now.

I'm Bryan by the way," he added, extending his hand to each of them. "So, where'd you find Boon?"

Maggie and Noah exchanged a look. Then Noah gave Bryan a sheepish grin. "I'm not certain, but it's possible that I may have stolen him."

Bryan frowned in confusion. "What?"

Noah briefly explained his temporary amnesia situation without going into too much detail. "I know that I was outside this shelter sometime Friday night. And somehow, I met Boon then."

Bryan rubbed a hand along his jaw. "Well, that lines up with when he went missing. I was on duty Friday night. We'd just gotten in a particularly anxious rescue, a puppy. So, I stopped by to check on him. I let Boon and a couple of the other big dogs out to do their business in the fenced-in yard out back. When I was ready to leave, I went to get them all, but Boon was missing. I freaked out!"

"I'm sorry," Noah said.

"No worries, bro," Bryan said. "At least he's back now, safe and sound."

"So, I take it Boon is a rescued dog then?" Maggie said, as she slowly ran her hand over Boon's soft head. The dog lifted his chin and closed his eyes in appreciation.

"Yeah, yeah," Bryan said. "We got him in a few weeks ago."

"What's his story?" Noah said. "He seems like a smart, well-behaved dog. How did he end up here?"

"It was kind of a strange fluke," Bryan said. "He was originally being trained as an emotional support dog for people dealing with severe anxiety."

"You can get a trained service dog for that?" Maggie asked.

"Oh sure," Bryan said. "If the dog's owner starts showing signs of an impending anxiety attack, the dog can be trained to get medicine or bring the owner a telephone to call for help. They're also trained to do stuff like cuddle up next to them or start doling out kisses. It often helps stop the attack and allows the owner to relax and feel safe."

Maggie exchanged a look with Noah and burst out laughing. "Well, that explains a lot!"

Noah looked back at Bryan. "You said Boon was *originally* being trained to be a service dog?"

"Yeah," Bryan looked down at Boon. "Unfortunately, he was the victim of a perfect storm of bad luck."

"What do you mean?" Noah asked.

"Well, more than half of service dog candidates don't complete their training. And Boon fell into that category. He was overly sensitive to humans under stress, causing him to overreact. And he also would get aggressive with certain people that he didn't take a liking to, for seemingly random reasons."

"Maybe they just weren't nice people," Noah murmured, thinking of Nick and Johnny.

Bryan shrugged. "I dunno. Anyway, after he flunked out of the program, he was sent to a service dog organization with an adoption program for failed service dogs. He got adopted pretty quick. But he was only in his new home for a few months when the owner died unexpectedly. Boon was brought here, and we were making arrangements to send him back to the original adoption organization. There's a big demand for failed service dogs because of all the training they receive."

Maggie had been absently running her hand along Boon's silky coat, but she stopped and looked up at the young man. "So, Bryan, does Boon *have* to go back to the service dog organization for adoption?"

The young man frowned. "Huh?"

Maggie locked eyes with Noah and he knew what she was thinking. Because he was thinking the same thing.

"What we mean is, what if we'd like to adopt Boon?"

"Ohhh," Bryan said with another toss of his hair. "Lemme ask my mom."

An hour later Noah and Maggie walked out of Mitten Mutts with a handful of paperwork making them the official owners of one floppy-eared German Shepherd mix named Boon.

"Is it weird that we have a baby even before our first real date?" Maggie said, making Noah laugh.

"Not any weirder than how the past few days have gone," he replied, opening the back car door so Boon could hop in. Then he reached for the handle of the passenger side door for Maggie, but before he opened it, he turned to her and said, "Speaking of our first real date…"

"Yes?" She was smiling up at him and he couldn't resist. Heedless of the passersby, he bent his head and kissed her. Her lips answered his, soft and yielding.

His head was still spinning when he finally drew back to whisper in her ear. "My apologies for such short notice, but are you free for dinner tonight, Ms. Milena?"

"I think I can squeeze you in," she whispered back, and rising up on tiptoe, she kissed him once more.

Chapter 25

Noah drove them to a tiny lakeside restaurant that offered outdoor seating and a special dog-friendly menu. They were delighted to get a table right by the water, the rolling white-crested waves a brilliant Caribbean blue in the sunlight.

As she slipped into the seat across from Noah, Maggie could hardly contain the joy overflowing within her heart. Even with all the unbelievable things that had happened to them over the past weekend, for her, this was the most unbelievable and miraculous of all. She was sitting across the table, on a date, with the man she'd been in love with her whole life. And now she knew without a doubt that he loved her too.

She adored watching his dark curls dance in the breeze as he studied the menu. The way the warm sunlight caressed the angles and features of his handsome face whenever his gaze drifted out over the water. And above all, how her insides would ignite whenever his smoky gray eyes locked with hers, reflecting a deep desire that made her breath catch in her throat.

They ate and talked and laughed together as they watched Boon devour his special doggie dinner of grilled chicken and brown rice followed by a scoop of peanut butter ice cream topped with a peanut butter cookie.

They lingered over their own meals, their fingertips playing with each other across the table as they reminisced over past memories and shared future hopes.

When they finally rose to go, Noah asked if she'd like to take a walk along the beach.

Thrilled with the idea of prolonging their date, she quickly agreed. "But what about Boon?" she asked.

Noah grinned down at her. "I got a babysitter; it's under control."

Maggie was surprised when Noah led her and Boon to a fenced-in yard behind the restaurant that served as a small dog park for their doggie diners. A staff member supervising the area took their information and promised to watch over Boon until they returned.

"How did you know about this place?" Maggie asked, impressed. Her heart fluttered with delight when she felt him reach for her hand, the warmth of his fingers enveloping hers as they began to stroll along the silky sand.

"When you have two dog-loving brothers living in this town, you learn all the tricks," he said with a grin.

They strolled in silence for a bit, weaving their way past children splashing in the waves, couples lounging on beach towels, and snowy white seagulls strutting along, picking up scraps of food left by picnickers.

At one point, Noah stopped and turned, pulling her close into an embrace. They had removed their shoes and now stood at the edge of the water, the foamy waves sliding gently over their feet and swirling at their ankles. She felt warm and safe in his arms.

"The sun won't set for another hour or so," he said. "Should we—"

The rest of his sentence was cut off at the sound of a sharp whistle.

"Hey there, sugars!" They both turned in surprise to see Rita McKay seated on one of the benches the village had set up along the backside of the beach. Next to her sat none other than George Fairfax, with Rita's arm hooked possessively through his. And on the bench next to theirs, sat Gretchen and Margot.

Maggie and Noah walked over to greet the group, and Maggie noted the glowing smiles on the faces of Rita and George. They looked really happy, despite the fact that Rita's flamboyance and George's reserved nature made them seem like quite the mismatched pair.

George was dressed conservatively as usual, wearing a pair of khaki dress pants and a light blue cotton button-down oxford. Rita was a flashy jewel in bright white Bermuda shorts and a highlighter-pink top that hugged her generous curves. Large apple-green hoops bobbed from her earlobes.

Rita immediately rose to give Noah and Maggie each a warm embrace. Then she sat back down to instantly reclaim George's arm. He gave her a pleased smile, which she returned with a flash of her ruby red lips.

"Sooo, what's going on here?" Noah asked with a bemused smile, indicating their locked arms.

"What's goin' on is that McKay successfully snookered this poor guy," Gretchen said, jamming her thumb in Rita's direction.

Rita lifted her chin and patted her fluffy hair. "Actually, Georgie here just finally saw the light," she said, giving George a sidelong look. "He finally realized what a great catch I am."

George laughed, and his expression softened as he looked at her. "Honestly, Rita is absolutely right." He looked at Maggie. "Even after all this time working with you, Maggie, you know I never thought I'd date again after my Sarah passed away. I told you that over and over, didn't I?"

"You did," Maggie agreed.

"But I could never have predicted the force of nature that is Rita." He looked tenderly at her. "I guess there's room in my heart for more love in a lifetime than I thought. I mean, Sarah will always be in my heart. But I know she'd be happy that I found Rita."

"Oh, George, that's wonderful!" Maggie exclaimed. "I'm so happy for you guys."

Noah echoed her words.

"So now it's your turn to give us the scoop." Rita leaned forward, her eyes alight. "I heard y'all been busy roundin' up mobsters?"

"And kissin' at concerts," Gretchen tossed in, causing Margot to sigh dramatically.

"All true," Noah said with a grin.

"Really?" George said.

"Start with the mobsters," Rita said.

Maggie began explaining—with Noah interjecting bits here and there—until together they brought the small group up to speed on everything that had happened.

"Whew!" Rita said, shaking her head and making her earrings bump against her neck. "You two have been on quite the adventure."

"Definitely," Noah agreed.

"Now let's get to the good stuff," Gretchen said, her small dark eyes moving from Noah's and Maggie's faces to their joined hands. "What's the story with you two? Did you finally convince another innocent victim to go on a date with you, Noah?"

"Gretchen!" Margot cried, looking appalled. "That's so rude! Besides, you can't just pry into people's private affairs like that."

"But is it an affair?" Gretchen said, narrowing her eyes.

Margot let out another exasperated breath.

"Oh, it's definitely an affair," Noah said, smiling at Maggie. "I not only convinced Maggie to go out on a date with me, but now we've adopted a baby together."

"What?" Margot cried in surprise before covering her mouth with her hand.

Noah laughed and quickly explained about Boon.

"Awwwww, that's wonderful news," Rita said.

"Speaking of news," Margot said, looking smug and smoothing a hand over her dress. "I'm really glad we ran into you. I was going to call you tomorrow, Maggie."

"Really?" Maggie said. "Why?"

"I finally figured out the source behind all your mysterious bad reviews."

"I still can't believe it's her," Maggie said as Noah parked in front of the Little Lakeside Bookshop.

After learning about Margot's discovery, Noah and Maggie picked up Boon and immediately left the beach to drive to the quaint shop.

"Margot's research seemed solid," Noah said.

"But I've never even had her as a client. And I didn't really know her at all when we were at college together."

"Well, for some reason she's got it in for you, Mags," Noah said.

Maggie took a deep breath. "And I'm going to find out why. Wish me luck," she said, preparing to exit the vehicle.

"Uh, what do you think you're doing?" Noah said, laying his hand on her arm.

"I'm going to go talk with her. And I need to hurry before she closes the shop."

Noah gave her a look.

"This is about my business," Maggie said, looking back at him. "There's no need for you to get involved."

Noah sighed and shook his head. "First of all, I doubt you could have gotten any deeper into my business than you have this weekend. And second of all, I think we've already established the fact that I love you, Maggie. Your business is my business. Besides, we have no idea if this woman is some kind of psychopath. I'm not leaving you alone with her.

"Hmmmm," he added with a glance at the dog in the back seat. "I wonder if we should take Boon in with us."

Maggie laughed. "I'm sure dogs aren't allowed in the bookstore. It's tiny, and his tail is a weapon that could clear the shelves."

"All right, but I'm coming with you no matter what."

The bell above the door tinkled as Maggie pushed it open. Inside the tiny shop, the shelves were high and packed with books, all neatly labeled by genre. They made their way up one of the narrow aisles to the back of the shop where the register was located.

Amy Jude sat behind the counter, typing on a laptop. She looked up as they approached, her friendly smile melting away at the sight of them. "I'm closing," she said sharply.

"We're not here to buy anything," Maggie said, coming to stand in front of the counter. Amy's hazel eyes radiated hostility from behind her black-rimmed glasses as she looked at Maggie.

For the life of her, Maggie couldn't imagine what she had done to offend this woman.

"Look, I'm going to get right to the point. I know that your name is Amy Jude and that you're the one who's been sabotaging my business by leaving bad reviews under multiple pseudonyms." She paused a moment, letting it sink in. "I haven't gone to the police to press libel charges against you yet. But I plan to."

"I—I don't know what you're talking about," Amy said, but her voice quavered.

"There's no point in denying it," Maggie pressed on. "IP addresses don't lie. The...er, investigator I hired assured me that every one of the negative reviews, regardless of the reviewer's name, leads back to an IP address at this location.

Amy opened her mouth, then closed it. Maggie watched with interest as Amy's expression transformed from hostility to uncertainty to fear. The color had leached from her face, and she was now the color of paste under the fluorescent store lighting.

"Do you have anything to say for yourself before I go file a report against you?" Maggie pressed on.

Amy's lips tightened, her expression turning bitter. "Oh, go ahead and file it. It's not like you haven't already ruined my life."

"What are you talking about?" Maggie said. "How have I ruined your life? We barely know each other!"

Amy kept silent for so long that Maggie was about to give up and leave. Then Amy spat out, "You stole my love."

"What?" She looked at Noah. But he looked as surprised as she felt.

"Not him," Amy said with annoyance, following her gaze.

"Then who?"

"Jack."

"Jack? You mean Jack Knightly?"

Amy sighed and sat back on her stool, pushing a stray strand of her mouse-brown hair behind her ear. "We were on the chess team together in college," she said. "I'd been trying to get him to ask me out for months. Then you come along and introduce him to that...that blond bombshell!"

Maggie was shocked. "I had no idea."

"Yeah, well..." She shrugged. "Once Miss Barbie Doll was in the picture, it was like I didn't even exist anymore."

Maggie took a deep breath. "Amy, I'm...so very sorry."

At her simple apology, Maggie saw some of the anger leave Amy's face. She sagged on the stool, looking as if the air had been let out of her.

Maggie studied the woman across from her. She took in the rumpled blouse and the way her short hair was pulled back into a low, tight ponytail at the back of her head. She realized Amy could actually be pretty with a better haircut and more fashionable clothes.

She leaned onto the countertop, subtly closing a bit of the space between them. "Listen, Amy, I have an idea. Will you let me do something to make up for how I hurt you?"

"What can you possibly do?" Amy said. "He's happily married with a family now."

"Yes, he is," Maggie acknowledged. "But why don't you meet me for coffee tomorrow? I'd like to offer you a complimentary membership to Matches by Maggie. If you let me, I'd love to help you find your own happy ending."

Amy looked shocked. But Maggie could see the hope reflected in her eyes. "You'd do that for me, after everything I did?"

"I will," Maggie said. "As long as you promise to leave me an honest review afterward."

"But what if it doesn't work?" Amy said.

"Oh, it will work," Noah said, grinning down at Maggie. "If there's one thing this woman knows, it's how to help people find their happy endings."

One year later

Noah had been acting strange all day. It had started with their hike in the state park that morning. They were celebrating the one-year anniversary of their first official date by spending the entire day together.

It was a perfect summer day, the heat tempered by a cooling lake-effect breeze. During their morning hike through the state park, bright sunshine had shone down from a cloudless deep blue sky, its golden rays gleaming off verdant green leaves and releasing the scent of fragrant pine needles. Despite the beauty of their surroundings, Noah had clearly been distracted. He'd tripped over tree roots and forced her to repeat herself numerous times because he kept missing what she said.

After the hike, they'd treated themselves to ice cream for lunch at the Dairy House. And while she polished off her double dip cone of Moose Tracks, he'd sat there daydreaming so long that his ice cream melted all over his hand and he ended up tossing it out without finishing it.

Now, they were at the beach enjoying time with Noah's two siblings and their wives. They'd all played in the late-afternoon waves and shared a lovely picnic dinner in the adjacent park. But again, Noah had been out of it throughout most of their conversations.

All three couples had brought along their dogs. And Maggie laughed as she watched how Noah's brother Wade and wife Cassie's tiny white fluffball, Angel, had proven very successful at eluding both Boon, and Jake and Alex's golden retriever, Rex, in a game of tag. The little dog pranced and hopped around, totally controlling the game as they chased each other around the picnic tables.

It was close to sunset now and everyone was starting to clean up. The other two couples offered to watch Boon so Maggie and Noah could take one last walk along the shore.

"It's your anniversary!" Alex said, shooing Maggie away as she attempted to clear off some of the remaining paperware. "And this is the most romantic time of day. You two should spend it together instead of standing here cleaning up with us old married couples."

"There's only a little bit more to do," Maggie protested. "Besides, I think if anyone should stop cleaning right now, it should be you." Maggie eyed Alex's tired expression and large, rounded belly.

Alex grinned and gently smoothed a hand over her pregnant form. "Baby Boy Riley is just fine in there. Too fine. Maybe my moving around will encourage him to finally move out. We're so ready to meet him."

"Yes, we are," Jake said, joining the group and kissing the top of his wife's head.

"I still can't believe I'm finally going to be an uncle," Noah said, tossing a handful of trash into the garbage can.

"Well, you are, bro," Jake said.

"We *both* are," Wade added as he finished scraping off the grill.

"And I'm going to be cool Aunt Cassie," Cassie said, grinning from beside her husband.

"Yes, yes," Alex said, sitting down awkwardly on the picnic bench where they'd eaten. "But you guys are all distracting me from my original point to Maggie."

"Which was?" Noah said.

"That you should take your lovely lady here for a walk before the sun sets or you'll miss it."

"Yeah, bro," Jake said. "I mean, one year of successful dating with nobody dying, losing a limb, or ending up in jail? Now, that's definitely something you should celebrate."

Noah lunged toward his brother, but Maggie laughed and grabbed for Noah's hand, pulling him back toward her. "C'mon! I want the sunset stroll you promised me this morning."

"Okay, okay," Noah said, tossing an "I'll deal with you later," over his shoulder to his brother.

Slowly, the two of them made their way up the shoreline. The crowds from earlier had thinned. And now there were only a few scattered families and couples left, many of them sitting on the benches that faced the water as they prepared to watch nature's nightly show.

Maggie gazed up at Noah. Even after a year together, when she looked at him, he still took her breath away.

They walked in companionable silence up the beach and out to the end of the lighthouse pier to look down at the waves crashing against the base of the massive structure. It wasn't until they were on their way back up the beach again that Maggie finally spoke.

"Jake's right, you know," she said. "You have totally crushed your FDF record."

Noah grinned down at her. "I have, haven't I? We've had some pretty special times."

And they had. During the course of their year together, he'd taken her on some of the most romantic dates she could have imagined: candlelight picnics under the stars, a hot air balloon ride at sunrise, a chocolate making class for two, and even a surprise weekend getaway to a beautiful resort in the mountains. Maggie had discovered that Noah was a true romantic. He'd gone above and beyond to make their times together unforgettable.

"We have," Maggie agreed, her voice soft. "But you know what? It's not just about the grand romantic gestures. It's...all of it."

They'd rediscovered shared interests, tried new things together, and the love that had been borne during their high school days together had matured, growing deeper, richer. That first bloom of love was only a whisper in comparison to what she felt for the man standing beside her now.

For Maggie, an added bonus to their relationship had been getting to know Noah's siblings, along with Cassie and Alex. Although they all had such different interests, his family had seamlessly welcomed Maggie into their fold.

They were almost back to the group when Noah stopped, turning her to face the horizon and wrapping his arms around her. Maggie leaned back against him and sighed with contentment as they soaked up the view.

The sky was a rich canvas of color, awash with hues of rose and tangerine, while deep amethyst clouds floated at the horizon. The sun's fading light danced on the water's surface, casting a glittering path that stretched into the distance. A soft breeze drifted over them, mingling the tang of the lake with the sweet scent of nearby blooming night jasmine, reminding Maggie of that first night when Noah had sung to her, and they'd confessed their love for each other.

The sun dipped lower and lower. When it was just about to touch the horizon, on impulse, she spun around in the circle of his arms and rising up on her toes, kissed him soft, slow and sweet.

"What was that for?" Noah whispered against her lips.

"I'm just so happy," Maggie said. "I love you so much."

He was quiet in response, and Maggie pulled back to look at him. He wore an enigmatic expression on his face.

"What's wrong?" she asked.

Instead of responding, Noah turned his head and gave a whistle.

Boon was suddenly bounding across the sand toward them. He was quivering with excitement, his pink tongue lolling.

"Boon, no, boy! You're not allowed on the beach!" Maggie cried.

"He's got special dispensation," Jake called out. Maggie glanced over and saw that their initial small group had grown in size. In fact, it had swelled considerably. She now saw J.P., Tilly, Rita, George, Hugo, Ani, Jaime, Jack, Gretchen, and Margot had joined them. And they were all walking toward the shoreline where she and Noah stood.

Her gaze swept the group in confusion then returned to Noah. "What's going on?" she said.

He cleared his throat. "Boon and I have a question for you?" he said. He ordered the wriggling dog to sit down beside him, and then dropped to one knee right there on the sand. It was only then that Maggie noticed a new blue kerchief bunched up around Boon's neck.

She watched in shock as Noah smoothed the kerchief out with trembling fingers. The words on it read, "Mommy, will you marry my Daddy?"

Maggie gasped and her heart skipped a beat as Noah pulled out a small, velvet ring box. He pried it open to reveal a gorgeous marquis diamond that glittered in the glowing light of the sunset.

"Maggie Milena," he said, his eyes locking with hers. "I love you. Will you marry me?"

She felt as if her heart was going to pound its way out of her chest as she exclaimed, "Yes, yes! A thousand times, yes!"

Noah broke into a wide grin, his face lit with joy as he leaped to his feet. Maggie threw her arms around his neck, kissing him all over his face as he lifted her off the ground. The rest of the group erupted into cheers, and soon they were surrounded by barking dogs, glowing smiles, and a symphony of enthusiastic well wishes.

Amidst the hubbub, Noah leaned close and whispered into her ear, "Maggie Milena, you are and always will be my dream girl. Thank you for making my dream come true.

Then she whispered back, "And thank you, Noah Riley. For finally giving me my very own happy ending."

And they all lived happily ever after.

A Note from Holly...

Reviews...they're critical! Reviews help authors more than you may realize. If you enjoyed *Forbidden Whispers,* I'd be grateful if you'd consider leaving a review on Amazon. Thank you!

Plan to read them all!
Other books in the Secrets of Whispering Pines series:

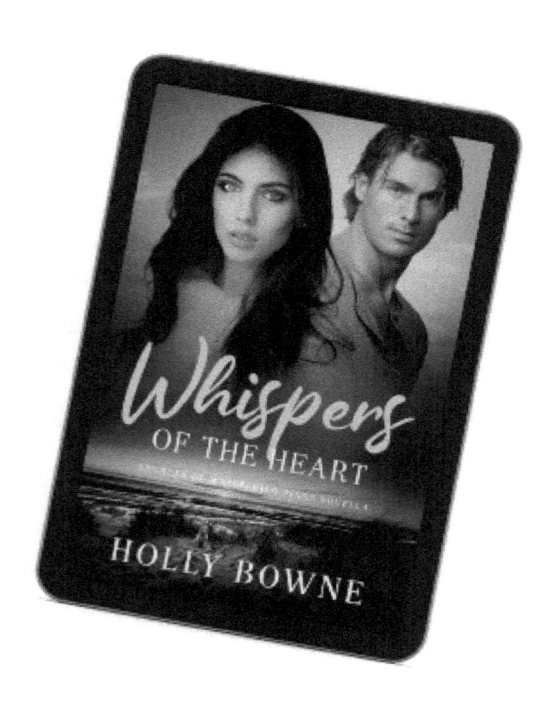

***Whispers of the Heart (Series Prequel)** – Would you like a FREE book?*
An artist driven by dreams. A businessman chasing profits. When their worlds collide, will they risk everything to follow their hearts?

Whispers of the Heart (a prequel to Alex and Jake's story) is available for FREE here: hollybownebooks.com/free-book. Along with your free book, you'll also begin receiving my occasional newsletter offering exclusive content, sneak peeks on new releases, and information on special giveaways.

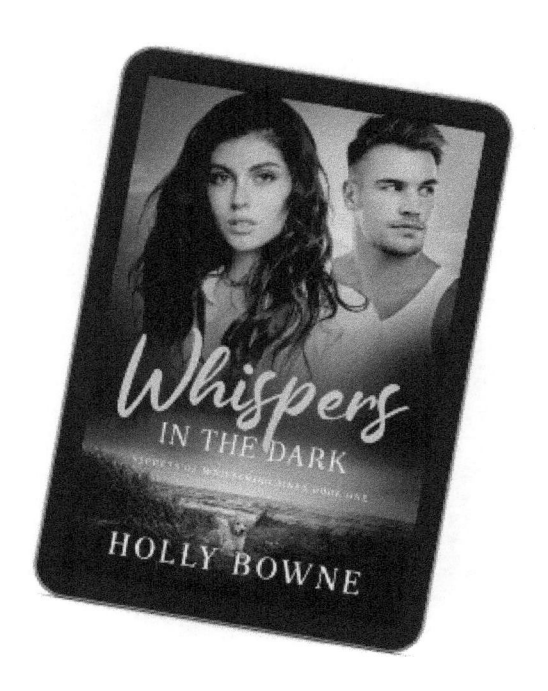

Whispers in the Dark (Book 1)

She can't stand him. He can't leave her alone. Especially when a sinister force threatens her safety. As Jake Riley and Alex Fontaine unite to solve the mystery, will their fiery connection lead to love or plunge them into even greater danger? Available on Amazon and Barnes & Noble.

Whispers of Redemption (Book 2)
He's a dedicated police officer, committed to upholding the law. She's a woman who wrestles with authority issues. When a mysterious art theft draws Cassie Sherwin and Wade Riley closer together, they find themselves caught between their convictions and an undeniable attraction. Available on Amazon and Barnes & Noble.

Acknowledgements

First and foremost, I want to thank God for blessing me with a passion and gift for writing. Glory to him!

And once again, I am indebted to my brother-in-love, David Schreiner, for helping me to stay accurate about police procedure stuff.

I also want to thank my entire family for your never-ending patience and encouragement in the face of my constant whining about how I would never get this series done. You guys were right. I did it!

♥ Holly

Meet the Author

Holly Bowne is the author of the Secrets of Whispering Pines romantic suspense series. She's worked in advertising, journalism and as a freelance writer. And she finds inspiration everywhere, from movies, TV series, the news, conversations with her friends and conversations she's eavesdropped on (shhh!). She currently lives on a beautiful lake in southeast Michigan where she dreams up new stories, falls down research rabbit holes, and witnesses the beauty and song of God's creation every single day. She's happily married to her college sweetheart, mother of two grown children along with a daughter- and son-in-love, and passionate Gigi to three adorable grandchildren. And she's not biased about this at all.

You can learn more about Holly and her books – and sign up for her newsletter – at www.hollybownebooks.com

Milton Keynes UK
Ingram Content Group UK Ltd.
UKHW010514250624
444652UK00005B/390